The Shade

Joseph F. Montoya

Copyright © 2009 Joseph F. Montoya

All rights reserved.

ISBN-10: 1481247670
ISBN-13: 978-1481247672

To my supportive and loving wife who inspired my writing and all the hours she has spent assisting me in every way, including the very writing of this particular book, I am forever grateful.

ACKNOWLEDGMENTS

Ted Montoya, what would I do without you. George Rinaldi, thank you, Christine Miller and Joceyln Wolf for editing, Dr. Raymond Lansing, my daughter Rhonda Palmer and her husband Dave, Candy Crawford Kunz, Tiffany Jarvis, Janet Hood, Debbie Hodges, Ed and Myrna Hewitt, Tony Petersen, Patricia Browning, Martha Wilson, Janice Wolf, Betty Cooper, Gary and Carol George, Virginia Jones Smith and Lynn, Jimmy and Helga Marr, Dean and Trina Adams, Dave and Bobbie Emerson, Sandra Sugg Arce, John Hunter, Don Jones, Richard Merriman, Kimber and Marshall Gingold, Kim Johnson, Janice wolf, my mother Lucy, sisters, Marion Montoya, Dr. Angelina Lansing, and Nancy Bownan, Lucy Lansing, Ollie Bowman, Joe and Janet Riggs, all my brothers Lee, Fred, Jess and Elaine, Dick, Tony, Bob and Nowella Ackerman. Thank you Beta Modic for your very kind words. Thanks to Kevin Alvidera for helping me on Microsoft Word.

Marco Martinez for putting me in the Wenatchee World, Wilfred Woods, Chairman of the Board of the Wenatchee World for his kind words about my family and allowing me to advertise in his paper for free. Thank you sir. I'm sure I've forgotten someone. My thanks to you all.

CHAPTER 1

Ever hear of Wenatchee, Washington? If you're an apple or cherry aficionado, you probably have. Otherwise well, I guess it's understandable.

Wenatchee is a small, predominantly agricultural town in the middle of the state. Incidentally, Wenatchee is almost geographically the center of the State of Washington.

In the fifties, most of the population in Washington State was to be found in Seattle, Tacoma, and Spokane. There were only about five million people in the whole state at that time. In any case, only about 18,000 of them lived in Wenatchee in 1954.

Alcoa had a plant in our town; it was the only industrial concern at that time. They made aluminum cans. But it was mostly the orchards, apples, cherries, pears, peaches and prunes, and oh yes, wheat fields in the hills surrounding the town, that employed the residents and fueled the economy.

This little town was my whole world. It was a time when "media" meant radio, or newspaper, and all we knew of the outside world arrived via those two mediums.

I'm telling this story from memory, and although it's far from photographic, it's pretty good when it comes to the events that follow.

Oh, yes, the Columbia River runs through town. On one side is Wenatchee, and on the other, East Wenatchee. Mom wouldn't let us play or swim in the river because her current was too swift. Every once in a while she would grab some unsuspecting innocent and pull him down and away forever. Sometimes I would stand on her shore and think about taking "just a little dip" who would know? but as I watched her roil and ripple with the current, I knew Mom was right. I was honestly afraid of her power.

Anyhow, I'm getting ahead of myself. I grew up and went to school from the first grade through Wenatchee High School. Later, a friend of my mom later told me that we…my generation, grew up in the most ideal period in recent history, and I believe her. The innocence, the cars, the clothes, the music… all of it served to create an atmosphere of change, of growth, and of freeness. As kids, we could go out after dark to play at a friend's house, to the movies, or to the drug store to get a coke, and never have a worry. I guess I should introduce myself since I'll be telling this story. My name is José Jimenez. No, no not really, but do you remember him? My name is Anthony Marinquez, but everybody called me Tony.

My parents couldn't have picked a more perfect place to finally settle down and raise us kids, all twelve of us. Most people probably feel that way about their hometowns, I guess, but they don't know Wenatchee. I remember once… it was a warm evening in May when Oren Brown and I walked down Yakima Street to the Plaza, down by Orondo and Okanogan Streets. The Plaza was a small convenience store that sold magazines, ice cream, sodas, sandwiches, cigarettes, and candy bars. You remember those little places? Had a counter with six naugahide-covered stools along its length? One time Oren and I bought a White Owl cigar here and smoked it behind the store and really got sick. We both threw up. Right across the street behind a small park, complete with a cannon on the Orondo Street side sat the courthouse. All right, so I digress. Anyway, we were walking down Yakima Street when Oren asked, "Hey, you want to get a tomato?" Now this was big stuff in those days, nothing destructive, just borrowing some fruit, yes, tomatoes are fruit and getting away with it.

"Yeah, sure. Is there a garden around here?"

"Next block, but Tony, you gotta follow me close, cause there's a droopy clothes line right next to the tomatoes."

"Is it dark enough, Oren? We don't wanna get caught."

Now Oren was a lot braver or maybe he wasn't braver, but more adventurous, or crazier or whatever. Anyhow, he looked around and decided we should go get our Coke first. So we did, and afterward we went back. There it was. A small garden behind the house, and the tomatoes were beautiful. Even in the darkness we could see their redness, beckoning us. I could almost taste them already. We slowed our pace and checked all the neighboring houses to make sure no one was sitting on their porch, or looking out a window. Not a soul in sight, so we crept quietly into the yard of the light green house.

"Watch out for the clothes line," Tony whispered. "You see it?"

"Yeah."

"I think I see a couple of orange ones." He liked tomatoes best just before they got ripe, so he was scanning for orange ones. "Stay here and I'll go get us a couple."

While he was gone, I was so nervous I was shaking. Didn't think he was ever coming back, but just before I bolted, he appeared out of the darkness.

"Here, hope it's ripe enough." Oren handed me a huge, firm, sinfully red tomato. It was gorgeous! "I brought a salt shaker." That's Oren for you, always thinking.

We stayed low and made our way over to the back wall of the house, leaned against it, and savored our pilfered treasure.

"Hey, Oren, look!" I whispered excitedly, and pointed to the light that had just gone on in the back of the yellow house that faced the house where we were. The light cast a shadow on the roll-down shade, and it was, the silhouette of a woman, and she appeared to be naked.

"The shade's up a couple of inches. Let's go over and look, Tony."

See, I told you he was crazier. Anyhow, I stammered "OK," and we crossed the yards slowly and ever so quietly. Went right up to the window. The opening between the shade and the sill was just about our eye level. We looked in.

There she was, naked as a jaybird, just sitting on her bed, reading a magazine like it was the most normal thing in the world.

It was me, Mr. Cool, started to giggle. I clamped my hand over my mouth and stepped away from the window, so she wouldn't hear me.

"Shhhhhh," he warned.

"Sorry, couldn't help it," I whispered.

We stayed up against the house, just beside the window, and waited for me to compose myself. I mean, I understood. A beautiful woman naked right in front of us… it was just not to be believed. Things like this just didn't happen in our world every day.

When, our control returned at last we resumed our peeping. From our narrow viewpoint, we could see her, where she lay on her bed, the adjacent room and down the hall to the front door. The only light was in her bedroom, and the front door was in almost complete darkness, but we thought we saw movement, a shadow, someone else in the house.

I grabbed Oren's elbow and pulled him away from the window. "There's somebody else in there," I whispered nervously.

"I saw it too. Wonder who it is?"

We went back to the window, and what we saw then - - well, we were petrified. There was a man in the doorway. When she saw him, she jumped up, covered herself with the bedclothes, and screamed, "What are you doing in my house? Get out or I'll call the police."

"What? You don't remember me?" he crooned, with a sardonic smile.

Oren poked me and pointed down by his feet. There was a big black and white cat, purring, and winding around his legs.

"Oren," I whispered, "look." He returned his attention to the room. The man was getting closer and closer to the bed. He looked up, scanned the room and, his eyes seemed to stop at the window.

As one, we bolted for the street; Oren stepped on the cat's tail and it let out a scream. That was it. We were both out of there just as fast as we could go, - - maybe faster. We hit Yakima Street at a full run and didn't stop till we got to the corner of Alaska and Spokane.

We were shaking, breathing hard, and couldn't talk. I don't think my heart had ever beaten so fast, or so hard. We were scared, embarrassed, and didn't have a clue about what we had just seen. But in the days to come, we would find out. Now, though, we just looked at each other. After I caught my breath enough to talk, I asked, "Have you ever seen that guy before, Oren?" Oren, still panting, hands on his knees, looked up at me and shook his head. "Do you think it was her boyfriend?"

"Don't know, Tony. But she sorta sounded serious about calling the police."

"Ahhh maybe they were playing some kind of game, or something. I didn't hear anything after we ran. She didn't scream or nothin'."

"Yeah, you're probably right. We would have heard something if he wasn't supposed to be there."

We convinced ourselves that they had been playing some kind of "adult" stuff, and went on home.

Well that's how the story begins, and I'll let the events tell you the rest.

CHAPTER 2

Police Chief James Allen was in his office going over what they knew so far about the Yakima Street murder that occurred last night, when John Brees, his primary homicide detective, joined him. "What can you tell me, John?"

The detective had been first on the scene. Lilly Jo's father had called the department after finding her that morning. She hadn't come in to work, and wasn't answering her phone, so the poor man had gone to check on her, and had found his worst nightmare.

John had quickly scanned and secured the scene, then gone to the morgue with the coroner in order to get, first hand, whatever preliminary information he could about the cause of death.

"Doesn't look like a forced entry. No windows broken, and the locks don't appear to have been tampered with. I'm thinking maybe she knew her killer," he ventured.

"Well, that could be, but everybody leaves their doors unlocked here, John. It's a small town. Everybody knows everybody."

John considered the chief's comment for a moment. "True enough. Well then, Lilly Jo was a beautiful woman. Maybe somebody was jealous. Ex-boyfriend? Rejected suitor? Admirer from afar?"

"But her father said she didn't have a boyfriend. Not that he knew of, anyhow, and her mother said the same thing," the chief mused, "so there wouldn't have been anyone to get jealous."

"She was no doubt raped. We'll know positively after we get the report from the coroner, and maybe we can get a blood type."

"Run it down for me."

"First, she had contusions on the front of her neck that suggest she was held down, probably from above, probably with considerable force. Second, there were stains on the sheets, probably semen. We'll know soon. And, third, there was a hell of a struggle in that room, and on that bed. I'm hoping the coroner will find something under her fingernails that can help us out."

"OK, have you interviewed the neighbors yet?"

"That's next on my agenda, Chief. I'm hoping somebody saw or heard something. Anything."

CHAPTER 3

It only took a few minutes for Detective Brees to arrive back at the Zilke residence. He checked his briefcase to make sure he had everything he would need and entered the house again, just to double check. Maybe he had overlooked something the first time around. Things had been a little hectic.

There was little furniture, and few personal items. Only the bathroom and bedroom gave any indication she had even lived here. He found nothing new.

As he was leaving, he paused at the front door and looked back down the hall at the shaded window in the bedroom. *Hmmmmph,* he thought, and walked slowly around the house, scanning for anything out of place. When he arrived at the back of the house, he noticed the shade was not completely down, and peeked in. There was enough of an opening for a clear view of the bedroom, and straight down the hall to the front door.

Careful not to destroy any evidence, he squatted down and studied the ground below the window. It appeared the lawn had been watered yesterday, and the ground had been soft. There were several distinguishable shoe prints that looked like they had been made by tennis shoes. From the placement, it appeared someone had been looking in the window, but when? Could it have been the perp? On closer inspection he determined there were at least two different print patterns. *Gonna have to get the lab guys back out here to make casts of these, and see if there's anything on the sill, maybe prints?* he thought.

CHAPTER 4

"There's been a murder in Wenatchee," Sam, my oldest brother, said to no one in particular. That's kind of the way it was in our house. There were so many of us that if somebody had something to say, they just said it. Somebody else was probably listening.

"Where?" Mom called out from the kitchen. Back then it seemed she was always in the kitchen.

"In Wenatchee," he said again.

"Where in Wenatchee, Sam?"

"Oh, sorry. Let's see. Oh yeah, here it is. On Yakima Street."

Mom came into the living room and sat near Sam as he continued to read the article in the Wenatchee Daily World. "Helen Wently lives on Yakima. She goes to the church," she murmured.

By the way, the Maringuez were Catholics and Mom knew all the ladies in the whole diocese. So Mom would probably know this person if she were Catholic. Anyway back to the story.

I'd been upstairs, cleaning my room, when I heard Sam announce that someone had been murdered on Yakima Street. I joined them on the couch and listened while Sam read the whole article for Mom.

"Does it give an address?" I asked, casual as you please, which wasn't the easiest thing to do since my insides were rumbling.

"Who do you know on Yakima?" my big brother wanted to know.

"Nobody."

"Hmmmm. Well, they didn't give an address, but there is a name. Miss Lilly Jo Zilke, age 23. Name sounds familiar."

"Oh no," slipped out before I could think.

"Tony, do you know her?" he asked again, a little suspiciously.

"No. No, I don't know her," I managed to get out without squeaking, but I was pretty sure that girl, Lilly Jo, was the girl we were watching through that blasted window. I was really tempted to tell Sam what Oren and I had seen. The bad thing was, I would have to tell him why we were peeking in the window in the first place. What if he thought we did it? Oh my God! I decided that I'd be better off not saying anything.

CHAPTER 5

Detective Brees had worked with the tech from the lab, and was pleased the casts had turned out pretty well. As they had worked, his attention had been drawn to the houses that backed up to the crime scene. *That's my next stop*, he thought as they packed up their supplies.

"Hi, I'm John Brees, with the Wenatchee Police Department. May I ask you a few questions?" he asked the woman who answered his knock.

"Yes, of course. Please come in. I'm Danielle Stumply. Guess you're investigating the...the murder? I saw you out back of her house."

"You have a pretty good view of that area from here? Could you show me?"

"Certainly." She took him through her small living room directly to a bedroom door. "Two nights ago I came into this spare bedroom to open the window. It had been a warm day, you know, and I raised the window to get some fresh air in here. This room gets stuffy. I mean, I wasn't spying on her or anything, just wanted to air out the room."

She was wringing her hands and looking at the floor. John knew she was nervous maybe she had seen something.

"Understandable, ma'am. So, that night, you could see her house pretty clearly?"

"Well, it was around 8:30 or 9:00 when I came in here to open the window and get my book. I had left it right there on the bed, so I didn't need to turn on the light. I was just gonna grab the book and go back to the living room."

"Uh huh," he murmured, mostly to himself. "Please, ma'am. Tell me, what did you see?"

"It was dark by then, you know, and there was a light in her bedroom, almost directly across there," she pointed, "so it kind of stood out, you know? My house sits back a little further from the street and it gives George and Nelda a view at the window too. You might want to talk to them too."

"What's George and Nelda's last name?"

"Plant.

"Thank you, I'll do that. Now you were saying something about a light in her bedroom."

"Yes, well it stood out."

"Yes, I can picture that. Mrs. Stumply, you're doing great. Now, please think carefully. Picture the scene, and tell me exactly what you saw. Did you see anything unusual?"

She was nervous, her eyes kept darting around the room, and it was obvious she had something to tell him.

"It's really important, please, tell me, did you see anything out of the ordinary?"

"I did," she said finally, "I'm not absolutely sure, but "

"Go on."

"Well, like I said, the light was on, and, oh yes, the shade was pulled down, but not all the way. There was a gap, just a few inches where the light was quite bright, and I think I saw the top of two heads, moving around out there, in that strip of light, like maybe somebody peeking in."

His heart rate bumped up a few notches, "Uh huh," he murmured encouragingly, but she didn't volunteer anything more, just turned and moved slowly to the living room. John followed her. "Mrs. Stumply, you didn't do anything inappropriate. We're curious critters, us humans."

She relaxed, ever so slightly, and smiled weakly "I suppose so." He waited patiently as she struggled with her conscience. "I...I think I saw those two shadows, but then, just like that," she snapped her fingers, "they were gone. It was almost umm... subliminal. I wasn't positive, but well, it was there. Can you understand why I didn't say anything about it?"

"It's dark, you see a light, maybe the shadowy movement of someone on the shade, maybe someone looking in, blocking out the light from inside, and then it's gone. And it all happens unexpectedly, and it's only there for a few seconds. Yes, ma'am, I can understand and I appreciate that you've shared it with me. It could be helpful. Did you know Lilly Jo very well?"

"Just to wave to. I saw her coming and going from time to time, but we never really talked. Since my husband passed, I've kept pretty much to myself, don't socialize much."

"Did you ever notice anyone visiting her? Boyfriends, anybody?"

"No…not that I remember. She was quiet, and I didn't notice she went out much at night."

"Thank you. If you think of anything else, please don't hesitate to call me." He gave her his card and turned to leave.

Mrs. Stumply, followed him to the door and waited, worrying the business card he had given her, when he turned, and pulled something from his pocket. "Oh, almost forgot, have you ever seen this before?"

She pursed her lips and her forehead wrinkled. "Just a cheap salt shaker, pretty common looking. It's not mine, too small. Sorry."

"Thought maybe since you have a garden, you might have taken a shaker out there. My mom used to take one out to her garden and have a tomato or cucumber while she watered."

She smiled. "My husband loved our little garden, and he would pick a tomato or cucumber, wipe it off with his hands, and have at it. He loved them warm from the sun, but he was on a low sodium diet toward the end of his life, so no salt shaker."

"Sounds like my kind of guy, Mrs. Stumply." John smiled warmly. "Thanks again for your help."

CHAPTER 6

Oren and I had gotten up our courage, or our curiosity had, and we were actually walking down Yakima Street. We saw a black '53 Ford parked in front of the **green house**, and somebody was walking around in the yard.

"Think that's the police?" Oren whispered.

"Yeah, gotta be."

We kept walking though, images of what we had seen running through our heads. It was so hard to keep them away, the images, the thoughts, the fear. But I'll tell you, we were both working at it, at pretending it had never happened.

"Hey, wanna go to the Midget and get a float?" Oren suggested lightly, but I could hear the strain in his voice. He was trying to sound normal, and he almost did…as normal as Oren ever sounded anyway.

"Sure, let's do it. Uhhh, you got any money?"

"Well, some, enough for floats anyhow."

We went to the Midget and found our friend, John Randall Jefferson III, reading some kind of history magazine.

"There's Mr. Encyclopedia. Hi, John."

"Well, if it isn't my two favorite basketball players." He greeted us with that same old line every time we ran into him.

"How come Bob lets you read the magazines when he won't let us do it?" Oren wanted to know, a tad petulantly.

"Well, do you ever buy any? I probably buy enough to keep his bread buttered. You might want to try that sometime." He nudged Oren in the ribs and laughed.

"Why do you read so much? Seems like every time I see you, you've got a book under your nose."

John shrugged, "I don't know. All kinds of things interest me. Maybe it's because of my mom and dad. Dad's always researching something, and Mom reads best sellers. Guess it's environmental."

"What's that you're reading now?"

"Look at this! A guy named Roger Bannister just recently broke the four-minute mile. Gunder Hagg had the record for nine years before that. This is history, guys!"

"Geez, what was his time?" Oren was enthralled; track was one of his passions. Not that he was a star, but he never stopped trying.

"Three minutes, fifty nine and 4 tenths seconds."

"Wow! Don't think I'm gonna be any competition for him, but it's something to shoot for."

"You've got a few years yet, Oren. Just keep at it. So, what are you guys up to today?"

"We're getting floats. Oren's treating." I got a punch on my arm for that one. Oren treated a lot. He usually had more spending money than I ever did. I tried to pay him back in the summer though. That's when my older brothers and I worked in the orchards, picking cherries or apples. Wherever we could get hired on.

"Oren, would you consider allowing me to treat you both? A float would hit the spot right now," John offered.

Now John was a whole different breed of cat. His mom was a teacher, and his dad was some kind of scientist. The Jeffersons had a beautiful home, and it was always quiet and cleaned to a sparkle. Even though they had a lot of money, John was just one of the guys. Well, OK, so he used better English, had better manners, and dressed better than the rest of us. But he was just a good guy, he fit in.

Well, we got our floats and sat at the counter with John telling us all kinds of stuff. Not that much of it would stick, but it seemed like he knew about everything, and I mean everything. Stuff like: Joseph Stalin died on March 5, and some guy named Georgi was gonna succeed him: Ernest Hemingway won a prize for a couple of books, I think one of them was "The Old Man and the Sea"; Rocky Marciano beat Jersey Joe Walcott; President Eisenhower didn't give clemency.

John glanced at his watch. "Oh my gosh, I gotta go. I'm gonna be late," he called out as he dashed off.

"He didn't even finish his float." Oren mused. This would attract his attention, cause Oren never left a drop. "Left forty five cents for our floats though."

We spooned the last of the ice cream from our glasses, and left the Midget at a more leisurely pace.

CHAPTER 7

Mary poked her head into Chief Allen's office. "Chief, there's a detective from Chelan here to see you."

"OK, Mary, tell him to come on back," he advised confidently, knowing Mary would have checked his ID before announcing him.

Detective Rotter strode into the room. The two exchanged names, and handshakes.

"Chief, thanks for taking the time to see me. Sorry I didn't call first, but I was in Wenatchee on another matter, and well, thought I might touch base with you on the Zilke murder."

Chief Allen scrutinized Rotter a little more closely. *What's his interest?* he wondered. "Well, we're just getting started. Don't have much yet, but I've got a couple of detectives working it full time. What, may I ask, is your interest?"

"Fair question. Two years ago, next month, we had a murder/rape in Chelan. It's still open. I worked it for over a year before I ran out of leads.

"I was thinking maybe there might be some similarities. Could be the same guy? It's a shot but, well you never know."

"Ummm. Well, if we find something that looks like it might tie in, we'll share, Rotter, but it'll have to go both ways. Work for you?"

Rotter nodded. "Works for me, Chief."

"Good. The lead detective, John Brees, is on scene at the moment. How 'bout you give me your number and I'll have him tag you when he gets back."

"Fair enough." Rotter turned to leave. "Chief, can you tell me the cause of death?"

"We don't have the coroner's report yet, but it sure looks like the COD was strangulation."

"Thanks, Chief," Rotter said quietly, "I have a sinking feeling I'll be seeing you again…soon."

Mary Corley watched Rotter leave the parking lot, and then went to the Chief's office. "Chief, do you know who that is?"

"Ummmm-…the name has a ring, just can't place it. He live around here?"

"Guess he did in '48. That was when Wenatchee High was ranked number one in the state polls. You know, small town, great football players. Jim Rotter was their star running-back, even got a scholarship to Washington State."

" Oh, yeah, I do remember that. Well, well…looks like he could still take on a defensive line," he chuckled, and felt a tad more comfortable about the detective from Chelan.

CHAPTER 8

Well, there we were again, headed down Yakima Street, this time to church. Everybody in my family went to church, at the very least on Sunday morning. Mom went most every day, and sometimes I helped out you know, cleaning the pews, putting the missals back in the racks. But today was different, I was nervous. I mean, what was I gonna say to Father O'Sullivan in confession? What would Oren say? First of all, though this was the least of my worries, we had stolen a couple of tomatoes. But then, we had gone and peeked in that lady's window. We saw a naked lady! No doubt that was a sin, maybe even a mortal sin.

How could we say anything, even in confession? Maybe if we said something the priest would have to tell the police. Wouldn't what happened to her make it wrong for the priest not to tell? I mean, I know what you say in confession is just for the priest's and God's ears, but that lady was killed!

Everything in my head kept going in circles, and getting more tangled up. Just about the time I decided to "get sick" and go back home, Oren grabbed my arm and pointed up the street. "Hey, Tony. What kind of car is that? The green and black one up there, blowin' all that smoke?"

"Looks like a '47 Hudson. Why?"

Oren was pale as a sheet, and his eyes were bulging. "I think that's the bastard that killed her," he whispered.

"You sure?"

"Well, no, not for positive. But it looked like him. Tony, I keep seein' that face. Guess maybe now everybody I don't know looks like him. I even dream about it. This whole thing is getting to me. Sometimes I don't even want to fall asleep."

Right then a horn sounded right behind us. Talk about heart failure!!! We both jumped 'bout out of our skins. Slowly, I looked over my shoulder, and breathed a sigh of relief. "It's just Norman Jack," I squeaked to Oren. We waved, and tried to look casual as he passed.

"Man, I love that car," Oren intoned wistfully. It was a deep blue, '42 Pontiac, lowered in back (which was mandatory for all "tough" cars) with twin, chromed exhaust pipes, through which a deep throaty rumble seemed to tumble and fill the air. You could feel that beautiful sound in your chest man oh man, what a car!

We were a few blocks down, on the opposite side of the street from the **green house,** trying our best not to look at it, at leastI was. Oren poked me with his elbow, "Hey, isn't that Dickie's dad? He's a cop, isn't he?" he whispered.

"Yeah, I think so," I said as I sneaked a peek, trying not to look like I was looking. Mr. Troop wasn't paying us any mind though; he was standing on the lawn beside the green house deep in conversation with some woman.

CHAPTER 9

Detective Daryl Troop didn't notice the boys stealing glances at him as they walked in his direction. He was busy conferring with Josephine Beach. "Would you mind going over that again, Mrs. Beach?" he asked politely. He was taking notes, and wanted to be sure he had every detail down, and down right. Neither the Chief, nor Detective Brees would be pleased if there were gaps or inconsistencies.

"Well, the young lady who lived there," she inclined her head toward the **green house,** "kept pretty much to herself. No loud parties or anything like that. I believe Danielle Stumply told me she was from um Egypt, or Morocco. Not sure about that though."

"Could it have been Turkey?"

"Yes! It was Turkey. You already knew that?"

"One of the other detectives brought it up at a briefing."

"I guess they have very strict upbringing in those countries. Not like here these days. People don't seem to have the time nor the inclination anymore. Just plop the kids in front of the TV and forget them," she huffed.

"Yes, ma'am, maybe so." He wanted to get her back on track. "You were telling me about something you thought you saw?"

"Oh, yes. Well, I was sitting out on the porch because my husband was listening to some western music program on the radio. It wasn't anything I wanted to listen to," Josephine said primly, "so I came out and was just enjoying the evening quiet when something caught my eye. I think it was a young lady coming up the street. First she was on this side, then she crossed the street, right there, right by the street light, and walked up to that poor girl's house."

"Are you sure it was a female you saw?"

Josephine frowned, closed her eyes, and thought back. "You know, now that you ask, I'm not altogether certain it was a girl. Isn't that strange? At the time, I didn't stare that would have been rude, you know, but there wasn't a question in my mind it was a girl. Now that I concentrate, I can't be certain, I mean I didn't see anything that would tell me for sure, you know, physical attributes."

John studied her face, and felt she was being truthful. "Would you do me a favor, Mrs. Beach?"

"Well, young man, it would depend on what it is."

"Would you sit here, where you sat when the person walked by?"

She nodded, walked over and sat on the front porch swing.

"Now, would you close your eyes again, and try to remember everything about that person, from when you first noticed, uh, him or her? As the person comes into your mind's eye, tell me everything you see. Every detail."

Josephine sat quietly for a little while, then said, "I can't see her whole face, but the profile makes me think she's young."

"What about hair?"

"It's short. Yes! Short and curly."

"What is she wearing?"

"I think it's a short coat. But it could be a sweater, it's black or maybe charcoal grey and wool or flannel slacks."

"You're doing great. How 'bout shoes?"

"Hum. Can't see her feet, but as she crosses the street…looks like flats, maybe loafers. She's walking rather slowly, like she's just out for a stroll."

"Anything else?"

"Yes, maybe. I think I notice hips, not much, but looks like a slender girl's hips, not a boy's."

"How tall?"

"Maybe 5'5" or 5'6"."

"Do you see a purse?"

"I I don't see one."

"What about "

"Oh my God. I just remembered something." She jerked herself erect in the chair, and covered her face with her hands. "She had been to that house earlier! I saw her go up to the door, wait a few minutes, you know, like she had rung the bell and was waiting, then she left, like there had been no answer. But that can't be right! Lilly Jo was home! I saw her come home. I know she was there!"

Troop was on full alert now. *This could be something!* "The same person? Are you sure?"

"Yes. Oh, my. Yes, it was her! That's probably why I didn't really think much about it when she returned later."

"About what time was it?"

"Hard to say, maybe about an hour before I saw her the second time, and that was around 8:30 or so, my husband's program starts at 8:30. Every Wednesday night at 8:30, that blasted program comes on, and he never misses it."

"Did she go in this time?"

"Let me think. Oh yes, my husband called me just then, and I went inside. I just didn't see where she went, Detective."

"Mrs. Beach, thank you. You did very well."

She beamed at his praise. "It's very interesting that well, that I could remember all of this, just by closing my eyes and reliving it in my head."

"I'll tell you, some people are better at it than others, but you're one of the best I've seen. Now, if you think of anything else, no matter how small you may think it is, please, call me," he urged sincerely as he handed her his card.

"I hope you find whoever did this. She was a nice girl," Mrs. Beach said quietly as tears welled in her eyes.

CHAPTER 11

We watched him get into his black '53 Ford Fairlane and pull away.

"Do ya think he'd talk to Dickie, Tony, maybe tell him stuff about what the cops find?"

Tony shrugged.

As they passed Mrs. Beach's house, they saw her watching them through a gap in the curtain. Oren was as jittery as a mouse, "Do you think she saw us out there, Tony? "

"Maybe, I don't know. No, I don't think she saw us, Oren. Calm down, you're gonna have a stroke. If she'd 'uv seen us that night, she'd 'uv told the cops, and they would've come after us. That's why! Now cool it!

"Oren. Have you said anything to anybody ya know, about what we saw? Maybe your aunts?"

"No way! They'd call the cops for sure. You tell anybody?"

"I don't know anybody I'd trust enough," Tony replied sadly.

By unspoken agreement, they dropped the subject and continued on their way.

CHAPTER 12

Chief Allen had called John Brees and Daryl Troop to a debriefing on the Zilke case. Brees and Troop had given their reports, each adding bits of information. These bits and pieces, when placed in context and order, would become the framework into which new bits and pieces could be woven. He entered each piece of information into a matrix he had created on a spreadsheet. The chief had developed the matrix years ago, when he was a detective, and found it was helpful in organizing his thoughts.

Now it was the chief's turn, and he was able to fill in some blank spaces in the victim's profile.

"The family is originally from Turkey. Father's name: Ahmet Zilke, mother's: Kara. There's a brother too, he's thirteen, adopted just before they immigrated. They owned a lot of land in Turkey, grew olives. The political climate was heating up and he sold out, came to the U.S., and settled here, in Wenatchee. That was about twelve years ago. They own a pear orchard in Cashmere, an apple orchard in Pateros, and several houses, one of which was the one Lilly Jo lived in. Mr. Zilke is the manager of the Wenoka Packing Plant. He speaks English Kurdish, and Arabic. Kara has a degree in Chemistry from Oxford. She worked in the food processing business near Ankara, the capital of Turkey. The son, named Ted, goes to school here, gets good grades, and works in the orchards in the summer. Lilly Jo graduated from Wenatchee High at the age of fifteen and attended Seattle University on an academic scholarship. She graduated in two years with a degree in business. At the age of twenty she had earned an MBA from the University of Washington. She was 5'8", brown and red hair, 118 pounds. Not outgoing, but friendly. Beautiful, and she knew it, but wore it with humility; pleasant, and had a smile for everybody. Had an aversion to small talk, always kept herself busy, according to her mother. She had a friend from Seattle U. who came to visit on occasion. His name is Sudhir Kulkrani. Their friendship was platonic, again according to the mother. Had no boyfriend the parents were aware of, few friends, period. Didn't chum around with anybody from work. Her father was her boss. The evening of her death, she had worked late at Wenoka and probably got home somewhere around 7:30 or 8:00."

The Chief, his data shared, paused, sighed, and slowly shook his head, "We will catch the son of a bitch that killed her," he hissed through clenched teeth.

"Did she attend church, Chief?" Daryl queried.

He consulted his notes, "They were non-practicing Sunni Muslims, so…no, she didn't."

"Umm, Chief did she like men? You know?"

"Don't have any info one way or the other, John, but I'm sure we'll find out eventually."

"Reason I asked was the info Trooper got from one of the neighbors. Unknown female went to the door, then left, but came back later. I kinda pictured some kind of tension there. Neighbor said Lilly Jo was home, so either she didn't want to answer, or the other female couldn't get up her courage to ring the bell. Could be a lover's quarrel?"

"Well, John, guess it could be, but at this point there's nothing to support it. We'll not rule it out, though. We'll not ruling anything out, yet. If she did go in the second time, it would put her in the house just before the murder. But I'm leaning towards a male killer."

"Why's that, Chief?"

"Lilly Jo wasn't petite, and put up quite a fight, but the perp was able to overpower her. She broke a couple of nails, might get a blood type, if we're lucky, and the perp might have scratches on his arms or face. The bruising indicates fairly large hands, could be a woman, but more likely not. Females don't, as a general rule, strangle someone with their hands. Maybe a garrote, and maybe by surprise from the back. But the larynx was crushed under the thumbs, so this was done face to face. The bruising was deepest over the larynx and where the fingers interwove at the back of her neck. Big hands."

Detective Troop listened, but was deep in thought. Then he spoke up, "What if this mystery girl was in the house when the killer came in? What if she saw him? Or what if they were working together?"

Mary knocked lightly and came into the room, "Chief, the coroner just called. Seems he found something they'd overlooked before. Looks like a lock of her hair had been cut. Looked like it could have been cut with a knife, not scissors. Might not mean anything but, he wanted you to know. It was cut from the back of her head, and so close that it wasn't, well,part of her hairstyle. They went back over the bedclothes and found some tiny bits of her hair there too. He's sending you a picture and a supplemental report."

"Thanks, Mary."

"Trophy? Souvenir?" John mused.

As they digested and logged this new piece of information, Mary returned to advise the Chief that his meeting with the Detective from Seattle was in five minutes. He excused himself, went to his office and just sat for a minute. I think I'm getting too old for this stuff, he thought sadly, then brushed the thought away as his mind returned to the puzzle at hand. He was a puzzle "freak" and worked all different kinds; maybe that's why he really loved his job. At times it was just one big puzzle after another.

He heard movement in the hall and turned to see Mary showing a sturdy, rather tall, very attractive black woman into the his office.

"Chief Allen, this is Detective Delia Louise Fontaine," Mary announced, as Detective Fontaine extended her hand.

"Nice to meet you, Chief, and thank you for meeting with me on such short notice."

"Detective Fontaine, pleased to meet you. Have a seat and tell me how I can be of assistance to the Seattle Police Department."

"Oh...well this is on more of a personal level, Chief. I'm in Wenatchee to question a person of interest in one of our cases. He moved to Wenatchee recently. Turns out he has an ironclad story, and couldn't have been involved. I volunteered to come over because my parents have always talked about Wenatchee, and how much they liked its tranquility. Guess it's not quite as tranquil as they remember, from what I read in your paper last night."

He chuckled, "This isn't something that happens very often around here. But, well, anywhere you've got people, you've got the same problems. It's just a matter of scale."

"All too true," she agreed quietly. "I'm here because I promised my mom I would check into the Wenatchee Police Department, see if you have any vacant positions, or maybe something coming up. I wanted to get a feel for the atmosphere here. I know I'm a novelty as a detective, heck, even as an officer. But I'm not looking for any slack. I'm good at my job, work hard, and pull my own weight, sir. So I guess you could say that I'm just touching base, to see how you might feel if I were to apply for a position here."

The chief considered her quietly, and looked her straight in the eye. He studied her as he gathered his thoughts.

"You're a pioneer in the field, Detective Fontaine. Since you have progressed to the rank of Detective, I can assume you were a good Officer. I can also assume that you have endured all of the demeaning treatment that goes with being a rookie, and the sly comments, innuendos and pranks that can be directed at a woman rookie. It was probably worse in the larger PD than it would have been here, but still. it goes on, to some extent, everywhere. Add to that those who take your color as some kind of permission to be abusive. In spite of surviving what must have been more challenging than many Officers could tolerate, I sense no resentment in you. You appear to be comfortable with yourself, and mature beyond your years."

Fontaine cocked her head, "You're right, Chief. I've had run-ins with my share of bigots, from both sides of the color line. My father is black. He's on the job too, and my mother is white. I am what I am. I grew up learning to respect myself, and ignore the hate mongers, of all types. It's pretty hard to get my goat." She grinned wryly.

Chief Allen considered the self-assured, attractive, soft-spoken young woman who was telling him she could handle most anything thrown her way.

"Detective Fontaine, are you happy with your job in Seattle?"

"I love it, Chief. But I've lived there my whole life. A change of scenery wouldn't hurt, and with my parents talking about getting a summer home here, or maybe Chelan, well I thought if I liked this area, it is a little warmer and dryer than Seattle, maybe I could make a move over here. I'm a good cop, Chief. Dad says I've got the hide of an alligator, and Mom thinks I've got the patience of a saint. So, back to my question, how might you feel about my chances if I were to apply for a position here?"

He chuckled, "You are direct, aren't you? Let me put it this way, if your name were to come up on a hiring list, I would consider it a pleasure to interview you for the job. It is my aim to put the people best able to serve the community on the streets of Wenatchee. In my book neither gender, nor ethnicity adds to, nor detracts from, a good police officer's qualifications."

"Thanks, Chief Allen. I appreciate your time, and your candor." She hesitated at the door, and turned back, "I hope you get a break in your case and find your bad guy soon. I know how tough it can be when you know they're still out there."

Delia stopped at Mary's desk and asked where she could get an application.

"I've got some in my desk, Detective. Just a sec." Mary placed a couple of forms in an envelope and handed it to Delia, along with a warm smile.

"Who was that?" Daryl whispered to Mary as he watched her cross the parking lot.

"That," she whispered back, "is Detective Fontaine. Quite a looker isn't she?"

"Boy, I'll say! She could stop traffic without even trying."

"Hey! You're married, Daryl," she teased.

"True. But I'm not dead."

CHAPTER 13

Four weeks later. Thursday, June 10, 1954. Oren had just wandered over, and we were looking for something to do. The fruit picking season was 'bout over and I didn't have to go to the orchard today.

"Mo-o-o-o-m, we're gonna go get a Dusty Burger. See ya later."

"You riding your bike, Tony?"

"Yeah."

"No riding on the handlebars. You hear me?" Mom ordered sternly.

"Yeah, I hear ya."

"I mean it!"

"How come she always tells you that?" Oren asked quietly as they left the house.

"Oh man! Once I gave Peter a ride and he was messin' around and fell off. We thought he'd broken his arm. So…no more rides on the handlebars, for anybody, any time, anywhere."

We took off down the street, I was riding my bike and Oren walked beside until we turned the corner. Then he jumped up on the handlebars and we were off down Chelan Street.

"Is this a JC Higgins bike?"

"Naaaaa. It's a Schwinn, you dummy. They're the best. Saved up and bought it new 'bout two years ago. Cost $24.95," I told him proudly.

"Man! Where did you get that much money?"

"Mowing lawns mostly. Helped my dad top some trees, and then what I earned picking fruit. Took a long time to save that much, but it was worth it."

Now, it wasn't that Oren couldn't hold on to a dime. Like I said, he usually had more spending money than I did, but he usually spent it as soon as he got it. Like today, he had just gotten his allowance and suggested we go to the movies. We rode by the Vitaphone theatre and saw "Singing in the Rain," starring Gene Kelly. Then by the Liberty where the movie "Citizen Caine," was playing. We didn't want to see either one. I asked Oren what he thought of Orson Welles.

"I dunno. Guess ya gotta be older to understand him. Way over my head. Mrs. Owens, ya know, the art teacher, she thinks he's great. I mean, I can understand Gene Kelly better. He sings, and he dances great, and looks like he's havin' a good time. But Orson Welles, he just talks, and I don't understand half of what he's sayin'."

As we approached the Owl drugstore we spotted Fred Weston leaning against the building, his foot up behind him, against the wall. I said "hi," but he just looked at us like we weren't really there.

"You know him?" Oren whispered, surprise in his voice.

"My older brothers do, and I've heard them talk about him. His dad's a doctor, and I think he owns the Owl."

"Must be rich."

"Yeah, I guess."

Then we ran into Steve Balder. We'd pal around with Steve sometimes, and he was OK. He wanted to know what we were up to. We told him, and he asked if he could go to Dusty's with us. We walked with him to the Buster Brown Shoe Store to pick up his bike. As we walked past the Cascade Hotel, we couldn't believe our eyes when we saw Doreen Morrow, the Apple Blossom Queen, coming toward us. Man oh man! She was a beautiful sight in her red dress and high heel shoes. Near took our breath away.

"What a babe!" Steve whispered, as she got closer. "She could be a movie star."

"Yeah, a movie star," we agreed from the depths of our near trance.

"Hi," she purred as she floated past the three of us, just standing there with our mouths hanging open. Well, they probably weren't hanging open, but it sure felt that way when a semblance of reason started to return.

When we were able to think again, we headed for Dusty's. Steve wanted to stop in Penny's. He was under instructions from his mom to bring home some T-shirts.

"Just don't take too long, I'm hungry, man."

He picked up on the annoyance in my voice and shot back "Hey! I'll just be a sec. OK?"

That was Steve Balder, all right, he was one of those guys that always had to do something when he tagged along. I mean here we were going to Dusty's to get a burger and he asks to come along, but he's gotta stop to get something. The last time he did this was when we saw him and we were going swimming at the big pool by the river and he had to spend forty five minutes looking for a nose plug. Anyway that was Steve Balder, always holding us up.

My eyes rolled, but Steve was already headed through the door. "I mean, he invites himself along, then, like always, has to do something that slows us up. Right, Oren?"

"Seems like it."

We cooled our heels on the sidewalk outside Penny's while I fumed, and Oren kept quiet.

"Look, Tony. There goes one of the Gwinn twins. Man, I love that Olds. Can you believe that that's the original paint job? I mean it's a '49 and it looks like new. He told me he has some kind of special wax he uses. Prob'ly waxes it every week."

"Someday you'll have a great car, Oren."

"Think so?"

"Sure. I heard Sam Dale got a '41 Ford on his birthday, from his dad. Cherry all the way."

"What about you, Tony? What kind'a car you gonna get?"

"Don't know. Cars aren't really my thing, tho. Guess I'll just borrow one from one of my brothers if I ever need one."

We started down the street when Steve came out the door and he ran to catch up. "Guess who I saw in there?" he asked with a smug grin.

I rolled my eyes, "dunno. Who?"

"Ted Zilke!" he announced.

Well, that got our attention! I shot a glance at Oren, as he shot one back at me. Then we both zeroed in on Steve, but he wasn't looking our way. Darn good thing too, we looked like we had seen a ghost.

"So?" Oren had recovered enough to ask with a show of nonchalance.

"Well, that's why I took so long. Know what he told me?"

"Steve," I said, trying to put a note of annoyance in my voice, like I really didn't care, but my insides were knotted up tight as...well, I don't know what, "how the heck would we know what he said?"

Now he got closer and looked over his shoulder, ya know, like he didn't want anybody else to hear. Definitely playing it up for all it was worth, cause there wasn't anybody else on the whole block. "He said the police found a bunch of footprints around his sister's house. Some of 'em were under her bedroom window too."

Oren looked like he was gonna barf, turned kinda green, and I probably didn't look much better. My heart was pounding almost as hard as it had been on that night.

"Ted said they came to his house and looked at his shoes, mostly his tennis shoes. Looked at all of his dad's too."

"Oh my gosh! Why'd they do that? They weren't" Oren blurted, but managed to cut himself off when he looked at me.

"Cops said they needed to 'eliminate' 'em. Guess that means rule 'em out. Anyway, they still don't have any new leads or anything. Poor guy, he's all torn up."

Well, we went on to Dusty's and ate, but my heart wasn't in it anymore, and that beautiful, juicy, fat burger could have been a sack of rocks.

We got there later than we had planned and had to settle for a booth inside. "What's wrong with you guys?" Steve wanted to know. "You keep looking like you're gonna, gonna, I don't know, explode or somethin'. What's up?"

"Nothin' wrong with me," Oren sort'a sneered, "maybe it's you."

They glared at each other across the small table. "Hey. Guys. Cool out. Let's just play some music and have some lunch," I urged, as I dug in my Levi's for a quarter.

The tension eased as we looked through the choices on the small music selections box on our table, and finally agreed on which three songs to play. The big old Wurlitzer across the room came to life, pulled out the first record and "Sha Boom, Sha Boom, ya da da da da da da da da da boom Sha Boom," soon filled the room.

Barb, a schoolmate who worked at Dusty's part time, came over to take our order. "Hey guys, what are you up to?"

"Just came down to see you, Barb," Steve crooned with a sly smile.

"Wise ass," Oren whispered, as Barb headed back to turn the order in.

"Just jokin', what's the problem?"

"Barb's a sweet chick. She doesn't like that shit, Steve."

"I didn't mean nothing bad. I think she's kinda cute."

"Hey, guys, check out the Stude that just pulled in. I think it's a '48," I interjected as I watched the car pulling into the lot.

"I heard that a '48 Stude took Matthew's '53 Olds on the Avenue last week," Oren chirped, "wonder if that's the one."

"From a dead start?"

"Yeah? Nah. They were on the Avenue, down by the roller rink. Matthew just kept egging him on and finally the old guy in the Stude just stomped on it, so did Matthew, and away they went. The Stude pulled ahead and was out in front when they got to the curve just before the bridge. That's where Matthew broke it off and came back, laughing his head off that he had been taken by the old guy."

We worked our way through our Dusty Burgers and fries and looked at the check. Steve checked his pockets and asked, "Can I borrow thirty cents from one of you guys?"

"You gotta be kidding," Oren said indignantly.

"Well, no. I've only got three cents in my pocket."

"And that's our problem?" I responded irritated.

"I'll pay you back. You know I'm good for it."

"You still owe me five cents for a Mound's bar I got you."

"OK, so I'll owe you forty cents. I'll pay you back. Promise."

"I'll cover it," I jumped in. Anything at this point, just to keep the peace. I pulled out thirty-five cents and passed it to Steve. "Don't forget, now you owe me thirty-five cents, and Oren a nickel," I shook my index finger in Steve's face, underscoring the reminder.

"Hey Tony I thought we were friends," Steve whined.

"Yeah, we are. Just don't forget."

"Hey, Tony! Did you get up on the wrong side of the bed today? What're you jumpin' all over me for?"

Oren was looking out the window, acting like he wasn't involved. Steve's gaze went back and forth between us. Then he slid out of the booth.

"Oh, sit, Steve. I know you'll come up with the money. It's just that I'm kinda broke right now. That's all."

"Sorry, Tony. I'll get it to you in a couple days. You got a job for the summer?"

"Yeah."

"What're you gonna do?"

"Pick cherries with my brother, Renie."

"How do they work that? I mean, how do you get paid? Like, by the hour, or what?"

"By the pound."

"So how do they know how many pounds you pick?"

"Come on, Steve," I sneered.

"Seriously, I don't know a thing about picking cherries. How does it work?"

"They pay five cents a pound. You pick the cherries, put 'em in a bucket, empty the buckets into a box called a lug. They hold 'bout forty pounds. No more or the cherries get bruised. When you fill a box, they weight on a scale under your name and at the end of the day, pay you $2.00 a box."

" How many boxes can you pick in a day?"

"Depends. If the trees have a lot of fruit we can pick thirty-five or forty boxes."

"That's a lot of cherries! Ever fall off a ladder?"

"Yeah, and out of trees, too. Sometimes ya gotta climb on the branches to get to the cherries on the inside. But never got really hurt, always finished out the day."

Oren, clearly bored with Steve, and the conversation, stood and stretched to convey his thinly veiled irritation, "Hey, you guys 'bout ready to go?"

We were, and we did.

CHAPTER 14

That day, after we parted ways with Steve, we just couldn't stop doing the "what if" thing. You know, "what if they figure out some of those footprints are ours?" or "what if somebody saw us?" or "what if we went to the cops and told 'em what we saw?" But in the end, we just walked.

Down the street a ways, toward the bridge, we saw Jimmy Speed. Now Jimmy turned up now and again, always pulling a little red wagon, just like he was today. Maybe there's somebody like him in your town. You think of him when you see him, and if you don't, you don't. Nobody seemed to know where he came from, or where his family was. It was kinda like he just appeared, as if by magic.

Can't tell you how old he was, but he had whiskers, so he was older than us. Today he was wearing a Wenatchee Chief's baseball cap pulled down tight on his head so that his ears were bent over and sticking out. He had a white sleeveless T-shirt, tan shorts, and ankle high military type shoes with no socks. At about 5 feet tall and 150 pounds, he was a little stocky. Most of his bulk seemed to be concentrated around his middle.

As the gap between us closed, Jimmy smiled and stuck out his hand to Oren, and then to me. Kinda had to think twice about shaking it, but we both did, in the end. In the meantime, with his other arm he was gesturing toward something behind him, blithering in his other world language. It must have been funny, cause then he giggled I think it was a giggle, then went on with his almost word words. We didn't understand a bit of it. Abruptly he said something that could have almost been "bye" and waved as he hurried off toward town.

Oren chuckled, shook his head and asked if I knew where Speedy lived. I didn't, but once, when one of my brothers and I had gone down to the river to fish for Steelheads, I had seen him sleeping in a make-shift shack made of cardboard boxes, his little red wagon right beside him. As I remember, he was around for a year or so, then just…wasn't. Never knew what happened to him, maybe he went someplace a little warmer than here. I know I woulda if I had to sleep outside.

CHAPTER 15

"Hey, there's the neighbor," Oren whispered as we approached the Zilke house.

"Yeah. Think she's watching us?" I queried nervously. "Just act natural."

"Hi, there," Mrs. Stumply greeted us. Oren stiffened like he'd been hit by lightning, and I wasn't much better off, but we tried our best to look casual. "You boys must live close by. I've seen you before."

Now that was just what we didn't want to hear. Wild thoughts were running through our heads. When had she seen us? What was she up to? Get us to confess? Confess to what? Oren recovered first and offered, "I just live a couple blocks from here, at Alaska and Yakima."

"And you? You live close, too?"

By now Tony had regained the power of speech, "On Stevens and Cashmere, ma'am."

"Like I said, I've seen you before, but since the, um, um. Oh, I guess you've heard about what happened here," she inclined her head toward the Zilke house.

"Yes, ma'am," we replied in unison.

"Anyway, since then, I've tried to be a little more aware of who's in the neighborhood. Maybe get to know my neighbors better. A detective came by and was asking his questions, you know, and I realized I hardly knew anybody's name, so this is me trying to get to know my neighbors better."

We just nodded and stood there. Mrs. Stumply seemed like she didn't know what else to say and found herself looking at Lilly Jo's house. "Did you know Lilly Jo?"

"I think one of my older brothers knew who she was. They weren't friends or anything, though. He just remembered her from high school."

I think she sensed our discomfort. "Guess you boys are on your way to town, so I'll...oh my goodness, how rude of me. My name is Danielle Stumply." She held her hand out to us in turn.

"Tony Maringuez, ma'am."

"Oren Brown, Mrs. Stumply."

"Maringuez, that's a Spanish name, isn't it?"

I nodded.

"Does your mother go to St. Joseph's? Yes! Oh, yes, I've seen you before. You're an altar boy. You say Mass with Father O'Sullivan, don't you. You're one of Lucy's sons. She told me once how pleased she was that your friend, Oren, was also an altar boy. Ohhhh, she's very proud of you, Tony."

Mrs. Stumply seemed so pleased that she knew something about us, and invited us in for iced tea.

"Thank you, ma'am, but we really should be going," Oren stammered.

"Really? Oh, come on and have just a small glass. It is a warm day. Please come in."

We looked at each other, and knew we were trapped. Adults are like that, you know. Even when you have important stuff to do, like have a root beer float, or something, they can make you do what they think you should be doing. So off we went for iced tea.

There we were. Sitting in her tiny immaculate kitchen with small glasses of iced tea. Danielle went on and on about her husband and stuff while we tried to hold up their end of the conversation, when her eyes sort of glazed over and she seemed lost in thought.

HERE "That detective…he found a salt shaker in the back yard."

"A salt shaker? In your back yard?" Oren asked weakly.

"No, not mine. In that poor girl's yard. Now what in the world would a killer be doing with a salt shaker? They're probably gonna see if there are any fingerprints on it."

"You they, think it was that the killer's?" Tony ventured tenuously.

She looked at me blankly and then it seemed that she came back to herself, like she was awakening from a dream, …or something, "Would you like some more tea, Tony? I have plenty." She turned to the refrigerator.

Oren took that opportunity to mime desperately that the shaker was his. I nodded and turned my gaze back to Mrs. Stumply, "No, thank you, ma'am."

"Oren?"

"Uh, no, thank you," he was able to get out in an almost natural tone, but I'll bet his heart was pumping like it was trying to escape.

"Josephine Beach across the street was telling me she thinks she saw a young woman go into Lilly Jo's house that night. Can you believe it?"

Our eyes widened and we looked at each other in disbelief.

I recovered first, "Mrs. Stumply, should you be telling us this stuff?"

"Well, I wasn't told not to tell anyone."

"You're not thinking it was a woman that killed her, are you?"

"I don't know. But if Josephine Beach said there was a woman in the house, maybe it was. Women kill too, don't you think?"

"But, why?"

"Oh, gracious, jealousy, over a man, envy, hate, maybe even love. Why does anybody kill?"

"I suppose so, Mrs. Stumply," I said without conviction.

"I shouldn't be going on and on about it, but it was just such a shock when Detective Brees mentioned it," she said sheepishly as she rejoined us at the table, sat, and folded her hands in front of her.

"Today when I saw you boys walking by, I actually thought I might have seen you that night outside her window."

Wow, what a bombshell! If we'd been nervous before, now we were nearing panic. I was sure my terrified expression, though I think I got it quickly under control, had given us away.

"But when I learned who you were, I realized it couldn't have been you. I told the detective I wasn't sure I saw anybody at the window at all. It was just an impression. I'm ashamed of myself for even thinking it might have been you."

No one spoke for a few seconds, then, as if by mutual consent, rose in unison and Mrs. Stumply went to the door.

"I'm so glad to have met you both. Hope you weren't too bored by the chatter of an old lady, but I feel a lot better. Guess I just needed to say some of that stuff out loud. Again, thank you for being so nice to a blithering old lady, and do stop in for tea again. Any time. I'd be happy for the company."

We left quietly and smiled politely at the lonely lady, each making a personal commitment to stop by every once in a while, just to touch base.

"Wow! Can you believe that, Tony?"

"She actually saw us!"

"What about my salt shaker? What if they do find fingerprints?"

"What about the girl?"

"You know, Tony, I actually thought I saw movement behind that guy when he was coming down the hall."

"Movement? What kind of movement? Why didn't you say something?"

Now Oren looked ashamed. "I dunno. Wasn't sure. It was like maybe a door opened or closed just a couple inches. It was kinda like a shadow in the background changed…just a little. I'm not sure it was anything."

"Ya know? We gotta door does that when somebody doesn't latch it. Kinda opens and closes on its own, kinda like the house is breathin'. It's creepy!"

"Prob'ly out of balance or something."

"Maybe that's what I saw, or thought I saw. I was so freaked out it could've been nothing."

"Maybe, or maybe it was like a room or a closet."

A light went on in Oren's eyes. "Could be that lady hid in a closet when she heard that guy come in the front door."

CHAPTER 16

"Mornin', Mary. Would you tell the chief I'm going out to interview the Plants? They're back from …wherever."

"Sure thing, Detective."

John Brees left the station and drove through the peaceful, sun-drenched town to the Plants neat little house. There was a maroon '50 Ford parked in the driveway.

"George! There's a police car out front," Nelda called out to her husband, who was trying to enjoy his coffee and newspaper at the kitchen table.

She watched as the plainclothes officer got out of his car and started up their walk. "He's comin' here, George! Wonder what's going on."

"Maybe 'bout that girl got killed," George speculated, dourly.

"Well, I certainly hope so!"

"What's that supposed to mean?"

"Nothing, George."

"Woman, why do you insist on provoking me?"

"Keep your voice down, George! He's on the porch," she whispered, as she moved to open the door.

The detective was greeted by a tiny, rail thin bundle of curiosity, with short, perm'd white hair and piercing eyes.

"Good morning. I'm Detective Brees from the Wenatchee Police Department," he said quietly as he displayed his badge. "Might I have a few minutes of your time, Mrs. Plant?"

"Certainly, Officer. Please come in, "George, could you come in here, please?" she called.

Detective Brees watched as six feet and two hundred pounds of fuzzy faced, rumpled, grumpy George shuffled into the room.

"Morning, Mr. Plant."

"Yeah. What can we do for you, Detective?"

"I'd like to ask you about Lilly Jo Zilke, if you don't mind."

"Don't know nothing'," he snarled.

"Well, you might know more than you think, sir." He turned to Nelda, "Would you mind if we sat down?"

"Oh! Of course. Please," she gestured toward the worn sofa.

"Thank you. It's just easier to take notes that way." Brees smiled warmly at her.

"May I offer you a cup of coffee, Officer?"

"Thank you, ma'am. Black, please."

Nelda scampered from the room and Brees turned to the still-standing George. He would have his work cut out for him with this guy, but this was the kind of stuff Brees was good at, winning over the belligerent.

"What kind of work do you do, Mr. Plant?"

"Construction."

"What kind?"

"Lately, mostly at the Rocky Ridge Dam. Big job, that one."

"I've been by and watched what you guys are doin' out there. Fascinating! looks dangerous, all the ropes, and scaffolds, and heavy equipment. Wasn't there an accident up there recently?"

"Yup. But it wasn't one of our guys. Some concrete contractor got sloppy. Lucky he didn't kill his own crew. "I didn't kill that girl, Detective."

"Oh, no. I'm sure you didn't, Mr. Plant.

"Here's your coffee, Officer, and I thought you might like a doughnut to go with it," Nelda announced as she placed a tray on the coffee table.

"Nelda, he's not an officer," George rolled his eyes and corrected impatiently, "he's a detective!"

"Oh, my! Didn't mean anything, Off...Detective Brees. I'll try to remember," she promised as she arranged napkins, forks, and small plates.

"Thank you, ma'am, and that doughnut'll go good right about now." He winked at George. "Noticed you can see the Zilke house from your porch."

"Yup---well not all of the house. Mrs. Stumply's house is in the way," George responded.

Nelda piped up, "We can see it from the side bedroom, too. Let me show you." George rolled his eyes as she scurried to the doorway.

The room was sparsely furnished, just a bed, nightstand and a dresser. There was a window that faced Lilly Jo's, and only about fifty yards separated the two houses.

Brees moved to the window, and saw that the windows of the two houses were almost directly in line, one with the other. His eyes fell to the nightstand, and held there. Nelda followed his gaze and saw what had captured his attention.

"Oh, those. Those're George's. Calls them his 'night eyes', but he looks through them in the daytime, too," she grinned innocently.

John looked into the living room. George was sitting on the couch, his head laid back, looking at the ceiling. "Mr. Plant, could I ask you to come in here, sir?"

George struggled to his feet and shuffled to the doorway, "Yeah, what is it?"

"Are these your 'night eyes'?" Brees indicated with his hand.

"Nelda!"

"Well. That's what you always call them, George," she announced smugly.

"Yeah. They're mine. Like to look at the stars, 'n stuff, sometimes."

"It's OK, Mr. Plant. I was just wondering though, sometimes when you're looking at the stars and stuff, do you happen to see other things? Things going on in the neighborhood?"

"Well yeah, sometimes," he admitted sheepishly. "But I don't spy on nobody!"

"No, I'm sure you wouldn't do that. But maybe you happened to see something on that Wednesday evening? Something out of the ordinary?"

George tilted his head back and made a show of trying to remember, "Nooooo, not really."

"Geeeooorrrge," Nelda chided, and wagged her finger at him.

Poor George looked away, and around, and finally at the floor. "I didn't see anything in that house. The shades were down," he finally admitted.

"Go on, George," Nelda scolded.

"Well...this isn't for sure, understand, but I can tell you what I thought I saw."

"Please. Any little thing you can tell me could be crucial. It's really important."

"Ok. OK. I think I saw a couple 'a guys peeking in her window. She'd pulled the shade down, but there was a couple 'a inches at the bottom where the light was comin' through. Looked like two guys was peekin' in through that crack."

John's interest level soared. *This could be something!* "What were they wearing?"

"Couldn't tell, it was too dark."

"Hats? Were they wearing hats?"

"Nooooo. Don't think so."

"Anything else you can think of? Anything? Were they adults, kids, male, female, tall, short?"

"Only got a gut feeling, and that it was guys. Don't know nothin' 'bout how tall, or how old. Just wasn't enough light."

"Have either of you ever seen anyone at her house? Visitors?"

"Only one I ever saw was her father. He's a big shot down at Wenoka Growers, ya know," Nelda said with a smug grin, and a head bob.

Brees looked over his notes, making sure he had covered everything, when there was a knock at the front door.

"Hi, Danielle," Nelda greeted, as she ushered her into the house.

"Nelda, I need to speak to Detective Brees."

"Mrs. Stumply, it's good to see you again. You have something for me?" John prompted.

"It's probably nothing, and I was arguing with myself about coming over here at all, but oh, my. I feel ridiculous."

"No such thing. You never know what will turn out to be important.

Her eyes darted around the room, and she wrung her hands. John, a little slow on the uptake, realized she might not be comfortable talking with him here, in the Plant's living room. "Would you feel more comfortable at your house?"

"No no, that's not a problem. It's just that I'm not sure I should be telling this at all. I mean I know that small things can be important, but I don't see how this could be. She looked around trying to think if she should even be here. Finally.

"It was about six weeks ago. I had taken some cookies to Mrs. Stanley, and was walking home. It was about dusk, and I don't see as well as I used to, you know. Anyway, I saw this car parked on the street, facing south. Well there was a man sitting it that car. Just sitting there.

"Good grief, this is silly. It sounds so ridiculous now. He wasn't doing anything wrong, just sitting there."

"What kind of car was it?"

"Oh, well, that's easy. I noticed it 'cause it was the same model as my mother's last car, a Hudson, green and black. My mother's was a different color though.

"Guess one of the things that really brought it to mind after your visit, though, was the way he acted when I walked by. When I got up to the car, he turned his head away from me. I just got the feeling he didn't want me to see his face.

"The other thing is that last evening, while I was watering my garden, I saw a green and black Hudson go by, and I swear, it seemed to slow down when it went by Lilly Jo's house."

She took a huge breath, and seemed to relax as she let it out. "See! I told you it was probably nothing, but I do feel better for the telling."

Brees knelt in front of Danielle, took her hands and looked her straight in the eyes, "Quite the contrary, Mrs Stumply. I believe you may have given us a very important bit of information. Very important."

Danielle beamed.

CHAPTER 17

Harold Slick Jr. was seventy-two inches tall, with dark wavy hair, and coffee-brown, menacing eyes, thin and wiry but not skinny. Had a disposition like a stepped on rattlesnake. Junior was definitely a loner unless you liked to be disrespected.

His father had abused, taunted and beaten him even more fiercely from the time his mother quietly left the family, years before. She left without her sons because he had threatened her more than once that if she ever decided to leave, she had best leave alone.

"You leave, you leave alone, bitch, or I'll hunt you down and kill you," he threatened. She believed him.

When Harold, Jr. grew old enough to hit back, he did. He lived for the day when he would pay his father back for all the pummeling, the vicious tirades, the poundings with his feet, fists, or whatever he happened to have in his hands at the moment.

The story that went around, from those who knew the family, was that Junior had watched and waited for his father to get drunk enough, then, beat him to within an inch of his life. He took out all of his considerable, stored up rage, took Harold down to Malaga, laid him on the heavily used Great Northern railroad track, and just walked away.

Dewey Slick, the younger brother, wasn't around to assist his older brother. He surely would have, but he had been living in Chelan with their Uncle Bert, his mother's brother, for several years. Harold, mean bastard that he was, had enough sense not to try to face down his brother-in-law.

Dewey's mother had managed to get him out of the house when he was just twelve. She waited till the old man was well on his way to getting blotto, but still in an expansive frame of mind, then suggested Dewey should go visit his uncle.

Harold, not too swift to begin with, and feeling drunkenly

generous, went along with it. She packed Dewey up and got him to Chelan that night, and he had never returned.

Dewey lived a pleasant, if not a spartan, existence. He eventually learned it was OK to talk to his aunt and uncle. They didn't go ballistic if he happened to say the wrong thing, or laugh out loud. He did well in school, was good with machinery, always tinkered with whatever he could get his hands on. His dream, fostered by his uncle, was to become a truck mechanic. Those monster eighteen-wheelers drew him like a magnet.

Dewey worked hard, learned his trade, and got a job working on trucks. He saved his money and, after a few months, moved into a small cottage behind his boss's home. He was quiet, didn't have any friends, and was comfortable being on his own. Old Harold's early, violent lessons were still there, lurking just below the level of conscious thought. Although Dewey didn't really think about the whys, he felt it was just safer not to put himself in harm's way, and, somehow, contact with other people could be dangerous.

Harold Jr. and Dewey didn't have much contact, though they sometimes bumped into each other unexpectedly. Their relationship was distant; mostly due to Junior's outlook on life, which was too much like their father's. He was often in fights, and was no stranger to the jail. Though they were a few years difference in

age, as adults they looked very much alike, and were sometimes mistaken for one another, much to Dewey's dismay.

CHAPTER 18

Harold Slick Junior swaggered into the Lighthouse Tavern at the south end of Wenatchee Avenue and sat down beside an older man who was drinking an Olympia beer. Junior was feeling good today and, quite uncharacteristically, friendly.

"Buy you an Oly, old man?" he offered, noticing his bottle was almost empty.

"Sure. Thanks. My name's Ken Bell," the man said and extended his hand.

"Harold Slick, Junior. You can call me Hal or Junior."

"Yeah, you could be Harold Slick's boy," the man nodded as he looked at him more closely.

"You knew my dad?"

"I did—didn't like him much, though."

"Oh? Why's that?" Junior asked slyly.

"I don't mean no offense to you, son, but your dad was the meanest son-of-bitch I ever knew. Cold heart, fiery temper and just plain damn mean," the older man said.

Harold looked into the mirror above the bar and pulled a long drink from his beer. "Yup, you knew my old man all right. See this scar on my temple?" Harold pulled his hair back. "He gave me that when I was eleven years old; broke my left arm when I was thirteen; broke my nose more times than I can count; stuck a six inch knife through the left cheek of my ass, big scar there. Never had a full set of teeth till after he died."

"Heard he had an accident down in Malaga a few years ago."

"Well, you heard right. Guess he got so drunk he passed out on the Great Northern railroad tracks. The trains made hamburger out of him," Junior laughed and slapped the old man on the back. He was laughing so hard the man on the other side of Ken Bell leaned forward and smiled, " musta been a pretty funny joke."

"Yes sir, it was funny," Junior said still smiling, "You see Mr. Bell, I had been wishing for that to happen to my father from the first beating I ever got from that mean son-of-bitch 'til it finally happened. You know that saying, 'be careful what you wish for, 'cause it could come true?' Well, guess this time it did."

A small, pale, slightly mousy lady wearing a blue cape came walking down the bar, speaking to anyone who would listen, "God loves you, God loves all of us."

The patrons kept their backs to the little Christian lady, no one acknowledged her, hoping she would go away. As she reached the end of the bar, the bartender walked over to her.

"Miss," he called quietly as she looked over to the card tables, "Excuse me, Miss."

She turned and set her eyes on the man behind the counter.

"Either buy a beer and sit down or I'm going to have to ask you to leave the premises," he ordered.

She looked at the bartender, then at the young man sitting on the next to last stool, then back to the bartender. "I'll have whatever this young man is drinking, please." She hiked herself up on the barstool next to Junior.

Junior acted like he hadn't heard the conversation between the bartender and the lady.

"God loves you, son. You just need to let him into your life, that's all," she said softly to Junior. He said nothing and took another hit of his beer.

"When was the last time you were in a church, young man?" she asked, staring up at him.

"Lady, you're talking to the wrong guy here," he sneered as he started to slide off his stool and move to another part of the tavern. She reached over and put her right hand on his left forearm. He stopped cold and glared at her with hellfire itself burning from his eyes.

"Who is this God you're talkin' 'bout, lady?" he sneered.

She saw the hardness and the anger in his face. He looked like a wolf defending his kill. She seemed a bit chilled, but bravely responded, even though her voice trembled, "He...He sees all things, He knows all things."

"He sees all things?" Junior barked.

"Yes, yes he does," her eyes were welling up with tears.

Junior looked her straight in her eye. "Then he prob'ly saw all the damn beatings I took from my old man. All the times that bastard's belt turned my back to bloody welts. I can still feel that buckle across my face and my back, the cowardly, drunken, son-of-bitch. Your God watched all of that shit for years? Is that what you're saying lady? Is that what you're saying? All the times he kicked me? You sayin' He watched while I pissed myself every damn time that bastard opened the bedroom door 'n come in and pummeled me till he passed out? Is that your God that sees everything lady?"

"Put a lid on it buddy. You're getting center stage here, watch it, OK?" the bartender said quietly to Junior.

"Are you saying this God loves me?" Junior's glare pierced into the ladies wilting, tearing, sad eyes. "I don't think so, lady!"

Tears ran down her face and she began to inch her foot toward the floor.

"If your God loves me, why didn't he stop all that shit that happened to me? What kind of God would allow all that?"

Her foot found the floor and she slid off the barstool, walked quietly down the bar, sobbing, and exited the tavern.

Harold was so upset with that do-gooder he didn't even finish his beer. He stepped outside and his gaze followed the lady across the street. Should he trail her and find out where she lived? He decided it wasn't worth the effort, turned and walked waveringly down the avenue until he reached Skagit and decided to cross.

"You dirty bitch!" he shouted inappropriately to no one.

"You all right, Sir?" a man asked from behind him.

"Fuck you! What's your problem?"

The man retreated a few steps and watched Harold walk across the street. He decided to wait for the next light.

CHAPTER 19

I brought in the last of the groceries and set the bags on the kitchen table.

"Mom, I want to ask you a question…about the confessional box, OK? Now I didn't do anything bad or anything, it's for a friend of mine."

"Who, Oren?"

"Mom, not Oren, OK? Maybe I should go to Father O'Sullivan."

"So what's your question?"

"You know when you go to confession and you confess your sins?"

"Yes, yes, go on."

"Can a priest be forced to tell anyone, anyone at all?"

"No."

"Even the police, if they ask him?"

"No one, he cannot tell anyone."

"What if he goes to court and he has to swear on the Bible to tell the whole truth, even then?"

"Even then," Mom said looking into his eyes with that look only mothers can get. "Are you in some kind of trouble?"

"No Mom, I'm not. I told you, I'm helping a friend find out about confessing sins."

"Tony, the Catholic priests are exempt, I think that's the right word. Anyhow, they don't have to discuss anything said in the confessional box. Actually, they can't discuss it, period."

"OK,"I nodded. Thanks Mom, that's all I wanted to know."

"Speaking of, are you going to confession on Saturday?"

"I haven't done anything wrong to have to go."

"You go to confession on Saturday! Hear me? Don't you forget!"

"OK. OK. I gotta go, see you later."

"I want you to go to Communion on Sunday," she called as I scampered out the back door.

My mind was churning as I walked up to the Catholic Church on the corner of Chelan and Spokane. I stopped outside the rectory and suddenly felt the pangs of cold feet. What if Father O'Sullivan started asking questions like mom had?

Then, as if by fate, Father O'Sullivan walked out of the church. "Hello, Tony, did you come to see me?"

"Hi, Father. Well, in a way, I guess I did."

The priest stood there, tall and slim, with black graying hair, and his arms folded across his chest. Nobody's ever seen Father Sullivan smile. Even when he joke, it's wry and dry. And there he was, peering down at me, waiting. I suddenly felt even more apprehensive, looked down, scuffed my shoes on the pavement, then took a deep breath and just spit it out.

"Father, can priests be forced to tell anyone about what is said in the confessional box?" I looked up and faced the priest squarely.

"The seal of the confessional is inviolate," Father O'Sullivan, meeting my eyes unwaveringly responded.

I stood as if transfixed for a few seconds.

"I guess that means no, right, Father?"

"That is precisely what it means, Tony. Do you have any more questions?"

"Ummm, no, Sir, I don't."

The priest turned on his heel and went on his way, leaving me to ponder what I should do now. I decided the first thing was to go talk to Oren. After all, we were both at risk here.

"Oren, it's all right to make your confession to the priest and not worry about him saying anything to anybody."

"Did you talk to Father O' Sullivan?"

"Yup."

"All right!"

"Have you seen our murderer lately?" I asked.

"Not since I saw him that day in the green and black Hudson. Why?"

"Just wondered."

"He must live up here somewhere close, don't you think?"

"Maybe. How many green and black '47 Hudsons do you think there are in Wenatchee?"

"Good question."

"Suppose we're breaking some law by not saying anything?"

"We didn't really see anything that night I mean, we didn't see her get killed."

"No, but that guy sure looked like he was up to no good."

"Yeah, I know."

"And what about that girl Mrs. Beach thinks she saw go into the house?"

"What about it?"

"Maybe she killed Miss Lilly Jo Zilke?"

"Maybe. 'Bout all we saw was that bastard moving toward her, 'til that damn cat squealed."

Oren nodded and smiled. "Now it seems funny."

I nodded, "I guess."

"Shouldn't we tell the cops, or somebody, all that we saw? Maybe it would help."

"We'd have to tell, whoever we tell, what we were doing looking into the window in the first place. A couple of Peeping-Toms, you know voyeurs."

"What's a voyeur?"

"Guys that peek in windows at naked girls."

"That doesn't sound good."

"It isn't."

"Can we get in trouble for being, uh voyeurs?"

"I wondered the same thing, but I'm not sure I want to find out."

"Could you ask your older brother?"

"Are you kidding? I'd never hear the end of it, and he'd tell, sure as shootin'. Anyhow, I don't think we were real Peeping-Toms. Maybe we could be called opportunists."

"Opportunist?"

"Yeah, we were minding our own business, eating stolen tomatoes, when we saw the shadow of a naked woman and we just kinda took advantage of the situation."

"Is opportunist different than Peeping-Tom."

"I looked it up. Webster's says something about 'getting sexual gratification from observing others surreptitiously.' and that word means, 'on the sly.'"

"Oh man. That sounds bad!"

"Yup.

"But I didn't get…any you know…what they said. I mean it was exciting stuff, to see her nekked, but I didn't feel any…you know. That means creaming your jeans, don't it?"

"Yeah, I think that's what it means. I didn't get gratified, but I did get a boner," Oren admitted, laughing sheepishly.

"You did? Really?"

"Didn't you?"

"I think I was goin' there, but when I saw that jackass coming into her room, it kinda well, you know."

"She sure was beautiful," Oren sighed.

"She had the most beautiful body—all copper and smooth. She looked… unreal…or something. My older brother said she was real smart, even graduated from high school early."

"Did he know her?"

"Not really, just said she was beautiful and bright."

"She looked kinda foreign."

"Yeah, think she was from Turkey."

"Wow, where's Turkey?"

"Maybe Europe, I don't really know."

"Bet Mr. Taylor would know"

Tony shook his head and rolled his eyes. "Prob'ly, Oren. He wouldn't be much of a geography teacher if he didn't."

"So, I guess being honest about things can get you in trouble sometimes."

"Lately, seems like most times being honest gets you in trouble," I said grinning sadly.

"Then it's better to lie?"

I thought about the question for a few seconds. "In our case, I think it's better that we just don't say anything. We won't get into trouble by telling the truth, and we'll stay out of trouble by keeping quiet."

"And we won't be lying."

"You got it."

CHAPTER 20

Alice Baker rented a small apartment on Sunset Avenue, just off 5th Street, near Wenatchee Valley College, where she would be attending classes. She was from Spokane and had spent all her growing-up years in that northeastern Washington city. All through school, right up until her senior year at John Rogers High School, she had received good grades, but then she faltered.

That year she had dated a boy that changed the way she felt about herself. Alice had really liked this boy, oh yes! He was fantastic! Had everything going for him: handsome as Rock Hudson, popular, funny, and kind. Now she had dated other boys, but those dates were more like spending time with friends, strictly platonic. But Dan Bolten was special. Every girl in class had a crush on him. He was a good athlete, good student, and had this way about him that made everyone feel kind of special.

Alice really wanted to like him, and had almost swooned when he asked her to the Spring Dance. She couldn't believe he had chosen her. As the dance got closer and closer, she tried to picture what the evening would be like. She would be wearing her brand new gown, he would bring her a corsage (he'd already asked her what color her dress would be so the flowers would compliment it), they would make a grand entrance and everyone would applaud them (he was the Spring Dance King), and they would dance the night away. After the dance, he would take her to the 'in-kids' after party, and then, at some point when they were alone, he would kiss her.

Now, she had been kissed before by the other young men she had dated, but well, there was just no magic, and she wondered what all the fuss was about. But tonight she would be with Dan Bolton! She could hardly wait.

The dance was fantastic. She felt like they were in the middle of a fairy tale. Everything was perfect, and Dan was a dream of a date, considerate and attentive. The after party was fun, but a few of the kids had brought a couple cases of beer, and after a while things started getting a tad rowdy.

Dan took her hand and led her out onto the back patio. It was dimly lit and quiet. The only sounds were the soft murmurs of two or three other couples, and the gentle creatures of the night.

This is it! It's my turn, she thought. She and Dan chatted meaninglessly for what seemed like an eternity, then, he cradled her chin with his hand, looked longingly into her eyes, moved toward her, oh so slowly. He brushed her lips with his, then kissed her gently.

Hmmmm, she thought, *that's OK, but where's the fireworks?*

Just about then he pulled her closer, deepened the kiss, probed her mouth with his tongue, and caressed her cheek with his fingers. Alice was aware of each touch, each sensation, each movement, but she felt nothing. His kisses had done nothing for her. Something was missing.

She didn't see Dan after that evening, and began to question herself. What if there was something wrong with her? All the other girls had stories about that night. They seemed to be so happy, so flushed with excitement. Why didn't she? After all, she had been there with the hottest senior in the whole school, and she really wanted to feel what her friends said they felt.

She was at a complete loss with whom to discuss her situation. She was looking for a definitive solution to a perplexing mystery. Dan Bolten's kisses had not aroused in her any feelings, none. No fire, and from everything she had heard, or read for that matter, that just wasn't right. There must be something wrong with her.

CHAPTER 21

Alice's mother was no help, had no answers, and was uncomfortable talking about it. She tried to brush off the issue, and told Alice there was nothing to worry about; she was just a late bloomer. But Alice knew in her heart that was not so. After several days of watching her daughter mope about in tears, the only suggestion she could bring herself to make, and that was reluctantly…maybe she could see a psychiatrist. That thought frightened Alice even more, so she made a concerted effort to hide her fears and feelings when she was around her mother, tried to pretend everything was OK.

Her long-standing dream had been to attend Gonzaga University and study law, but in the waning weeks of her senior year at John Rogers, she felt she had to get away from Spokane. Alice and her mother had visited the beautiful Wenatchee area several times. She loved the spectacular Columbia River that ran between Wenatchee and East Wenatchee, which were connected by a single bridge. The town was only 150 miles from her home and easily accessible by car.

There, she would be free from the constraints of living at home under the watchful eyes of her mother. She could try to find out who she was, what she was. Certainly, there must be others who felt the way she did. '*Oh my God*,' she thought, '*what if there aren't? What if I'm some kind of a mutant, or something.*' Her best friend didn't act like there was anything unusual about her, at least she never said so.

Once, though, Betsy Davis had tried to discuss something with her, but at the last minute, couldn't. Told Alice it was nothing, and to forget it. Could it have been about this very thing? Whatever this "very thing" was.

Betsy had graduated the year before and gone on to Washington State. They had drifted apart after a few strained phone calls, and Alice had sorely missed her friend that last year of high school

The epiphany occurred when Delia Napolitano, on the last day of her senior year, was rushing around like a crazy person, kissing every graduate. When she hugged and kissed Alice on the mouth, she set off the fireworks Alice had been looking for with Dan Bolton. She was surprised and embarrassed by the way her heart pounded, and promptly flushed a bright red. Of course, Delia was completely oblivious. But for next few days, Alice's whole world was Delia Napolitano, who, of course, didn't even know she existed.

Well, the summer came and went, and the move to Wenatchee was uneventful. Alice had started to fall into a routine: classes, shopping, enjoying the small town life, and anonymity.

One day she went shopping on Wenatchee Avenue and stopped at Clausen's Drugstore for a coke. In just a few minutes the small fountain area had filled up and there were no available tables. Lilly Jo Zilke appeared with a Coke in hand, and nowhere to land.

"Would you mind if I join you? All the tables are occupied and, well, you appear to be alone too."

They talked about school and work and families, and found they had a lot in common. They chatted easily for over an hour, like old friends. Lilly Jo gave Alice a business card with her temporary address on Yakima Street written on the back, and suggested she drop by some evening for coffee or a soft drink.

Lilly Jo was beautiful, self-assured, and obviously very intelligent. Alice really liked her and felt comfortable in her company. She hoped, prayed, they could be friends.

"Just go down 5th Street till you get to Chelan Avenue and follow it towards the bridge until you get to Yakima, turn right and go up two blocks to 410—that will be me," Lilly Jo said with a warm smile.

CHAPTER 22

The closer she got to Lilly Jo's home the more apprehensive Alice became. *Maybe I shouldn't have come. What if she has company? What if she's married and has kids? No...she wasn't. She would have said something about a husband or children. Maybe she didn't mean what she said. People say things but don't really mean them. Why do I do this to myself? Stop it, Alice! Stop this "doubting Alice" routine. Stop all the speculation.*

She looked up at the house she was in front of, saw it was an odd number, and crossed to the opposite side. As she drew near the door she became anxious. What was she doing here? She scanned the neighbor's houses to the left and then the right. '*No one watching*,' she thought nervously. She was starting to perspire and then, to make matters worse, felt like she had to pee. '*Nerves, that's all. Pull yourself together you wimp,*' she admonished herself.

She stepped up on the porch and looked for the doorbell—no doorbell. Through the screen door, she could hear a radio playing softly somewhere in the house. The door was open. She knocked softly, and waited.

CHAPTER 23

Detective Jim Rotter was going over then now two-year-old murder file of Nadine Morrison; there had been few leads, all had dead-ended.

Nadine had been young, pretty, quiet, and kind of a loner. She was raped and strangled in her apartment. He kept thinking about the recent murder in Wenatchee. There were many similarities, and Wenatchee was only thirty- five miles away.

Back then he hadn't really considered it might have been an outsider, someone who didn't live in Chelan. Now it seemed more likely. Why had he been so tunnel-visioned?

Both times, the creep had strangled, raped, and killed a beautiful young woman who lived alone, and then just disappeared. It could be the same guy, and for some reason he couldn't quite put his finger on, his detective's instincts almost screamed at him that it was.

Not long before her murder, Nadine had been seen at one of the local taverns, Señor Frogs, to be exact. It was time to re-visit that place, with a different mindset.

Detective Rotter parked his car on Woodin Avenue, a short walk from the tavern.

"Morning," he said with a disarming smile, "I'm looking for Richard Montez."

"Well, you're in luck, he's here right now. Are you from the liquor board?" the man whispered conspiratorially.

"No, I'm not," Rotter said with a grin.

"I'm the manager, can I help you with anything?"

"I'd really like to talk to Richard Montez."

"No problem, I'll get him for you. Can I tell him who's asking?"

"Detective Jim Rotter, Chelan Sheriff's Department."

The manager strolled off and Jim settled in at the end of the bar.

"What would the Sheriff's Department want to talk to me about?" Richard asked with a smile as he stepped into the room and extended his hand.

"Well, I'm doing some follow-up on a cold case, and according to the profile we have on Nadine Morrison, she'd been to your tavern several times."

"Morrison, hummm, Morrison. That name does sound familiar. Why should I know that name, Detective Rotter?"

"She was murdered two years ago last month."

"Oh, yeah," Richard nodded, "I remember her. Murder isn't something that happens often around here. Have you found the guy that killed her?"

"No, we haven't, but I was hoping maybe you could remember something more than what you told us back then."

Richard chuckled, "I don't remember what I had for breakfast yesterday morning, Detective, and two years ago…well, that's a lot of water under my bridge."

"I understand, and you're right, it was a long time ago."

"I don't believe I could add anything to what I said then."

"Well, maybe you could think about her now that I've brought her up again," Rotter said extending a business card.

"OK, but I wouldn't hold my breath, Detective."

Detective Rotter headed for the door and was about to leave when Richard volunteered, "Maybe it was the same guy that killed that girl in Wenatchee a few nights ago."

"You never know, it could be," he replied sadly.

Richard couldn't help thinking about Nadine Morrison as he walked to the back of the tavern where his manager was readying hamburger patties for the lunch rush.

"Do you remember the gal got killed a couple years ago?"

"Nadine Morrison? Oh sure, one of the regulars and I were talking about her, because of the girl that got murdered over in

Wenatchee. I never heard anything about them catching the killer, did you?"

"They haven't. That's why that detective was here. Who were you talking to about Morrison?"

"George. You know, George Root."

Richard nodded.

"Guess the Zilke girl's murder is jogging a lot of people's memories, makin' them think more about lockin' their doors, too."

"You were working that night, weren't you, Joe?"

"Sure was. I may be seventy five, Boss, but my memory is still sharp as any twenty-year old. I told the Sheriff back then that she always came in alone, sat at the bar, had a hamburger and a beer, and left right after. Pretty little thing she was, and real nice. Couple of the regulars always tried to start up with her, but well, she just kind of wasn't interested.

"George and I were reminiscing about that night and between us both we recalled all the men, and most of the gals that were in that evening."

"Really, all of the men?"

"Well, not exactly. There were two we couldn't account for, two new faces. One was an old coot that kept falling asleep, and finally left when he spilled his beer all over his pants. The other was somewhere around thirty. Nice looking guy, but cold as ice. Seriously unfriendly, with the meanest looking eyes I've seen.

"He was sitting at that table back there by himself and I meandered over to see if he wanted another beer. Well, sir, he stood up and near knocked me over with the devil's own glare and said, 'I'll let you know when I'm ready for another one. Got that?'"

"That's all?"

"It was the way he said it, and the way he looked at me," he said, shuddering involuntarily at the memory. "Not many give me the tremors the way that guy did that night."

"Oh, come on, Joe, you? You can hold your own with the worst of 'em."

"This guy is coming from somewhere else, Rich, really."

"Does he still come in, have you seen him lately?"

"Haven't seen him since that night. Told George it was strange he hasn't been seen since the night the Morrison girl got killed, don't you think, Boss?"

"Probably just a coincidence."

"Maybe."

"How many transients do we get in here, Joe?"

"That's pretty tough to determine, bein' as how we get all them tourists, but that night we were pretty quiet. You know everybody hires extra people around that time."

"So, this devil-eyed guy might have been a transient?"

"Well, that's my point, he could've been a guy that was working as someone's extra and that was his last night, the night of the murder. Then again, like you said, maybe a coincidence."

"Did you tell the detective about this scary guy two years ago?"

"Can't honestly remember, but don't think I did."

"Here, Joe," Richard said as he handed him the detective's card, "his name's on there. Give him a call, tell him what you just told me, OK?"

CHAPTER 24

Alice started to walk away, then stopped abruptly, turned and went back to the door. "Lilly Jo," she called hesitantly in a whispery, quiet voice. No answer. She knocked again. Nothing. Without conscious thought, she opened the screen door, stepped inside, and stood motionless, barely breathing. Alice felt beads of sweat on her forehead, and the quiver in her arms and legs.

She found herself in a small, neat living room. There was a three bulb lamp with one low wattage bulb dimly lit, two cushioned chairs, and a small throw rug on a highly polished, brown stained pine floor. The floor creaked as she stepped softly toward the lit room at the end of the very dark hallway.

The shower, Alice thought, *she's in the shower.* She heard the water running. *"What am I doing in this house? Trespassing comes to mind, you dummy."* As she turned to leave, she heard a voice from behind her at the door, a man's voice, "Hello." Alice immediately ducked through the open bedroom door off the hallway and looked for a closet to hide in. The room was empty, thank goodness. She tiptoed quickly to the closet and stepped in, quietly pulling the door close behind her.

Her heart was pounding, pounding, pounding, and she could hardly breathe. Perspiration ran down her face in rivulets. *'Oh my God, what have I done?'* She began to tremble as she leaned against the door, which caused it to rattle. Her heart leaped as though trying to escape from her chest, and she scrabbled away from the door. The rattling stopped.

Alice just stood there, staring at the door, and shaking. *What will I do if he opens the closet door?* She felt dizzy. *What if she fainted? Who was out there? Boyfriend? Father?*

She felt rooted to the floor. There was that urge to pee again. It was so quiet; her breathing became frighteningly loud to her, and her knees were weak. Could someone else hear her breathing? For a few seconds she heard sounds coming from the hallway, or maybe the other bedroom.

Desperation was dictating she bolt from the closet and run out of the house. Driven by that urge, she put her hand on the doorknob, turned it slowly, and eased the door…just a crack. She couldn't see anything through the darkness, but could hear someone talking very quietly, sounded like it was from the room at the end of the hall.

Opening the door a little further, she stepped out of the closet, paused at the hallway door, looked to the right at the lit room, then to the front door. It looked clear! She moved like a sprinter, a sprinter on tiptoes, down the hall and out the screened door, taking care to close it silently.

From across the street, beneath a large willow tree, she turned to see if she had been noticed. Thank God, she saw nothing. With a deep, slightly shaky breath, she turned and took a few steps toward Kittitas Street when, abruptly, out of nowhere, an older woman with wild white hair stepped from behind the huge willow tree trunk and said quietly, "I see you, I see you." The woman giggled, and waggled her finger at Alice.

Alice froze. At that moment a voice from the house behind the willow tree called out, "Mother, come on in now, it's getting late."

The woman scampered off to the house, giggling and pointing at Alice.

"Who were you talking to, Mom?" Alice heard the daughter ask.

Oh my God. Now I've been seen! Why did I go into Lilly Jo's house in the first place? Why? Why? I must be crazy! she thought, *'I've never done anything so utterly stupid.'* Now that she felt like crying, wanted to cry, maybe needed to cry, she couldn't. The tears wouldn't come, just the shivers, and the urge to barf.

CHAPTER 25

Oren and I were just leaving Stallings Sport Shop, heading up Orondo Street to the YMCA to play some ping-pong. Coming down the street towards us was him the killer. We recognized him instantly. It had been a while, and his face was getting fuzzier and fuzzier in our memories, but when we saw him, we knew.

"Tony," Oren whispered urgently.

"Yeah, I see him," I responded quietly, as he looked down at the sidewalk. Making eye contact would not be a good thing! I knew what the man would see. Recognition and fear!

He was easily six feet tall, and then some, wearing a blue one piece uniform with a red logo, and his name sewn onto the left chest. He was looking at a yellow copy of a worksheet of some sort, and appeared to be lost in thought.

"Did you catch his name?" I asked as I chanced looking back to see where the man was going.

"No, did you?"

"No, didn't want to stare."

"Should we follow him?"

"Yeah, but we'd better hurry, he's crossing Orondo and heading south on the Avenue."

"Looked like those uniforms the car dealership's mechanics wear."

"It was the guy, wasn't it, Tony?"

"Sure looked like him, I swear."

We followed as he hurried down the block to the Cascade Hotel, where he crossed the Avenue and went into Wells and Wade. The big ole' store carried darned near everything.

We walked in, pretending to search for something, and canvassed the store. There he was, at the far end. We browsed our way toward him. The name, his name on the uniform was our focus.

The man was absorbed in his task, looking for some mechanical part, and never noticed us. "May I help you?" came a loud voice from out of nowhere. We almost bolted, but realized just in time it was a clerk.

"Oh, no sir, we're just browsing."

"Anything specific?"

"Well, no. We'll just look around, if that's all right, sir?"

He looked at us curiously, then walked over and offered his assistance to him.

"I'm looking for a part for a truck, do you carry parts for Peterbilts?"

"Some. Do you have a part number?" the clerk asked as he pulled out a parts catalogue. "Are you a mechanic?"

The man nodded.

"Well, Pete, you're in luck. The book says we have it in stock. Now I just have to find it. Be right back."

Oren and I were covertly taking in the whole transaction, all the while trying to look innocent.

"It appears to be your lucky day, Pete," said the clerk as he returned and set the part on the counter.

The man grinned sheepishly, "Actually, I'm wearing an ex-employee's uniform. My name's Dewey."

"Sorry, Dewey." He extended his hand. "I'm Rusty."

They exchanged a pleasantry or two, Dewey paid for the part and left.

"Did ya hear? Did ya get his name, Oren?"

"His back was to me, but I think the guy called him Dewey."

"I thought he said Louie."

"Well, did you boys find what you were looking for?" said Rusty.

" Uh no sir. Guess we need my big brother to come with us," I mumbled as we headed for the door, looking over my shoulder to see if the salesman was watching. He was, and he kept his eye on us all the way out the door.

Outside, Oren said, "This guy seems almost too nice, you know? There's something different about him. It's odd, almost like he's two different people."

"Yeah, yeah, maybe he changes from this nice guy and becomes a bastard when he wants sex. Like, "The Three Faces of Eve."

"Naw, this is the guy or else he's got a twin. We both saw his face, right?"

"You know, Tony, we should have followed him when he left the store. We're so dumb."

CHAPTER 26

Alice Baker's life had turned upside since her botched "covert mission" at Lilly Jo's, at least that was the way she tended to think of it. Even now, she couldn't believe what she had done. She had to talk to someone! Her mother was her only lifeline and now she was remembering one specific conversation.

"Don't hesitate to seek counseling. I don't have all the answers. You need someone more qualified than your mother---or your father. Alice, we can afford to pay for whatever help you need, so please, please go. If you want help finding somebody, call me and I'll check around for you. Don't think you can understand it all by yourself. There's way too much for anybody, and everybody needs to talk to an expert at sometime or other."

Today she sat by the phone, worrying her fingernails and contemplating calling her mother. The Daily World hadn't mentioned anyone having been in the house, other than Lilly and the murderer. Alice couldn't sleep, had not a whit of interest in eating, nor study, and generally felt like she was going to fall apart. She had to talk to someone. She picked up the phone and dialed.

"Mom?" she said wistfully.

"Hi, honey. How's my girl?"

"Mom, I'm in trouble and I don't know what to do," she barely managed to articulate through her sobs.

"Honey, honey, I'm here, talk to me, talk to your mother. Alice, honey, come on, talk to me."

"Mom." But Alice couldn't form any other words. They just wouldn't come.

Mrs. Baker crooned softly to her distressed daughter, like she had when Alice was just a pup, and had a scraped knee.

Alice smiled through her tears and gradually relaxed as

she listened to the long-remembered tones and words. Soon she was able to speak, almost calmly.

"Mom, you once said if I needed a counselor you would help me."

"Oh, honey, of course."

"I think I would do better talking to someone other than you."

"I understand perfectly."

"I mean, I love you. You're my favorite person, but I think I would do better with a counselor. Will you help me?" she sniffed.

"Sweetheart, all you have to do is ask and I'll do anything humanly possible to help my angel. I'll get on the phone right now and see what information I can drum up. Do you need anything, honey?"

"I already feel better just talking to you. I know there's help on the way. I'll be waiting for your call. I love you."

Alice felt spent, and guilty for dragging her poor mother into her suffering. Even at that, she absolutely felt better now, not so alone. Maybe tonight, at last, she could get some sleep.

CHAPTER 27

"Who do you know that drives a blue car?" Mom asked as she peeked out the front room window.

"Must be Lito's or Lorenzo's friend," I answered barely looking up from the paper I was reading.

"Looks like Oren getting out of that car."

"What?" I yelped as I jumped up and rushed out the front door.

"Hey, Oren, what goes?"

A big smile lit up his face, "I got my license yesterday."

"Wow, whose car?"

"Mine. The Aunties bought it for me…but I have to pay 'em back," he beamed, using his pet name for his mother's sisters.

"You're so full of it."

"No, it's true. Wanna go for a ride?"

"Are you kidding? Let me tell Mom." I started for the house at a dead run, but Mom waived at him from the door, telling me to go.

"Was the driving test tough, Oren?"

"I did OK on the written part, but screwed up on turning right. You know how you have to put your left arm out the window, bent at the elbow? Well I forgot to do that so he took some points off for it."

"Who took you down there?"

"My uncle, Ted."

"Wow, and you passed it the first time. Were you nervous?"

"Scared shitless! I gotta get some gas, Tony. Man I love sayin' that," he practically swooned.

"Where you gonna get it?"

"Uncle Ted told me to get it at the Rainbow station at the north end, right across from the Highway Patrol."

"I'll pitch in a dollar."

"Swell, I'll get eight gallons, then."

"Can I fill her up for you?" The attendant asked as he approached.

"Two dollars of regular, please."

"Would you like me to check that oil for you?"

"Yeah, would you please?"

We stepped out of the car and walked over to watch the attendant as he lifted the left wing of the hood.

"Looks like she needs about a quart."

"What kind of oil do you have?"

"Does it use oil?"

"I guess it does. I um I just got it."

"How about a quart of bulk oil?"

"How much is a quart?"

"Two bits."

"All right, put a quart in please."

"Is it a '37 or '39?"

"37."

"Nice little Chevy you have here."

Oren tried to play it cool, but inside I could tell that he was bursting with pride.

"Wow, Oren, he liked your car."

We were pulling out of the station when we saw the '47 Hudson going north on the Avenue,

"You wanna follow him, Tony? We've got plenty of gas?"

"Sure!"

We followed the Hudson to the Roller Rink. The driver went inside, and just as we were stepping out of the Chevy, he dashed out and back to his car, drove to the Avenue, and headed south till he got to Western.

"I'm not gonna follow him any more 'cause I don't want him to notice this car, Tony."

CHAPTER 28

"Come in, Mr. Zilke, good to see you sir," the chief greeted solemnly.

"I guess I should have called you, Chief, but I like to see a man's face when the subject is this important."

"I understand."

"My wife and I are anxious to know what, well, anything you might have found out about Lilly Jo's murder."

"I wish I could tell you that we have something, but we're still investigating. We do have a possible lead, but that's just what it is…a possible lead."

"Are you the only officer working on the case, sir?"

"No! There are two detectives, besides myself, Mr. Zilke. I assure you, we are doing everything possible to find the person who killed your daughter. We have very little to work with right now but we're turning over every leaf, and we will get to the bottom of it."

They sat quietly for a few seconds, Mr. Zilke perched on the edge of his chair, looking like nothing less than death warmed over. Chief Allen was at a loss for words. Mr. Zilke finally stood and extended his hand to the chief.

"Thank you, Chief Allen. I'm confident you're doing all that you can do. I apologize for interrupting your busy day. I'll leave you to your duties. Please, if anything turns up, my family would appreciate any news."

"I understand perfectly, Mr. Zilke, and please come by or call anytime you wish." They shook hands and Lilly Jo's father walked out.

"How's he holding up, Chief?" Mary asked as she stepped into his office.

"He's doing all right. He's a take-charge guy and has operated several businesses. He's used to getting results from the people he oversees, and it must be difficult for him to rely on someone else.

"Does he interfere?"

"No, but I feel he wants to put his hands on this case. Inside he's fighting with himself to leave the work to the police department. I respect this man."

John Brees walked up and joined them. "Was that Lilly Jo's father that just left?"

"What's on your mind, Detective?"

"Could we talk in your office?"

"Come in and close the door."

"Do you know Jeremy Brody, up in the Okanogan/Omak area?"

"So he called you."

"You knew he was going to call?"

"If you're looking for a good policeman in somebody's town, it's the right thing to do." The chief smiled, sitting back in his chair, hands behind his head.

"Do you think I could handle the job?"

"Absolutely, John. I wouldn't have given him your name if I didn't think so."

"Thanks, Chief."

"There's a big American Indian population up there. You might want to check out the area, maybe spend a weekend up there to see if you'd like to live there."

"That's a great idea, would you mind if I went up this next weekend?"

"I think we can work that into the duty roster."

Detective Brees gave him a huge grin and ducked out the door.

CHAPTER 29

"So why was John walking on cloud nine?" Mary asked cheerfully.

"They're looking for a new chief up in Okanogan and he's one of the candidates."

"Good for him! Oh yeah, almost forgot what I wanted to ask. How long will you be at the mayor's office?"

"Just need to fill him in on the Zilke case. Wish I had some good news to tell. By the way, have you seen Troop this morning, Mary?"

"I believe he's in his office."

The chief knocked on his door.

"Come in, Chief."

"Sorry to barge in, Daryl. Do you have anything new on the Zilke case?"

"I'm pursuing the '47 Hudson lead—I've got some names, but nothing else yet. I'm going through the phone book right now looking for numbers and addresses."

"Good! I'll check with you later." He started to leave but paused. "Wasn't the '47 Hudson lead Brees?"

Daryl stopped and came back.

"Yes sir, it was, but he didn't want to sit on it till next week so he asked me to run with it."

"Good, I was hoping I wasn't losing it."

Troop poked his head out of his office and called to Mary, "The chief with the memory of an elephant, is afraid he's losing it?" He rolled his eyes and smiled. "Well Mary, guess I'll go start knocking on doors."

CHAPTER 30

A young man, probably in his thirties, opened the door. "Good morning. I'm Detective Daryl Troop and I was looking for Ruth Wilson," he said, displaying his badge.

"I'm her husband. What can I do for you?"

"Do you folks own a '47 Hudson?"

Just then a black '47 Hudson pulled into the driveway.

"That's my wife."

"Nice looking car. Has it always been black?"

"Nope. We had it painted a couple years ago."

"Well then, that's all the questions I have. Thank you, and have a good day."

The next '47 Hudson on his list had been sitting on blocks for three months and had no battery. The last two were inoperable and were being stripped for parts.

Mary Corley radioed him to let him know that Nelda Plant wanted to talk to him. He made the Plants his next stop.

"Mr. Plant, how are you? Your wife called me this morning, is she around?"

"Come on in, Detective Troop. I'm afraid Nelda wants to lead you on a wild goose chase."

"George, let me explain myself, please," Nelda said sharply as she walked into the front room.

"She's lost some of her marbles," her husband whispered, circling his finger by his temple.

"Oh, George! Nothing of the kind."

"Who lost their marbles?" Troop asked, clearly confused.

"Mildred."

"George, would you go into the kitchen and allow me to explain, please? I'm the one who called Detective Troop," she said sternly, hands on hips.

"Yeah, yeah," he grumbled, and slunk into the kitchen.

"I'm sorry about George. I called you because June Alexander, in the house on the corner of Yakima and Kittitas, has a mother by the name of Mildred. Well, Mildred told June, her daughter, that she saw a young lady come out of the Zilke house on the night of the murder."

George leaned out of the kitchen behind Nelda, and again circled his finger around and around his temple.

Troop sneaked a quick peek at George and asked, "Is there something wrong with Mildred?"

"Well, she's got old people's disease, you know. Dementia or something."

"I see," he nodded and frowned.

"But June says she believes her. For real! Maybe you should go talk to her."

"That's a good idea, Mrs. Plant. I'll do just that. Thank you for calling me." He leaned back until he made eye contact through the open kitchen door, "and thanks, Mr. Plant."

"Good luck, Detective," he shouted from the kitchen.

Detective Troop walked to the front door and was about to knock, when it opened and June welcomed Troop inside.

"Nelda called just now and said you were on your way over. I'm June Alexander."

"Detective Daryl Troop. Nice to meet you ma'am."

"It's too bad about that poor girl across the street gettin' gettin'."

"Yes ma'am. I understand your mother believes she saw someone come out of that house on the night of the murder."

"That's what she said, Detective."

"I see," he nodded, "would it be possible to talk to your mother?"

"I guess it would be all right," she answered apprehensively. June started out of the room, then stopped and turned back to Troop. "I suppose I should tell you my mother has a kind of dementia, old people's forgetfulness. Nevertheless, there are times she's perfectly clear-headed. I've proved that – at least to myself," she whispered and glanced toward the kitchen. "I do believe she saw someone come out of that house on that particular evening. I'll go and get her." June escorted her frail mother down the hall. Mildred walked hesitantly, but with determination, face serious and an apprehensive demeanor.

"This is Detective Daryl Troop, Mother."

"How do you do? my name is Mildred Dern." she extended her hand. "Nice to meet you."

"Thank you for meeting with me, Mrs. Dern, I understand you might have seen something at the Zilke house a few nights ago."

"Well, I didn't see anyone in the house, but I did see someone come out of the house. She was tall, had dark hair, and seemed to be in a hurry." She paused and peered into his eyes to see if he believed her.

"Do you recall what she was wearing, Mrs. Dern?"

Now she beamed. He believed her! More confidently, she responded, "Pretty sure it was slacks, black ones, and I believe a big sweater, or a light coat. Whatever it was, it was red, and had a hood, and something on the back. Oh…what was it? Nope, can't see it just now, but it was there."

"About what time, would you say?"

She pondered the question.

"Early evening, maybe seven-thirty or eight."

"Is there anything else you remember about her?"

"Well, she was hid behind that big old willow tree in our yard, and she was peekin' 'round it back at Lilly Jo's place."

Daryl's heart rate spiked and he took a deep breath, trying to keep his voice calm, "And where were you, ma'am?"

"Well, I was standin' further back of that tree. Watched her come out of that house, run 'cross the street and, pretty as you please, just come up in our yard and under that tree."

"And you got a good look at her, at her face?"

"Surely did! Should'a seen her when I told her 'I see you.' Looked like she'd seen a ghost. Her eyes got so big. It was kinda spooky, but then she just ran off."

"Do you remember anything else about her, ma'am?" he asked softly.

"Well, not right now. 'Cept I think she was hidin' from that man that snuck in right before she came out. I know he snuck in 'cause he didn't knock or anything. I was watchin' him, so I know he didn't. Just opened the door real slow and tiptoed in." Her eyes turned far away, and she yawned. "It's time for my nap, but you come back and visit me sometime, young fella. You're cute." With that she winked, yawned again, and padded off to her room.

"See what I mean? Sometimes she remembers things. I believe she saw what she said."

"Ma'am, I believe her. "Daryl nodded. "I'll be contacting you again, probably sooner than later, and setting up a time to come back. It's important I talk with your mother again. It would be really helpful if you folks didn't try to discuss that night any more. You never know when a question or comment can plant a thought. The other thing I would ask you to do is write down anything you remember from that night, or anything else Mildred might have said about it. This could be very important June. Very important! Just don't bring it up to Mildred again. If she wants to talk, let her, and afterward, when she isn't around, write down what she said. And if it's alright with you, I'd like to send someone out to have a look around that willow. There might be evidence there no one saw, because no one was looking. But now we're looking. I can't tell you how critical this could be. It's wonderful you had enough faith in her story to give us a call."

CHAPTER 31

"Mom," I called, "I'm going over to see Mr. Applewood."

"Why you want to go see that old man?"

"Just to talk. He's my friend, Mom."

"He's crazy! The things he says…I don't trust that man, Tony. You be careful. I don't want to tell you 'I told you so,' you hear me?

"Mom I just want to talk to him."

"You be careful," she fumed as she made the sign of the cross.

"I will. I almost snapped, my irritation bubbling to the surface. Almost. It was not a good idea to snap at Mom, and anyway, it was true. *The guy is kind of a scary old man.* I thought, as I head out the door.

"Who is it?" a voice bellowed in response to my knock.

"Tony Marinquez, Mr. Applewood."

After a long minute, the door opened a crack and he peeked out.

"You alone?" he boomed.

"Yes sir." I stood there waiting to be invited in.

"Well, are you going to stand there all day? Come in, come in."

I entered the dimly lit room. There was a hint of Vicks Vaporub in the air. It was warm and stuffy, like a sickroom. Applewood was already seated in a large overstuffed tan chair. The matching divan was huge and took up most of the space. There were two standing lamps that emitted little light, and a large framed picture of sunflowers on the wall beside the door. *Dracula's room*, I thought and smiled inside, careful not to let Applewood see.

A large bookcase that almost touched the ceiling took up

the wall beside Applewood. "Are those all your law books?"

"No. I have more in the study. Did you come here to talk about my law books?" the old man snapped.

"No, sir, I didn't." I stood patiently by the divan, my eyes acclimating to the dimness, and waited. Applewood finally noticed, and gestured impatiently for me to sit.

He peered down his nose at me, as if he was wearing bi-focals. His condition caused him to drool at times, and now was one of those times.

"Would you hand me that handkerchief on the end of the divan, please?" He paused to wipe his mouth, then without meeting my eyes said softly, "I had a premonition about you and your friend."

"A what?"

"What did you see that you weren't supposed to see, you and your friend? What did you see?"

"I'm sorry, Mr. Applewood, I don't know what a promonition is?"

"*Prem*-onition, not *prom*-onition."

"OK. *Prem-onition*. What is that?"

I could see Mr. Applewood's hands were shaking perceptively. I'd never asked why his hands shook, and just as he opened his mouth to pose the question.

"I believe the dosage my doctor prescribed is not adequate to control my tremors," Applewood responded to the question I had not yet voiced. *"How did he know I was thinking that? Or did I say it out loud?*

"I really don't know the answer to that. I don't know if I'm guessing at what you're thinking, or if I actually can read your thoughts," Applewood responded sincerely, almost shyly.

"That's spooky," I shot back as I stood up.

"Sit down, Tony. What we have is very special; special in the sense that I'm not able to do this with anyone else…at least not that I know of. It's still new to me. Have you sensed things too? Like my wanting you to come here today?"

"That was my own idea!" I ventured, not quite sure it was true.

"Then what are you doing here? Why did you come?"

What indeed. What was I doing here? I remembered telling my mother I was going to see Mr. Applewood, but for the life of him, I couldn't remember making the decision, or why, I just knew that was what I should do.

"My mom doesn't like you."

Mr. Applewood was leaning forward and Tony could see saliva oozing from his mouth. He scowled and impatiently wiped it away.

"Which further reinforces my theory. Your mother doesn't like me, you're a little afraid of me, and yet here you are. He wiped his face with the handkerchief, with a very shaky hand.

"Are you all right, Mr. Applewood?"

"I'm fine, Tony, other than this God forsaken disease. I believe I can understand your fear of me. I must look like some vulture drooling bodily fluids, after gorging myself on some decaying wildebeast or zebra in the wilds of Africa."

"You are quite a spectacle, sir."

"Oh, so now I'm addressed with some respect?"

"Respect?"

"You addressed me with a 'sir'."

"Well, you really were a lawyer, weren't you?"

"Technically, I still am. I'm not as busy with my practice as I once was, but yes, I am a real attorney-at-law."

With a lot of effort and groaning he was able to rise from the chair and amble into his study. Rufus Applewood returned holding a diploma from Gonzaga University.

"Do you know what this is, Tony?"

"Looks like some kind of diploma from Gonzaga U."

"That's right my boy."

He replaced the document in his study, and returned to his chair.

"I stopped caring about what people thought of me a long time ago, Tony boy."

"Excuse me, sir?"

"You said your mother didn't like me, didn't you?"

He nodded.

"She has that right. It's the beauty of living in these United States. Believe it! In some parts of this world people can't voice their likes and dislikes in public."

"I've heard that."

"Do you believe in psychic powers, ESP, premonitions, things of the unknown, unproven phenomenon?"

"Well, I've heard of extrasensory perception."

"Good, we stand as equals on that subject."

"What about those other things you just mentioned…you know anything about 'em?"

He wiped his chin and looked up at me. "The terms are, at best, intriguing. There are no definitive answers, mostly just speculation depending on whom you read. Maybe in the future we'll learn more about them, but for now, they're just fascinating mysteries," he mused distractedly.

"My mom says you have some grown children."

Rufus stood with great difficulty, walked unsteadily toward his bedroom and came back with a picture of his whole family when he was younger. I studied the picture more closely under one of the lamps. I saw a once happy family. They were all smiling for the picture.

"The girls are both married and have children of their own. Both are lawyers in their own right." He stood and went to his study and came back carrying a couple more pictures. "This is Bonnie with her two children and this is Sarah with her only daughter."

"Your daughter's are very attractive, Mr. Applewood."

"Not bad for an old condor," he said through a wry grin.

"Your wife looks like Doris Day."

"Several people thought the same thing. That's the reason she started wearing her hair short."

"Wow, is this you?" I asked as he looked at a younger Rufus Applewood?

"You wouldn't know it now, but yes, that's me a Dennis Morgan look-a-like. There's no reason why you should know who Dennis Morgan was, but he was a movie star, a leading man in the forties and fifties."

I stood in awe of the pictures of Rufus Applewood's family and was especially impressed with how handsome Rufus had been. I snuck a peek over at the old man to see if he still possessed any of those attractive features.

Rufus was reaching awkwardly toward the tissues on the end table, allowing the tears raining from his eyes to fall on the glass top; I scurried over and grabbed the box. I held it up so Rufus could get a handful of tissues.

"Forgive me my weakness, Tony boy." he said, his voice faltering. "Grown men look foolish crying, but nevertheless, we do cry."

I sat quietly, allowing Rufus this time with his tears. *Men do look different crying,* I thought. It seemed more significant somehow. This was an emotional cry. He hadn't been hit or had ugly words thrown at him, hadn't been sent to his room. It was a picture of his family, an image of himself in happier days. The photographs were always there, but somehow, I knew, he hadn't looked at them in a very long time, and they had touched him deeply.

The nostalgia, the bittersweet thoughts of yesteryears, the happy times, a beautiful wife, adoring children, a prestigious position, the bounties of life. He grieved the loss of the happiness he had once known, long ago, and now, for the first time in ages, that loss rose up unexpectedly and almost overpowered him. It embarrassed him. "Maybe you should go Tony. I'm feeling quite vulnerable right now. It seems this melange of subjects has precipitated a rueful melancholy in me. At any rate, I need my pills. I see my tremors are beckoning me."

"Sure, Mr. Applewood. Is there anything I can do for you before I leave?"

"Just make sure the door is locked on your way out…and thank you, boy."

I thought about Rufus Applewood all the way home. I had a different opinion of him after that odd encounter today. He didn't seem so cold or indifferent, or scary. Strange how seeing the images of his family, and of him as a younger man, had changed my view of him. I chuckled when I remembered Rufus telling me he resembled a vulture. Oddly enough, he did look like a vulture now. Maybe he had glanced at himself in the mirror, and had seen himself as a raptor.

To this day, I still remember that glum mood I felt when I witnessed Rufus crying quietly from the memory of those pictures of his family. Just for those few moments when his memory pursued the past, and touched the present, it was more than he could handle. What he had been and what he was now. He was just a good man that loved his family; a warm, gentle man.

CHAPTER 32

I entered through the kitchen door and found Mom eating fresh peas from the pod as she filled a pan with the crisp green buds.

"So what did that crazy man have to say that was so important?"

I sat down and grabbed a hand full of pods, opened one with his thumb, raked the peas into his left hand then threw them into my mouth. "Umm, these are good. Where'd you get 'em?"

"A little stand down by Zittings grocery store."

"You're wrong about Mr. Applewood. He's not crazy. Did you know he's Catholic?"

"Of course I knew, he came to talk to the seniors at the church and I went with Mrs. Monda to hear him speak."

"What did he speak about?"

"Something about the law and something called a 'will'."

"I saw his diploma from Gonzaga University. It looked like a real diploma."

"I didn't say he wasn't a real lawyer, Tony. I said he talks crazy," she snapped.

"He said you have a right not to like him and to voice it openly to anyone that wants to listen."

"You told him what I said? Why would you tell him that?"

"He wasn't mad, really. He said you had that right."

"You shouldn't have told him."

"Mom, he's a real person, just like Mr. Monda. He's a nice man, just a little more serious, I guess. Did you know he has two daughters that are lawyers?"

"So?"

"Well, he has kids just like you and Dad, right? And his wife, when she was young, looked like Doris Day. She was real pretty, and he looked like some guy named Morgan. I don't remember his first name, but he was a movie star. Mom what I'm trying to say is that Mr. Applewood is a nice man, he's not crazy oh, and I saw him cry."

"You saw him cry?" she gasped, then made the sign of the cross on herself.

"Yes, I don't know if it was from me saying nice things about his family or him looking at the pictures."

"Did you see his wife?"

"No, Mom, he doesn't have a wife anymore."

"You see, a woman won't stay with a man like that. He's strange, Tony. You should be careful around a person like him."

"His wife died, Mom, and besides, he has some kind of disease that makes him shake."

"Well, that's too bad," she said, her voice softening.

"He thinks he looks like a vulture."

She smiled. "He does kinda look like a vulture."

"That doesn't make him a crazy person, though."

Mom stood and, apparently trying to close the conversation about Mr. Applewood, asked if I wanted something to eat, maybe a sandwich?

"Not hungry, thanks."

"Why do you like him?"

"I dunno. He's all right. Doesn't talk to me like I'm just a kid."

"Humph, you are a kid. How did you meet him?"

"I don't know if I should tell you that story, Mom. You already think he's crazy."

"What do you mean? You're my son, for God's sake. Jesus, Mary, and Joseph, you tell your mother," as she looked up to the heavens and rolled her eyes.

"Mom, don't be so dramatic! You know he lives on Highland Drive? Anyhow, he and I were at the Plaza at the same time, me for a Pepsi and a Hershey bar. I don't remember what he was buying. Anyway, I had dropped some change on the floor and bent over to pick it up when he came around the corner, didn't see me bent over there, and stepped on my hand. Well, that set him to try to keep from falling, but he landed squarely on top of me. He already has trouble with coordination because of his disease. He began shaking when he was trying to get off me and stand up. He slid off and was on his hands and knees. His whole body began to shudder or shiver, kind of. It was weird."

"He said, 'I'm sorry young man, but could I impose upon your good will to assist me to the vertical position?' He talks funny sometimes.

"I said sure, and asked if he was hurt. Then he wanted me to help him to a stool at the counter. Said only his pride was hurt.

"The clerk thought he was my grandfather." As I relayed the scene to Mom, I envisioned it in my head, and felt as if I were back at the store.

"He's not my"

"Would you like a glass of water? Should I call an ambulance?" the clerk interjected.

"Water would be fine."

"Hope you're not having a heart attack cause I'm the only one working here today," the clerk blithered, looking like he might have one himself.

"I don't think you should address yourself to my misfortune, you simple, obtuse oaf. My friend and I will now be exiting your miserable premise."

"Excuse me?" the clerk responded, bewildered.

"Precisely!" the old man cracked a faint grin as he ushered me out the door.

"My name is Rufus Applewood, and I'm trulysorry for my clumsiness, and for falling on you."

Tony had noticed the galumphy nature of Mr. Applewood's movements, and his dribbling. I wanted to ask him what his problem was, but couldn't bring myself to voice the question. I didn't want to offend him.

The old man peered at me through squinted eyes.

"Were you ever hit by car while standing on a corner?"

"Do you know me Mr. Applewood?"

"I don't even know your name."

"Tony Maringuez, sir."

"Well, Tony, I don't possess numinous powers, wizardry, sorcery, or black magic. I don't cast magic spells, or engage in mumbo jumbo, hocus pocus or abracadabra. I can only tell you that I saw you standing, waiting for the light to change. I saw your face clearly, it came to me when I fell on you."

I shook my head, and came back to my own kitchen. "Mom, how could he have known that?"

"He's a strange man, Tony," she said obviously spooked. "I told you he was a crazy man, now maybe you believe your mother."

"He's not crazy," I protested.

"You mean the story you just told me about Rufud Applewood is a lie?"

"Rufus, Mom, with an s, Rufus---no, it's not a lie."

"Tony my son, sometimes I don't think you know bunnies from bears."

"What the heck does that mean?"

"Well, do you know bunnies from bears?"

"Mom," I laughed, softly at first, then I was howling.

When I could breathe again, I looked at Mom, "Where did you get this 'bunnies from bears' thing?"

She pursed her lips to one side and winked.

"You're funny, Mom."

"I'm no dummy, Tony."

"I didn't say you were…you're just…cute."

"You want Momma to warm up some pinto beans?"

"Sure."

"You know Tony, one time many years ago, I made a mistake. I can't remember what year it was, and maybe just maybe, I made my second mistake today. You think?" she teased with a wry smile as she stirred the beans.

I walked over, put my arm around her, and kissed her cheek.

CHAPTER 33

Alice's mother gave the number of someone who might be able to counsel her on her "problem." Alice was hesitant to call it because she was so unsure. What would she say? What would this person, this stranger, think of her? She tried to play it out in her mind but was unable to imagine how she would bring up the subject. Like a coward, she ruminated over the possibilities again and again, but none sounded right. Her mother had emphatically assured her these people were trained to help, and were bound by law and professional ethics to keep anything said during the sessions in complete confidence. So what was her problem?

She walked over to the phone, grabbed it up before her resolve faded, and dialed the number. It rang four times. She started to hang up when she heard a voice.

"This is Angie Lansing."

Alice froze and couldn't breathe.

"Hello? This is Angie Lansing."

Complete silence for a long moment, then. Alice stammered, "Hell—hell---hello."

"Yes, this is Angie. Could this be Alice?"

Alice could feel her heart racing. "How did you know that?" she uttered.

"Well Alice, your mother called me yesterday to see if you had called. She loves you very much, you know."

"She called you?"

"She did. She's concerned about you."

"What, what did she tell you?" Alice managed to squeak out.

"Not a lot. Frankly, she did ask whether I was in tune with girls and boys who are…different."

"Oh well um"

"Alice, would you like to meet someplace? Or I can drive

over to your apartment. We could just chat…get to know each other. No pressure, I promise."

Silence.

"You would come to my apartment?" she eked out.

"Yes, I would, Alice. You probably live over by Wenatchee Valley College, right?"

"Yes."

"All I need is an address, unless you'd like to meet somewhere else."

"I think my apartment would be fine."

Angie Lansing arrived at the address Alice Baker had given her. She knocked gently on the door. After a long moment the door opened slowly. Angie was looking into the frightened eyes of a tall, pretty brunette who looked like she might bolt at any second.

"Hi, I'm Angie Lansing, you must be Alice Baker?"

A reluctant smile, hardly perceptible, lined Alice's face. "Yes."

They stood in awkward silence.

"May I come in, Alice?"

"Oh, of course, I'm sorry, please come in."

Angie stepped into a sparsely decorated room with a fluffy cushioned chair, a small love seat and a short coffee table. There was an attractive landscape painting on the wall behind the loveseat.

"I'm a little nervous, Miss Lustoff. Please sit down."

"Just call me Angie. And I'd like to call you Alice, if it's all right with you?"

"Oh, sure. That would be fine. Would you like some coffee or a soda?"

"No, no thank you."

The conversation died for several long seconds as Angie settled onto the loveseat.

"You said you were nervous," Angie spoke softly.

"I'm very nervous. I'm more than nervous. What comes after nervous?"

Angie chuckled.

Alice clasped her hands and kneaded one thumb against the other. "I suppose Mother told you that I'm...I'm different."

"Different?"

A long pause.

"Yes, I'm different." Alice squirmed on her chair and looked down at the carpeted floor.

"Do you want to talk about why you feel that way?"

"Yes, I think maybe...I...well...I'd like to try," she said with a hint of relief.

"I'm glad." Angie smiled warmly. "Let's set up a time when we can chat again and get to know each other. I do have an appointment right now, and don't want to be late." She handed a business card to Alice.

"Oh my gosh, you're a psychiatrist?"

"Yes. Your mother didn't tell you that?"

"No...well...I guess she figured I would know. I mean, I thought you were a counselor...or something. Oh my gosh and I called you Lustoff. It's Lansing. I'm sorry."

"That's all right, Alice. I've been called lots of things, and some of them that weren't very nice. Lustoff is polite."

Alice laughed openly, and Angie got the impression that she was feeling good about their visit...maybe even liked her.

"I'm glad you came over here, Angie...thank you. I probably would have chickened out if I'd had to go to your office."

"I'm equally glad we were able to meet, and I think we're going to be all right. When you're ready to talk, call and make an appointment. OK?"

"Yes, and thanks again."

"I'm sorry to rush off like this," Angie apologized as she

stepped out the front door. She extended her hand and Alice took it in both of hers.

"I believe I feel better already."

CHAPTER 34

Chief Allen was reviewing everything in the Zilke case. Lilly Jo's father was on his way in for an update. John Brees and Daryl Troop arrived together for the meeting.

"Let's use the conference table so we can sort out everything we have so far," Allen instructed as he came around his desk.

"Chief, I really don't have anything new in my file," Brees said dejectedly.

"Let's see now, John, you've done the neighbor interviews, right?"

"Right Chief. And we're still working on the '47 Hudson lead. I believe Daryl was running down every Hudson we could find."

"Where did you get that information, John?"

"Mrs. Stumply gave it to me when I was talking to her neighbors, the Plants."

"Good." He looked down at his notes. "Didn't one of you guys tell me there was a neighbor that saw somebody peeking in the victims back window that night?"

"Yup. That was Nelda and George Plant. He was looking through his binoculars that evening and just happened to catch a glimpse of the silhouette of a young woman on the drawn shade. We believe she was nude, maybe just out of the shower. Anyway, that's when he noticed the top of two heads. Said it looked like someone peeking through the space at the bottom of the shade."

"Do we have anything on who it could have been?"

The two detectives looked at each other and shook their heads.

"So what do you think, Daryl?"

"Well, you know how when people plant little gardens

in their yards, we get irate calls from homeowners because kids steal the tomatoes, cucumbers 'n stuff from their gardens? It's possible a couple of kids saw the garden from the sidewalk, decided to have a tomato, and were in Mrs. Stumply's backyard. She has a nice little garden behind her place, with lettuce, carrots, tomatoes, cucumbers and even some corn. I think I saw squash and watermelons too. Anyhow, we know it was already dark when they would have been there, so they could have been eating a cuke or tomato. Remember, I found a little saltshaker back there? It didn't match anything in Lilly Jo's house, and Mrs. Stumply didn't recognize it.

"Now just imagine. They're sittin' in the dark, munching on their take and a light goes on in the house across the way, right in front of them. Then they see the silhouette of a naked lady walk past the shade. Well now, you know they have to go check it out. See what they can see through the bottom of the window where the shade is up just enough to peek through."

The chief nodded.

"What do you think, John?"

"Well, it might have been kids out there. The footprints don't really tell us. Maybe it was an opportunist who saw the victim through the shade then cased the house to see if she was alone. When he didn't see anyone else, he might have gone to the window and peeked in, then gone to the front door and knocked. When no one answered, he was emboldened by the thought she was alone in the house, went in, and the rest we know."

"Hummmm. So you think someone might have been just walking by and noticed our girl flash across the shade and took it from there?"

"Yes Chief, or driving by. The other evening I went over there to see if I could find anything we may have overlooked. I left the light on in the bedroom and went outside to see what it looked like. If he was driving, and coming up that steep incline on Okanogan, his speed would probably have been about 25 or 30 miles an hour. He might have seen her shadow and, well, maybe he parked somewhere near and came back. Or, it could have been someone who had previously cased the place, knew the victim was alone and just waited for the right moment," John added.

"We really need to find those peeping toms. They may have seen something that scared them off, something that could help us," Daryl asserted.

"I think if we get lucky with our canvas of the shoe stores, we may be able to narrow down our search a little, and if we find the shoes, we'll be able to match them to the casts we took from under that window, John submitted.

"OK. What else?" the Chief muttered as he scanned his notes, "I also have something here about another woman who may have been in the house that evening."

"That's right," Troop spoke up. "I almost forgot about that. I'm not sure how much credence to give that information."

"Why?"

"Josephine Beach was the lady who told us that story and, well I'm not sure it's helpful. I believe what she told us is true, but Josephine didn't see her enter the house, just saw her at the door."

"Well, one of your notes here, has a different witness, who saw a woman come out of Lilly Jo's that night."

"Right, that's Mildred Dern, June Alexander's mother. June called Nelda Plant when she saw us over there, and told her that Mildred had seen a person come out of the house. Mildred has dementia, and can be lucid, or completely…well… out of it, according to her daughter. I'm not sure how much weight we can give to her statement."

"Does her account differ from the one that Mrs. Beach gave? I think she said she saw someone cross the street and approach the house."

"Josephine Beach is the one who gave us a pretty good description of the woman that approached Lilly Jo's residence. Mildred says she saw the woman go in, and then come out again right after a man 'snuck' in."

"Have we located this mysterious female visitor yet? Any ideas on whom she might be?"

"Nothing yet. Josephine's description was clear, but only went so far. What we have is too general to use to find her. It'll let us rule out some people, but there was nothing that would lead us to the lady." Troop explained.

"Didn't you just tell me Mildred saw her too?"

"Yes Sir, but"

"But what?"

"Well, she's kinda like my ball point pen here. Sometimes it writes and other times nothing."

"Do you think she saw her?"

"Yes sir, I do, but I don't know if it would stand up in a court of law."

The room got quiet while the chief mentally sorted and catalogued the information. "What about co-workers, school friends, church acquaintances, anyone that knew Lilly Jo. Do we have anything there?"

"Well, Sir, it's been kind of hard to work those interviews in. There haven't been enough hours in the day for everything. Like yesterday, I had to spend most of the day down at the South End Slaughter House, trying to find out who stole some beef from the secured freezer unit. Seems they had a lock that was supposed to be impenetrable, until yesterday. Whoever it was stole about three hundred pounds of meat."

"That sounds like a whole cow after it's been quartered for market."

"Yep. The manager thinks it was an inside job or a disgruntled ex-employee. He even thinks he might know who did it."

"I'll assign that to someone else, John, 'cause I want you on this case exclusively. Go talk to Lilly Jo's parents again and find out as much as you can about her. You know the routine. Same with you, Troop. I want you two on this case, and only this case. You follow up on the mysterious woman who may have visited that evening. All right, let's get back to the Zilke file."

"What about the perp? Do we have anything new on him?" Troop inquired.

Anything is possible at this juncture. We need to find out who was peeking through that window, and find out who was going up to her door. I believe we have enough independent witnesses to feel pretty sure there were people around the house that night. Now, Detectives, all you have to do is find them." He smiled ruefully.

CHAPTER 35

Oren drove up to the Maringuez home and walked up the five steps to the front door.

"Come in Oren. Tony's in the back tilling my garden soil for me." Mrs. Marinquez said from the kitchen.

"Oh, you got him working."

"Do you need him for something?" she queried.

"I was hoping he could go to Mills Brothers Clothier with me."

"Got some money that's burning a hole in your pocket?"

"Yeah, I guess so." He smiled.

"Go into the backyard and tell him he can go with you, but he has to finish tilling tomorrow."

"Your mom said you can go with me to Mills Brothers, but you have to finish tilling tomorrow."

"Hey, thanks. I guess I should have put gloves on, my hand has a blister already," I said looking down at my right palm. "What are we going to Mills Brothers for?"

"I wanna get a White Stag jacket like your brother."

"Wow, where did you get the thirteen bucks for a nice jacket?"

"I've been saving for a while. I'm dying to hear what you and Applewood talked about."

"How'd you know I talked to Rufus?"

"I called yesterday and your mother said you went to see the crazy ole man."

"Oren, he's not crazy. Believe me, as a matter of fact, he's very smart."

"So what did you talk about? did you say Rufus?"

"Yeah, his first name is Rufus."

"Come on Rufus?"

"Really, his name is Rufus Delroy Applewood."

"Yee gad, what a name."

"I guess he's Irish or Welch, maybe even English, I don't know, anyway he's a nice guy, really. Did you know he was a lawyer?"

"How would I know that, Tony? I don't know him at all."

"Well, he is an attorney. Went to Gonzaga University in Spokane. Real smart man, uses those dollar words.

"So Rufus is a lawyer."

"Yup."

"Someone said he's a queer."

"Aw, come on, he's no queer, who said that?"

"Don't remember, lives on Highland Drive?"

"Yeah, but he's no queer. That's worse than Mom calling him a crazy man."

"How come I heard he was?"

"I don't know, but he's not. Next time I go see him, you wanna go with me?"

"Let me think about that, Ok?"

We parked on Wenatchee Avenue and walked into Mills Brothers Clothiers.

"Can I help you gentleman?" a tall red headed young man asked as he approached us.

"Hey, you're handsome George, aren't you?"

The clerk looked at the two and smiled wide.

"My name is George." he said, nodding and looking a little embarrassed.

"I'm sorry George. My friend is looking for a White Stag jacket,"

"Oh sure, follow me. It's more of a windbreaker," he said, arriving at the section with all the coats and jackets. "You probably wear a medium. He extracted one from its hanger and assisted Oren in placing it on his upper body.

"I'll be back in a few minutes, guys. There's a mirror

over there," pointing to a large mirror against the wall.

"How does it look?" Oren asked.

" Swell. You look great, really."

"Does it look like it fits me?"

"Yeah, how much is it?"

"$13.49."

"Wow."

"This is a White Stag, right Tony?"

"Yeah, check the zipper."

"Is this it?" Oren pointed to a small deer mounted on the zipper.

"That's it all right."

"The real thing," he said proudly, wearing a big smile.

Oren paid for the jacket and we walked out to the car.

"So what did you and Rufus talk about?"

"I know this is going to sound crazy, but I think he knows something about what we saw on Okanogan Street, really, I mean it."

"Whoa, how could he know anything about that? Come on, he couldn't know anything."

"Yeah, Suddenly a startling realizaton blasted me. *"He asked me what we saw, that we didn't want to see."*

"What? That doesn't make any sense maybe your mom's right about him, there is no way he would know anything." Oren said shaking his head in disbelief.

"You know he asked me about ASP or ESP, psychic powers, unknown phenomena, stuff like that." Tony said mysteriously.

"Maybe he's a Martian."

"Martian?"

"Yeah, from another planet," Oren said smiling wryly.

"Hey, can we listen to Nat King Cole?" as he turned the volume up.

"Guess so."

"KPQ, right."

I sang the song along with Nat until the last word.

"Wow, you really like King Cole."

"Well yeah, but it's the words too."

"You don't even have a girlfriend, I don't get it."

"It's just Nat King Cole, singing 'Because of You,' what else can I say?"

"You must have heard Applewood wrong or he was referring to something else," Oren said returning to our earlier conversation.

"What did you see? What did you and your friend see" That's what he said Oren. No wait, 'what did you see, that you and your friend weren't suppose to see? That's what he said."

"So what did you say, then?"

"I don't remember, I think he started shaking. He's got some kind of disease that causes his hands to shake, so we talked about premonition, I remember that, I went home and checked it out with Webster."

"Who's Webster?"

I laughed. Webster's Dictionary, that's who."

"Smartass."

"Aw, come on, Oren. Just kidding. Anyway, premonition means 'an intuitive anticipation of a future event; presentiment.'
"

"So what the hell does 'intuitive' mean?" Oren growled. I could tell he was getting a little annoyed.

"Right, I looked that word up too---it means 'to know or understand by intuition.'"

Oren rolled his eyes up and said. "Well, no shit."

"Hey, that's what the Web said. 'A perception of the truth without any reasoning process.' "

"You mean, what you think, right?"

"Yeah, kinda," I said dubiously.

"So, what does premonition mean?" Oren asked again,

exasperated.

"Near as I can tell, it's a gut guess at something that's going to happen in the future."

"The future?"

"Yeah."

"Give me an example, Tony."

"Well, I'm just guessing, but let's say I tell you that Mary Beth is going to have an accident on Monday morning and then she does have an accident on Monday morning. That would be a premonition. I think that's what Webster is saying."

Oren smirked and nodded. "So, it's knowing something is going to happen before it happens?"

"I think so. Yeah, that's what it means. It's spooky."

"Tony, you want a Dusty Burger? I'll treat."

"Sounds great." I lightly punched Oren on the shoulder. We parked on the dirt and gravel in Dusty's parking lot.

"Isn't that Gary Mathew's car?"

"Well, his dad's car, yeah, I think it is."

We walked into the seating area.

"Well, look what the cats drug in. What are you two birds up to?" Gary asked from the depths of a deep red padded booth. He moved over so we could join him.

"Oren just bought a White Stag windbreaker at Mills Brothers."

"All right! Oh, that's right, you're starting high school this fall. Movin' into the big time," the slightly older boy teased.

We placed our order for burgers.

"What's the word around where you live, Oren, about the Lilly Jo murder?"

"The word?"

"Yeah, what do you hear from the people around there? They talking about the murder of one of their neighbors?"

The look on Oren's face made me think he was wondering why Gary was asking about Lilly Jo's murder.

"I don't know anything about it, Gary." he glanced at me.

"So why the guilty face? What do you two know about Lilly Jo Zilke? I'm just kidding. You guys sure look guilty about something, though. It's not like you were there."

"Well, we could ask you the same question. Why are you so concerned about her murder?" Tony snapped.

"Hey, I don't think you killed her, so stop getting all uptight, guys, geeze?" Short pause. "The reason I was asking about her is because my dad has been to several business conferences with old man Zilke. I just thought you might have heard something I could relay to my dad, something new. That's all."

"Your dad is in the fruit business?" Oren queried.

"Yeah, he's one of the founders and ex-presidents of the Washington State Fruit Growers Association."

"Wow, that sounds pretty impressive, Gary," I replied.

"Well" Gary said as he stood, "I gotta go, nice talking to you two birds, enjoy your burgers."

We watched Gary leave, then looked at each other and burst out laughing. They weren't laughing at Gary though, it was purely and simply the release of tension.

"It's not like you were there. Isn't that what he said? Wow," Oren wailed. "He's really a swell guy, though. I didn't know his father was a big wheel with the fruit industry."

"You know Oren, we don't know much about anybody, really."

"What do you mean?"

"I know your aunts have a little store and they take care of you, right?"

"Yeah, so."

"You have an uncle named Ted who was in WWII, and he has some pictures of naked French whores in his wallet. Right?"

"Yeah," Oren laughed.

"My dad was a logger, you knew that."

"No, I thought he worked at that place down by Malaga, a metal place, across from Alcoa."

"Well, yeah, that's what he does now, but he was a logger for years. I know that Timmy's father leases a thousand acres of wheat land and Timmy tills it every year. His dad makes his own beer. Jon's father has been dead since I've known him and his mother works at the hospital. That's it. I don't know anything else about any of our other friends. We just know them."

We finished our burgers and were sipping our cokes.

"Do you think we're poor, Oren?"

"Never thought about it."

"Have you ever gotten anything from the church?"

"What do you mean, money or what?" Oren frowned.

"Well, once in a while we get boxes of clothes from the church and my dad knows a guy that gives us clothes."

"That doesn't mean you're poor, Tony."

"No, I didn't say it did."

"Hey, you have a big family and people give things to big families, that's just the way it is, right?"

"I guess."

"Don't get sad on me Tony, come on, let's not talk about poor or clothes, OK?"

We sat silently and looked around, while we finished our cokes.

"Let's get out of here," Oren said as he stood, his back to the door.

"Isn't that the Apple Blossom Queen coming in?" I whispered.

We sat back down. She walked by and gave us a big, beautiful smile and a soft hello.

We slid out of the booth and walked out to the car.

"Do you think she eats oatmeal for breakfast?" I mused

dreamily.

"What? What the hell kind of question is that?" Oren said. He grinned and slapped me on the back. "I think that Dusty Burger was too much for you, Tony."

"No, really, what kind of breakfast do you think she eats?"

Oren pretended to think seriously about the question for a few seconds, then offered patiently, "I suppose she could eat oatmeal, cream o wheat, pancakes, eggs, ham, bacon, corn flakes or almost anything else. Who knows?"

"You're right, that was a stupid question. Maybe that burger did made me goofy."

Oren punched my shoulder as we strode to the Chevy.

CHAPTER 36

"Hey, there goes that '47 Hudson again." I pointed as the car drove by us heading the opposite way. We turned and followed the car up Orondo Street.

"Maybe we better not follow this guy anymore. What if he finds out we're on to him?"

"So?"

"Remember when you stepped on that cat at the Zilke house and we ran like hell? Suppose he remembers that, and puts that together with us following him now."

Oren drove to the side of Miller Street and stopped the car. "We don't even know if he killed her," he said skeptically.

"True, we don't know for absolute sure that this is the guy. They say everybody has a twin in this world. But it sure looked like him, I swear. Let's see now. We, or rather you, saw him the first time on Okanogan Street. Then we followed him to Wells and Wade. Now, you saw him when we were on Chelan Street and we chased him to Miller. Do you think he might begin to see us too often?" I said.

He probably doesn't even know we exist," Oren said as he glanced down the street.

"Then do we agree, we don't want him to know or think he knows us?"

Oren nodded solemnly.

"Have you seen anything in the paper about the murder?"

"No I haven't, and I check every day. Aren't the damned police doing anything to solve this poor girl's death?" Oren grumbled.

"I have an idea, but I'm too chicken to do it myself," I said feeling pretty gutless.

"I'm not sure I want to hear your idea, oh brave one. So what's this idea that you won't do, but you think I will?"

"No, I don't know if you'll do it. If I haven't the guts to

do it myself, I certainly don't expect you to," I assured him.

"All right, so tell me your idea."

"It's pretty simple, really, we call the cops and tell them what we know about the guy in the '47 Hudson."

"Oh really, just pick up the phone and call the cops and tell them what we know about the guy and the '47 Hudson, just like that? Oh sure, that sounds simple, and what, call from my aunts house?"

"No, I wouldn't expect you to call from your house."

"Your house?"

"No, not there either. I think we could call from a phone booth."

Oren thought about that for few seconds. "All right. I think I could do it, Tony."

I studied Oren's face and smiled. "Don't you want to think about it? That was pretty fast. You surprise me, I didn't think you'd want to do it, only thing is, I don't know if they can tell where we're calling from."

"You mean like trace the call?"

"Right."

"How can we find out if they can do a trace, or whatever it's called?"

"I think I know who we could ask."

"Not your queer friend."

"He's not queer, really, don't say that please. He's smart, I think he would know stuff like that cause he's a lawyer. You want to go down and see him?"

"Honestly, no I don't, but I'll drop you off there, OK? Some other time I might be up to it, but not right now. He lives on Highland Drive, right? We're on our way."

"The third house on the left," I said flatly.

"I hope he knows if they can trace."

"Aw, come on in, please," I begged.

"Let me know what he tells you."

"OK, thanks for the ride, see ya later."

I strolled up to Rufus Applewood's door and knocked lightly. I turned around to gaze at the houses and lawns on the block. It was one of the nicer areas in the southwest corner of Wenatchee. Applewood's home was well cared and the lawn looked like a golf course.

"Can I help you?" came a voice from inside. I turned to face a woman at Applewood's front door.

"Ah, is Mr. Applewood home?" I asked nervously.

"He is. May I ask who's calling on him?"

"Tony, Tony Marinquez."

"I'll tell him you're here, Tony."

I nodded.

"I'm Bonnie Bush, Rufus's eldest daughter. Nice to meet you, Tony," and she extended her hand, and I shook it awkwardly. "He's in the back yard, you want to go around the side of the house or walk through?"

"I'll just walk around, thanks."

I headed for the yard, thinking I shouldn't have come over now. Too much trouble and his daughter is here to be with him, and here I am taking up her valuable time.

"Hi Mr. Applewood. Catching a little sun?"

"At my daughter's request I'm indulging in some much needed fresh air and yes, some sun. What's up with you, boy?"

"Well, I do have a purpose in coming here today, sir. I think you might be able to answer a kind of legal question for me. My friend and I were having a discussion and we were a little confused about the authority that the police have or don't have."

"Authority about what? Your question isn't very clear. Sit down, Tony boy, and clarify. Don't be nervous, you should know by now, I don't bite."

"Yes sir. I know that. I thought for a moment, "can police umm, is the police department able to trace a call from a citizen? Would you know about something like that—that kind situation?"

Rufus tried to peek into my eyes like he was trying to figure out why I would ask such a question, but I kept my head turned away.

"Tony, can you assist me to stand for a minute, please?"

"Oh yes sir." I walked to Rufus and stood in front of him.

"If you will just stand there and extend your hand out as if to shake hands with me, I can do the rest."

Rufus scooted forward in his chair and then reached out and held my hand as he raised himself out of the chair.

"Thank you boy, that was a great help. If I sit too long, I get stiff and become immobile. That's not a good thing."

"Dad, would you and Tony like a glass of lemonade?"

I nodded.

"Sounds good."

Bonnie Bush came out with two glasses of pink lemonade.

"She's nice, Rufus." I said after Bonnie vanished back into the kitchen.

Thank you, she is, and very bright."

We stood in silence, sipping our lemonade for a few seconds and Rufus sat down again.

"The answer to your question, if I heard it correctly, is yes. However, they must maintain the connection for at least four to five minutes."

I reckoned Rufus Applewood hadn't heard my question or had just forgot about it.

"So, if I call the police department and talk for at least four or five minutes, they could trace where I was calling from? A house or telephone booth, right?"

Rufus nodded and I could feel his eyes boring into me.

"Does this have anything to do with what I thought I saw you see?"

"Oh boy, Mr. Applewood. I am really, really confused. How could you know what I saw? I mean, it doesn't make sense. I told my friend, Oren, what you said the last time we talked, and he got spooked. Really spooked."

"I agree with you, my boy. Your doubt is not unfounded. However, this is not reasonable it has no explanation. It just is. I can't make sense of what have I saw. Have you ever heard of the phenomenon of people walking on hot coals barefoot, without burning their feet? How can that be possible? Certain events are beyond our understanding. Maybe in the future, someone will be able to figure out the whys." Rufus sat tapping the fingertips of his left hand to the to the tips of his right hand and held a blank stare. I sat, caught up in the same gaze, then stood and told Rufus I had to leave.

I walked home in a cloud of confusion. How could Rufus have felt or seen what Oren and I had seen? I'd never heard of people walking on hot coals without getting burned. I walked into the kitchen, the visit to Rufus still on my mind.

"Don't forget you have to finish tilling the garden tomorrow," Mom reminded me she stirred the homemade chili she often made.

"OK."

"You got a lot on your mind, Tony?"

"Uh huh."

"You wanna talk about it?"

I looked at Mom. Did I want to argue with her about my friend Rufus Applewood? I didn't feel up to that right now. I did need to talk, though.

"Just talked to Rufus Applewood."

"No wonder you have a lot on your mind."

"Come on Mom, I don't want to argue about the man. I have to call Oren."

"Oren didn't go with you to see him?"

"No, he didn't."

"He's afraid of him, isn't he?"

"No he's not."

"Then why didn't he go with you?"

"He doesn't like Mr. Applewood. All right, Mom? Is that OK?"

"Don't you raise your voice at me young man!"

"I'm sorry, I didn't mean to, I just don't want to talk about this anymore."

"You're probably the only person I ever heard of who likes Applewood," Mom called out as I headed for the phone to call Oren.

"Oren is coming to get me so we can go downtown for about a half hour. OK Mom?"

"Why don't you two have some chili and tortillas before you go?"

"Could we have some after we get back?"

"It's warm now. In a half hour you'll have to heat it again."

"Maybe Oren has already eaten."

"All right. Do whatever you want." She threw up her hands and left the kitchen.

Oren arrived, smelled the chili and his eyes pleaded with me. So we had a bowl of chili and warm tortillas.

"Thanks for the chili, Mrs. Maringuez, it was delicious and so were the tortillas."

"You're welcome, Oren. I'm glad you liked them," Mom crooned as she raised her eyebrow at me.

"I would never turn down your green chili."

I smiled at Mom and shrugged. "We'll be back soon."

We were headed down Chelan Street and found a telephone booth across the street from the post office.

"Do you want to call from here, Oren?"

He nodded and pulled over to the curb.

"What are you going to say?"

"I'm going to say they should talk to the man that drives that '47 Hudson." He took a deep breath and dropped the coin in the slot.

"Police Department, this is Sandy," said the voice on the other end of the line.

"Aaaa, hello, could I speak to the chief, please?"

"May I have your name, sir?"

"Do you need my name?"

"Well, it would help."

"Well it's Bud Dillon."

"I'll connect you with his secretary, Mr. Dillon, One moment, please."

The phone beeped, then another female voice answered. "Good afternoon this is Mary. May I help you?"

Oren asked again to speak to the police, and when pressed, told the secretary it might be related to a murder.

Mary laid the phone down and hurried to John Bree's office.

"John, there's a young man on the phone that wants to talk to the Chief. I think he stepped out for a minute, would you take the call? It may be important."

"Oh sure, Mary, put him on."

She rushed back and transferred the call.

"This is John Brees, can I help you?"

"We think----ah, I think you should talk to the guy that drives a green and black '47 Hudson."

"I see. What would we want to talk to him about?"

Oren put his hand over the mouthpiece. "Tony, he wants to know why they should talk to him," he hissed at me, in a whisper.

"Tell him it's about the Zilke murder," I said.

"It's about the Zilke murder," Oren repeated into the

phone as beads of sweat broke out on his brow.

"Could I have your name, sir?" requested the officer on the other end of the line.

"It's not important."

"Two minutes," I whispered, pointing to my watch.

"I gotta go now, but you should talk to the man that drives that '47 Hudson." Oren quickly hung up the phone.

"OK, we'll…" but Brees was suddenly listening to a dial tone. Chief Allen walked into the office.

Allen sat down and waited for Brees to elaborate on the call he should have received. John Brees frowned, shook his head, and told the chief, "I think that was one of the 'bobbing heads'."

"Bobbing heads?"

"Yes sir, the bobbing heads Danielle Stumply and George Plant think they saw behind the Zilke house that night. I don't know for sure by any means, but that's my hunch."

"Go on, John, tell me why you thought, this man on the phone was one of the bobbing heads?"

"Thing is, while he was talking to me, he paused for a couple of seconds. I believe he put his hand over the mouthpiece and spoke to someone close by. He said we think you should talk to the man in the '47 Hudson. John Brees paused for a few seconds. That's right, when I asked him why we should talk to the guy in the '47 Hudson, that's when he paused. Then he says, because it's about the Zilke murder." The detective sat for a few seconds thinking something else. "Be right back, Chief," he said over his shoulder as he walked out of his office and went to Mary's desk. "Mary, what were the exact words you said to me when you asked me to take that call?"

Mary thought for a few seconds, "Well, I had seen the chief go down the hall towards the restrooms and knew he was unavailable. I knew you were available, John so I walked down to your office and said, 'John, there's a young man on the phone that wants to speak to the Chief but he's unavailable, would you mind talking to him.' I think that's what I said."

"That's right, you said, 'young man' and I believed I was talking to a young man, because of how you introduced him and his voice… did sound young."

"Yes," Mary chimed in.

"I can't know for sure he was with someone else at the phone when he called in, but I truly believe it was the other 'bobbing head.' Thank you Mary, you have a good memory."

"Maybe we're starting to get somewhere with this case," the chief, who had followed John down the hall, ventured optimistically.

CHAPTER 37

During the tenor of the next two years the Zilke case was inevitably inched to the back burner as no new leads surfaced.

The Chief of Police, James Allen, had a stroke and was replaced by a policeman from Seattle, who failed to adjust to the Wenatchee Valley and left after only a few months. His replacement was from Spokane, but he was being actively pursued by the FBI and ultimately accepted their offer. He was gone after ten months.

The third candidate was from Yakima. He liked the new surroundings and immediately set to work, using his knowledge of police procedure as well as his years of street level experience to stabilize the shaky police department in Wenatchee.

John Brees had moved to Omak and become the Chief of Omak and Okanogan.

Daryl Troop, at the request of his wife, resigned from the police department and they moved to Seattle.

Mary Karen Corley, the secretary, maintained her position through all the transitions.

Several detectives came and went; some came with the new chiefs and some departed with them.

The unfortunate period of musical chairs resulted in dust setting on the Zilke case until Detective Kelli Finnigan arrived. She could have been a high fashion ramp model. Gloriously auburn hair, deep blue eyes and long legs, topped off by a classically beautiful face, made her very serious demeanor come as a surprise. She was intrepid, martial arts tough, and could talk "the talk", if need be. But if you disrespected her, the normally easygoing manner disappeared, and you paid the price.

Her father had been a sergeant on the Kent Police Department, just like his father before him.

She had already heard everything that could be said about a woman in her ten years on the force and then some.

Tolerating a joke was part of the uniform. Penetrating the "blue wall" even though your father was a policeman, didn't cut you any slack. Working around men compelled her to become somewhat of a loner. Her patience was often tested and she could be heard quietly reciting a Hail Mary or Our Father.

Kelli had been looking at the two-year-old files on the Lilli Jo Zilke murder, and thought it could be solved. Why had it been sitting idle for so long?

With the file in hand, she approached the Chief's office, ready to commit to solving the case.

"Patrick, I'd like to work on the Zilke case if it's all right with you."

"You would, would ya? I think that's great. Just last Thursday I talked to Mary about it. She thought you might be just the detective to crack it."

"How long has she been working here?"

"She came with the building when they erected it."

She smiled weakly at his attempted humor.

"I'd like to talk to Ahmet Zilke. Would that be a problem?"

"Do you have anything else on your desk?"

"Nothing I can't work around."

"You have my blessings, then. If you need any help, Mary knows everything. Really. She knows where all the skeletons are buried."

Kelli called Mr. Zilke and found him at home. He had a slight cold and his wife insisted he stay where he was. She asked permission to come to and talk with him, which he granted.

Kara Zilke answered the door. She was polite and gracious, though slightly guarded. She led Kelli to the lovely front room, where Ahmet was already seated. He stood and extended his hand cordially.

"You have a lovely home, Mr. Zilke. I'm sorry we have not been able to work on your daughter's case for so long."

"I believe I am able to understand the shortcomings of the police department, with the staff upheavals these past few years. I'm a businessman and have some of the same problems. Having said that, I am very disappointed with the total lack of progress by the PD, concerning my daughter's unfortunate passing. I assume you are a new detective at the PD. "It has been two years---" He stood and was unable to speak; his eyes welled with tears. "My perception of---" he choked up, pulled a handkerchief from his pocket and wiped his eyes, and started again. "My perception of justice," he sobbed, "is clouded by the ineptitude displayed by the PD. Maybe because I'm Turkish, the wheels of justice don't turn as easily."

Kelli watched him empathetically, unable to say anything in her defense. She waited quietly for his sorrow to run its course before going any further. He brought himself under control and was able to speak more clearly.

"I was going to hire my own detective and have him work exclusively on my daughter's murder. My wife was opposed to this idea and felt we would alienate the Wenatchee PD. I feel that the department was unable to find my daughter's murderer because of the lack of interest," he said wearily.

"You have every right to feel the way you do Mr. Zilke. I suppose I would feel the same way if I were you. The Wenatchee PD has had a turbulent few years, from what I have heard. I'm sure you're aware we've had three Chiefs in the interim. Since there were no new leads, nothing was done on your daughter's case. Our new boss, Partick Duffy, has given me free rein on the file and that's why I'm here, sir. I plan to make this my priority."

Kelli waited for Ahmet to speak. He looked her in the eye and Kelli felt he was trying to decide whether or not to get his hopes up, after all this time whether or not to trust her. When he reached his decision, he spoke softly, "I suppose I shouldn't kill the messenger in this case you, Miss Finnigan."

Kelli scrutinized Mr. Zilke closely. He was an average sized man, swarthy skin, dark brooding eyes, mustachioed, intelligent and perceptive, and he spoke English very well, as did his wife. Kelli felt he was holding back what he would really like to say. He was a gentleman.

"I think I understand, sir."

"You will be working on my daughter's case on a more consistent basis?"

"I will," she nodded.

"Then I am your captive. How can I help you?"

They spent the next two hours reviewing every detail of that night, and anything he was aware happened on the days immediately prior.

Kelli Finnigan left the Zilke home feeling good about the relationship she had cultivated in those two hours.

CHAPTER 38

"So what do you think of this detective, Ahmet?" Kara asked her husband.

"She appears to care and seems sincere, but she's a woman."

"Ahmet! Yes, she's a woman, but not just any woman. She's a detective. How many women do you see in the police department? She's special! She's smart like your Lilli. And didn't you say, more than once, your Lilly would exceed you in business some day because she was special? This woman is special, you'll see, just like your daughter."

"I have no choice. They send me a woman to find my Lilly Jo's killer. I will trust they know what they are doing, Kara. I have no choice, however, I will give her my confidence, as you wish."

The detective approached the secretary's desk, still preoccupied with everything that was discussed at the Zilke residence.

"Kelli, Patrick informed me I am to make myself available to you, at your discretion, as long as I can stay close to my office here. Will that work for you?" asked Mary.

"Oh absolutely! That's fantastic! Let me put some of my things in the office and maybe we could confer for a few minutes while it's on my mind. I just came from the Zilke home."

"I hope I can be of some help."

"Mary, I've been going over some old files on the Zilke case. I understand you took a call for Chief Allen from a young man about two years ago."

"I thought you might ask me about that. I remember it like it was yesterday. The call was for Chief Allen but he had stepped out of his office and I transferred it to John Brees. He's now the Police Chief up in Omak/Okanogan. Anyway, the question we had was whether the person that called and talked to John was a juvenile. Both John and I felt it was probably a young person, maybe fourteen, fifteen, sixteen years of age. We definitely were guessing at the age."

"I see from John Brees notes he thought it might have been one of the 'bobbing heads' the Plants and Mrs. Lumply had seen. Is that what you thought, too?"

"I don't pretend to know all the details on the Zilke file, but I did hear some chatter to that effect."

"Do you recall the name?"

"I don't, but the phone operator is the one that asked for and got the name. I'll call her and see if she remembers it. Isn't that information in Brees' notes?"

The detective scanned through the notes for a name, nothing. "There is a name scribbled on the edge of a page. Does Bud Dillon mean anything to you?"

"Yes, that's right, Bud Dillon. Now I remember, Bud Dillon. There is a boy by that name. He is a real person. John did check him out."

"And what did he find out?"

"Brees talked to Bud Dillon and discovered he was a popular young man and knew just about all his classmates. He was the class president, played basketball and tennis. He was an honor student. Just a nice young man, liked by everyone."

"I guess that means he denied ever calling the PD."
Mary nodded.

"So one of his many friends used his name? "

"Isn't this information in John Brees notes?"

"I didn't see it in here."

"There was another detective working on the case at that time, and they exchanged notes constantly.

"That would be Daryl Troop."

"Right."

"Some of his notes are in this folder too."

"They worked well together, so it doesn't surprise me," Mary said, nodding again.

The phone rang and Mary excused herself. She listened for a few seconds.

"I'll have Patrick call you when he gets in, Mayor," Mary said as she hung up the phone up and met Kelli's eyes.

"The Mayor?"

"Glad you're working on Lilli Jo's file. This new Mayor has been pressing Patrick for results."

Hmmm, she thought, *Patrick didn't push the pressure off on me; he only said he was glad I was going to be working on the case because he and Mary thought I would bring fresh eyes to the old case.*

"You know, Mary, I think I'm going to interview Bud Dillon again. It's been two years and maybe he'll remember something now he didn't think of then."

"Good luck."

Kelli had been at the Dillon residence for about an hour, going over every tidbit of information with Bud. He certainly was the person Brees had described as a popular young man, and she felt he was in the clear because of his alibi, which was verified by his mother.

"I think you're going to like Central College in Ellensburgh, Bud. I had a friend that couldn't say enough good things about the school. It's small and personal, more one on one. Thank you for taking the time to go over all of it again. If something, anything, about this case comes to mind, please give me call or drop me a note. The Zilke family is still devastated by their daughter's death and I would like to give them some kind of closure, even though it won't bring her back."

He promised he would. She stood and thanked Mrs. Dillon and Bud for allowing her into their home for this second interview. She extended her business card to him and left.

"Wow, mom, wasn't she just great?" Bud bubbled.

"She looks more like a model than a police detective, and seems quite sincere about finding out who did this thing."

The following morning Bud Dillon was telling a couple of girls about his interview with Detective Kelli Finnigan when Oren stopped by.

"I was just telling the girls that I had the most beautiful policeman woman, come by the house yesterday. You should have seen her, Oren. Tall, auburn hair, just beautiful."

"Oh yeah, why was she at your house? What'd you do?"

"Wise guy! She's the new detective on the Zilke murder. Remember the girl that was killed two years ago?"

Oren's heart flipped. *Oh man, they're still working on that?* He made an excuse and left quickly

How could he forget! He wished he could forget. We should have gone to the police the next day but we had too much fear. The church, aunts, moms, and brothers. How silly, he thought. Now, two years later it seemed different. He and Tony hardly ever talked about it. Out of sight, out of mind. *I wonder why some one is bringing it up again. Gotta talk to Tony about this see what he thinks.*

CHAPTER 39

I found Tony at the Y shooting pool.

"Hey Oren. Why the sour face? What's up?"

"Wanna go down and get a coke at Laufren's XXX?" Oren asked, concern in his voice and eyes.

"Sure, what's up, guy?"

"What?"

"It's written all over your face. You look like you swallowed a frog." I pointed out.

Oren smiled weakly, "I saw Bud Dillon today talking to some girls about a detective, that was at his house asking questions about the Lilli Jo thing. The detective is a woman and I guess she's a knock out, that's what Bud said anyhow. Tony, what do you think about us telling this new detective what we know. This whole thing has been bothering me for two years. It's not right."

I nodded. " I agree, it's like a rock in my shoe. It's always bothering me too. You want to go to our telephone booth and call her right now while we both have the balls to do it?"

Oren turned right on Wenatchee Avenue and headed down Chelan Street to the phone booth across from the post office,

They walked over to the booth.

"What are we going to say?" Oren asked.

"We're going to tell her about the guy in the '47 Hudson."

"Are you going to call this time, Tony?"

"Sure, why not, it's my turn."

We dropped the coin in the phone.

"Police Department, can I help you?"

"Yes, I'd like to talk ah, do you have more than one woman policeman working there?"

"Excuse me, sir, what's this call in reference to?"

"The Zilke thing," I said nervously.
"One moment, sir."

"Mary, this is Sandy, the operator. There's a young man on the phone, sounds like our young man from two years ago. He wants to talk to Kelli, do you want to talk to him first?"

"You bet, Sandy. Put him on."

"This is Mary, who did you want to talk to?" she said in her sweetest voice.

"The woman detective, if she's in."

"May I ask your name, please?"

"Well, ah, I'd rather not say, but it's about the Zilke case."

"All right, I'll put you through to Detective Finnigan," she said, trying to contain her excitement.

She ran over to Kelli's office and told her one of the "bobbing heads" was on the phone and wanted to talk to her.

This is Kelli Finnigan."

"Hello Miss Finnigan, I just want to tell you that the person that drives a green and black '47 Hudson could be responsible for the Zilke murder," the voice on the line rattled out like a .30 caliber machine gun.

There was silence for a few seconds.

"Miss Finnigan."

Pause.

"Yes."

"Did you understand me?"

"Yes, I did. Could I ask you why you would make such a statement?"

"We just know that, OK?"

"You realize you would not be in any trouble if you were to assist the PD in solving this two year old murder. In fact, your assistance would be sincerely appreciated by the Police Chief and me, not to mention the grieving family."

"Yes, but we knew this two years ago, wouldn't we get in trouble now?"

"Absolutely not. Did you kill Lilli Jo Zilke?"

"Wow, no way. Why would you ask that?"

"Because that's the only way you would be in trouble."

"We didn't kill her," he said emphatically.

"Look I'm trying my hardest to solve this crime, and if you have some bit of information that would assist this cause, I would be so grateful. Please help us. Could we meet somewhere and discuss what you know? At your convenience, of course. I know you're trying to help and God knows I need to hear anything you might know, please."

The line was quiet for a few seconds.

"Can I call you back tomorrow?"

"Yes, you certainly can, and you can call me direct." She gave him her direct line number. "My name is Kelli Finnigan. You won't get in any trouble, and you could help us crack this case."

"OK, Miss Finnigan. Tomorrow."

"Just call me Kelli."

"OK, Kelli, I'll call you tomorrow."

Kelli sat at her desk and thought about what had just transpired.

Out of the blue, the 'bobbing heads' had contacted the PD, after all this time. *I hope they don't get cold feet over night. These boys really want to help. I felt it. They just need a little handholding. He said "we." They have to be the boys who were in the yard and had witnessed something in or around the house that evening. They'll call. I know they'll call*, she kept telling herself.

I was still a little shaky when I got off the phone, but the feeling of relief was quickly calming me.

"Wow Oren, she sounds great. I think we can trust her.

She wants us to call her tomorrow."

"I believe it was you who said you'd call her tomorrow."

"Oh yeah, that's right, it was me that said that. I just wanted to double check with you, make sure you were still OK with it. She needs help in solving this thing, Oren. We gotta help her. We're not gonna get in trouble, that's what she said and believe her. Like she said, we didn't kill Lilly Jo."

"That's true, but we were outside the window that night."

"Yeah, but we didn't kill her and more than that, we didn't see her get killed either. We really didn't see anything but a beautiful body, and then that guy that came in."

"Well, we saw a little more than that."

We mulled over the possibility they we'd be putting our young lives at risk, but in the end, decided we really had no choice. After all is said and done, we still had to live with ourselves. We would, indeed, call Miss Finnigan the following day.

You know it's funny what time does to a very scary situation. Oren and I had matured a little and we were thinking more like adults. The thought that we had been such cowards, now seemed ridiculous.

The following day around three, we made the call. Kelli Finnigan.

"I'm so glad you called. I was beginning to think you'd gotten cold feet."

"Sorry Miss…"

"Kelli," she interrupted.

"Kelli. We were at school till now."

"I see. Well ummm what shall I call you?"

"Tony. I'm Tony, and my friend is Oren."

"Tony, I would sure like to meet with you and Oren. Would you be comfortable coming to my office?"

"We were thinking the same thing but we don't want to

come to the police station. Sorry. We don't want anybody to see us."

"How about the Columbia Hotel? There's a small coffee shop off the lobby, and it's pretty quiet this time of day."

We discussed the suggestion in hushed voices, then agreed, "that would be all right, Kelli."

"Good. How about four o'clock?"

"See you at the Columbia at four," Tony responded.

CHAPTER 40

We parked across from Wells and Wade, walked the short distance to the front of the hotel and waited. Soon a black and white '48 ford, two door sedan, pulled up and parked. Out stepped the most beautiful woman we had ever seen. She was tall, with dark wavy hair. She walked straight toward us. She was wearing a black wool suit, white blouse, and black shoes with Cuban heels and had this great full figure. I'd guess she was aware of the effect she had on men and chose her clothing to minimize it. As she approached the two she flashed a friendly smile and extended her hand.

"I'm Kathleen Finnigan, but most people call me Kelli, which is my middle name. One of you must be Tony."

"I'm Tony," I said as I grasped her hand.

"Then you must be Oren?"

He nodded, "Yup."

"I am so pleased to meet you both."

We all stood outside the door for a moment in awkward silence.

"Let's go inside and find a table, guys."

Kelli ordered coffee. We ordered cokes and fidgeted as they waited for them to arrive.

"Now, for sure, we're not in any trouble and won't get in any trouble about what we tell you, right?" I asked quietly.

"That's right guys, I need some help in solving this case, so I'm not going to get you in any trouble. You have my word on it. You'll have to trust me."

"OK, what do you want to know?"

"Well, for starters, why should I want to talk to the person who owns a '47 Hudson?"

I glanced over, passing the baton to Oren, then down at my drink.

"We think he had something to do with the Lilly Jo thing."

Kelli waited for Oren to continue, and when he didn't, she prodded, "Guys, you're going to have to tell me more than that to help me understand."

I think Oren guessed where the answer to this question would lead us and decided to let me answer instead.

I sighed. It was up to me to open my mouth and get us involved. Once we told Kelli about that night, we would be in this case to the end. Kelli looked like she was about to ask another question when I took the plunge.

"We were at the window that night," I blurted out.

Kelli blinked and looked like she couldn't believe what she heard. "OK. How did you happen to be at the window?"

"You see, Tony and I were going for a walk that evening," Oren chimed in. " I think it was on a Wednesday, I mean, I know it was on a Wednesday. Anyway, we were walking by a house just down from Zilke's. I knew there was a garden in back of that house, so I asked Tony if he wanted a tomato. He says yeah, but it was still too light so we went down to the Plaza for a coke 'til it got dark enough."

"Is this a general practice of the young men here? I mean, stea... appropriating tomatoes from people's gardens?"

We bowed their heads sheepishly.

"About what time would you say this was?"

"Around six thirty or seven, somewhere around then," Oren guessed.

"It was just starting to get dark," I asserted, "I don't remember how long we were at the Plaza, but when we left, it was dark enough to go into Mrs. Stumply's back yard and get a couple of tomatoes."

"Mrs. Stumply's backyard?" she asked as she gazed at Oren, then at me.

"We didn't know Mrs. Stumply's name then, but it was her yard," I volunteered.

"I would like to hear the rest of that story later, but for

now, please continue with that evening."

"Yeah sure, well, we took two tomatoes and were leaning against the back of Stumply's house, which faces the back of Lilly Jo's house, eating them. Anyway, all of a sudden the light goes on, at the only window in the back of her house and we see a, a Tony could you tell her the rest?"

"Hey, thanks Oren," I smiled wryly. "Well, the light went on in the window, which was shaded, but we could see a woman's silhouette. Looked like she was naked, but we didn't know for sure. Oren, with his hawk eyes, noticed the shade was not pulled all the way down. It was maybe three inches up from the sill." I stopped talking and thought of how to word the next event.

"And?" Kelli prodded.

Oren and I had resigned ourselves to tell it all. I just hadn't known how hard it was going to be. He sighed and continued.

"We walked quietly over to her back yard, until we were right under the shaded window, with the gap. She was naked."

"Maybe from a shower?" Kelli interjected.

"We thought the same thing, or maybe just getting ready for bed."

"Go on, Tony."

"The shade was pulled down, but left about two and a half or three inches from the sill. But we could see inside the room."

I fidgeted in my chair. I was nervous, but boy was I talking, and there was no taking it back now.

"We'd never seen, well, you know, and Tony got the giddies and started giggling when he saw her. He had to step away from the window with his hands over his mouth, to keep from being heard," Oren explained.

"We're not perverts, Kelli. We just saw this shadow of a woman who didn't have clothes on. Not that that it makes it right, but I don't believe any other guy would have passed up looking at a pretty girl like…like her." I felt too guilty to say her name.

"We're not some kind of freaks," I said sorrowfully.

All at once I felt nauseous. The reality of Lilli Jo's death was resurfacing, just as strong as it had been two years ago.

"Tony," Kelli, cut in, "I believe you."

Oren and I glanced up, but we were both so ill at ease that we couldn't meet her eyes.

"Are we getting to the guy in the '47 Hudson?" She prompted.

"Oh yeah, well, we were watching her through the small gap in the shade, and by the way, the window itself was open about six inches," said Oren.

"Was she talking to anyone?" Kelli asked.

If you consider the front door as the South end, and the window we were looking through as the North end, it's easier to describe what we saw. When we approached the window, our only focus was Lilly Jo, but things started to happen. Out of nowhere, this man came walking down the hall into Lilly Jo's bedroom.

"There was light coming from a room to our left, off the hallway. As I recall, that was the only other light in the house, besides the one in her bedroom. From Oren's position outside the window he could see straight through to the front door. Maybe he better tell this part," I said.

"I thought I saw a door open, just a little, not wide open. I couldn't see the person, just kind of a shadow against the door, and the man walking toward Lilly Jo's room was blocking my view with his body." Oren looked up at Kelli. "Is this making any sense?"

Now Kelli looked stunned. "Are you saying there was another person in the house, besides Lilly Jo and this this man?"

"I'm not sure. But I truly believe there was. The hallway

light wasn't on and this guy walking towards us blocked the view of the hallway behind him. I thought I saw a door open towards me, just a little, right as he passed that point. I guess it could have been his shadow. That night I was sure of it, but now well I still feel it was a door, I'm just not as sure," Oren responded apologetically.

She was writing as fast as she could, would lift her eyes up as she thought, and then would write some more. "Did he say anything?"

"He did. We think he said something like, 'Don't you remember me? You said hello to me the other day.' She started shouting at him, but about this time a cat came over to where we were standing and rubbed against my leg, you know how they do, and well, it scared me out of my wits. I stepped back trying to get away from it and damned if I didn't step on its foot. It let out a scream that had us running all the way back to my house," Oren recounted, red faced and embarrassed.

"So you didn't see what happened after that?"

"No, we didn't."

"But you saw the guy that could have killed her, right?"

We nodded.

"And you think he's the guy that drives a green and black '47 Hudson. Why is that?"

I looked at Oren, squirmed in ny chair, then started. "We saw the guy again. Oren and I went to Stalling's and Conway's one afternoon and when we left there was this guy walking down the street toward us. We knew it was him. So we followed him. He went down to Wells and Wade, and we pretended we were looking for a part for my brother.

"We got a pretty good look at him in the store. He was wearing a mechanic's uniform, one of those one-piece coveralls with a name stitched over the pocket on his chest. I think it was light grey."

"OK. What else did you notice?"

"We think he might be a truck mechanic, you know, big eighteen wheelers. We heard some of what he was saying to the clerk, and it sounded like he wanted a truck part. They introduced themselves, so the guy at the store might remember his name, but we couldn't hear it clear."

"Anything else? Was he driving the Hudson?"

We exchanged glances, and Oren took over. "Well, we didn't see him in it that day, but two times after that we saw the same guy driving it in town. We uhhh, we kind of followed him for a while, both times, but we got scared he'd see us so we never got to see where he went."

"You guys are great! Any other little gems you want to share?" Kelli prodded gently. But we couldn't think of anything else.

CHAPTER 41

Kelli approached the Chief, Patrick, which is what he liked to be called, about her meeting with the "bobbing head" boys. She felt she had gained their confidence, and told him that the boys seemed to trust her, and she believed they were being truthful.

She gave him a complete report on their meeting and all the new information, and she requested permission to follow up on the leads the boys had given her. He was only too happy to grant her request.

Kelli leaned back in her chair and thought about truck mechanics. Her thoughts gravitated to the police department's older officers, the ones that knew Wenatchee well. She recalled Patrick telling her about Bob Dyer, a patrolman who had been on the force for twenty years and knew Wenatchee like the back of his hand. Patrick joked that Bob probably knew all of the 17,000 residents personally.

She headed down the hall, knowing his current assignment was administrative, but he wasn't there. She called Mary and was informed he was off today, so she called him at home.

"Hi Bob, this is Kelli Finnigan, sorry to bother you at home."

"No bother, Kelli. What can I do for you?"

"I'm working on an old case and I need your help."

"Fire away."

"Well, I'm looking for a mechanic, maybe a truck mechanic, that drives a '47 Hudson and thought-"

"That would be Dewey Slick." Bob interrupted.

Kelli was dumbfounded.

"You still there, Kelli?"

"I am. Glad I was sitting down. I just couldn't believe

you knew who it was, and so quickly. I guess it is true what Patrick said about you knowing every citizen in Wenatchee. That was almost psychic."

"No, Kelli. I don't know everybody by a long shot. You just asked the right question to the right person. I know the young man. He's a good mechanic and a nice kid. Well, maybe not a kid any more. He in some kind of trouble?"

"This Dewey Slick, you sure he drives a '47 Hudson?' she asked.

"Yup, that's Dewey Slick."

"I'd like to talk to him. Would you have his address or telephone number, by any chance?"

"No I don't, but he works for Allied Freightways down where Miller meets Austin Way. Allied has a good-sized building there. A warehouse I think. Their trucks are green and white. Anyhow, that's where Dewey works."

"How do you know all these things?"

"Kelli, I've been here for twenty six years and when you drive from one end to the other for that long…you get to know just about everything you can know about this town and you get to know a lot of the people, too."

"I can't thank you enough. I can't believe I've gotten so lucky today. Thanks again, Bob."

"Anything for the prettiest detective I know."

"Hey, I'm the only woman detective you know."

"Exactly. By the way, my wife would like to meet you sometime."

"I'd like that. Anytime would be fine with me."

"I'll have her pick a time. Good luck with Dewey."

CHAPTER 42

Kelli walked into the Allied Freightways office and up to the tall counter where a middle-aged woman was organizing freight bills and running an adding machine. She looked up and saw Kelli.

"Can I help you?"

"Hope so. Do you have an employee by the name of Dewey Slick working here?"

The woman stood and walked to the counter.

"I'm sorry, would you repeat the name?"

An older man walked out of the adjoining office and approached the two ladies. "I'll take care of this, Doris. Hi, I'm Bill Stanford, the manager. You would like to talk to Dewey Slick? We all know him here as Thorpe, cause he looks like Jim Thorpe, the legendary Indian sports star. May I ask who you are and what your business with Mr. Slick is?"

"I'm Detective Kelli Finnigan, and I'd like to ask him a few questions."

"I assume you have some identification."

She showed him her badge and ID.

"I didn't realize we had a woman detective on our PD. Has anyone ever told you, you're reminiscent of Ava Gardner?"

She smiled at the manager. *I couldn't tell if he sincere or was he hitting on me?* She thought, "No, that's a first."

He lolled on the counter and continued, "Except for the dimple in your chin, and you're a little taller, you could easily pass for her."

"Dewey Slick," Kelli repeated.

"Oh yes, Dewey. I apologize, I'll go get him for you, Miss Finnigan, sorry, Detective Finnigan."

The manager returned in a few minutes accompanied by a tall, swarthy man, with dark wavy hair. He was wearing a grey one piece uniform with a name on the left breast. He, looked

American Indian, and he was handsome, she thought.

"Is he in some kind of trouble?" the manager asked.

"I'm just trying to clear some things up and need to talk to him."

"You can use that conference room at the end of the hall."

"I can't imagine what I might have done wrong," Dewey said nervously as he opened the door for her.

"I don't know that you have done anything wrong, Mr. Slick." She gestured for him to sit down across the small table from her.

"You're a police woman?"

"Yes, I am; technically, a Police Detective. Mr. Slick. Do you own green and black '47 Hudson?"

"Yes," he answered, concerned.

"How long have you owned it?"

"Several years."

"More than two?"

"Yes."

She nodded and wrote something down on her notepad.

Dewey nervously pushed away from the table and stood.

"I haven't done anything wrong with my car, why am I being questioned?" he asked cautiously, like he was trying not to anger the detective.

"Please sit down, Mr. Slick. I'm just trying to get answers to some questions I have. Please sit."

He remained standing, now glaring defiantly down at her.

"I could have taken you to the police station to ask these questions. I'm trying to give you a break. Please sit down and I'll be done in no time."

He sat.

"Are you the only driver of your car?"

He nodded.

"Do you know a young lady by the name of Lilli Jo Zilke?" she asked and watched his face carefully.

He pondered the question as though he was trying to think if he knew the name or had heard it somewhere before. Then he shook his head and looked directly into her eyes, "I don't think I know the name."

"Are you sure? You hesitated."

"Somehow, I feel like I do know that name or I heard it before, but I don't know when."

She made a notation on her notepad.

"Thank you Mr. Slick. That will be all for now. I would like to get your telephone number and address in case I need to talk you again."

CHAPTER 43

Alice Baker sat in Dr. Angelina Lansing's office. The usual diplomas hung on the wall just inside the door. The furniture consisted of a small desk and swivel chair, a cushioned sofa, and a wooden chair with a cloth seat. Artificial roses in a china vase and a box of tissues sat on the end table next to the sofa. Above the sofa, a large landscape print displayed a floral setting with horses grazing in a sunlit meadow. An expansive set of windows opened the view to a lush green lawn bordered by diversely colored Lilies and a sparsely traveled road.

"Oh good, you're here," Angie said as she closed the door and took a seat at her desk. "I'll be with you in just one minute."

Almost to the second, she came over to the chair and Alice moved to the sofa.

"'Spoken, written, acted on, etc. in strict privacy or secrecy or secret.' I looked it up in Webster's. Not because I doubted what you told me, but for my own satisfaction," Alice said quietly.

"Confidentially, that pretty well sums it up, Alice."

They smiled at the play on words.

"I'm not going to tell anyone what we say here. That's part of my commitment to you, to all my patients. What you say here stays here. Please trust me on that. If we're going to move forward, you have to trust me."

"Angie, this is all new to me. I'm not used to pouring out my feelings or my thoughts to a complete stranger. I hope you can understand."

"I do understand. On the other hand, why not pick a stranger that does this for a living? I'm not biased because I'm your friend or a relative, or anyone that knows you. That way I can be more objective, thereby more constructive, more helpful."

"If I sound like a big coward, Angie, it's because I am. I

have no reservations about admitting it. So many things just piled up on me in such a short time. The feelings I'm having now must be what people feel when they start to lose their minds."

"Where are you going with this, Alice?"

Neither spoke. Alice crossed her legs again, picked up her purse, foraged inside, then set it down. She looked up at Angie, put both feet flat on the floor and looked her straight in the eyes. She had come to a decision.

"Do you know who Lilli Jo Zilke was?"

Angie thought for a few seconds.

"Well, I read the paper like everyone else. She was murdered, wasn't she?"

"Yes."

They stopped talking for what seemed like forever. Alice was obviously nervous about the subject she had initiated. Angie knew Alice wanted to say something and waited her out.

"I was in her house the night she was murdered," she said flatly.

There! She had said it out loud and she felt better. She felt relieved. The feeling reminded her of the time she had broken a beautiful Mexican vase while running down the hall, which she had been told repeatedly not to do. She had thrown away the pieces and said nothing. The following day her conscience had gotten to her, and she told her mother what she had done.

Her mother knew Alice had broken the vase and had hoped she would tell her. She had hugged Alice, told her she had never liked that old thing anyway, and had thanked her for 'fessing' up to it.

Alice reached for her purse and pulled out a small handkerchief.

"I haven't been able to sleep well since it happened. She was my friend, my new friend, and I just feel awful because I haven't said anything about it to the police or anyone else."

Angie sat quietly and listened.

"I feel so awful, like I let her down and she was so nice to me. She invited me to her home, she befriended me, she was my friend and I've done nothing. I thought that man was her boyfriend or someone she knew. I didn't know he was a killer. I might have been able to help her. I just thought she knew him and I was there when I shouldn't have been. I was in her house when she hadn't invited me in. I mean, I mean I was in her house!" She continued through her tears, "I mean, she did invite me to her house, but she didn't hear my knock. I could hear her in there, so I called out and went in without an invitation. Do you know I what I mean? And then when he came in I thought he was her friend or boyfriend. I thought she knew him. All I could think about was how to get out of there without either of them seeing me. If I had known, if I had known I might have been able to do something to prevent it. I could have run to a nearby house and alerted a neighbor, anything, except what I did."

Alice was embarrassed by her emotional outburst, her cowardice, and her admission to entering Lilli Jo's house without an invitation. She had finally blurted it all out and she felt miserable. But it was out. The bleeding had started, the catharsis, relieving the guilt like an over inflated balloon releases air.

"So you never informed the police you were there, in the house?"

"No, that's why I've been miserable lately. I've lost ten pounds because I can't sleep, and I can't eat. It's driving me crazy."

"How did you get in her house?"

"The door was open. The screen did have a latch, but it wasn't fastened. There was a little light from a small lamp in the living room, and a back room, her bedroom, was lit. I don't know why I just walked in. I'm so ashamed of almost everything I did that night."

Alice stared at the floor in front of her, as if she were reliving the awful night again. She squirmed on the divan as she desperately tried to forget.

"Oh Angie, I'm so ashamed, so ashamed. I wish I could die, just die. My life is mixed up. I'm so pathetic. If I had a gun now, I would kill my self. I feel so alone," she sobbed inconsolably. "What am I going to do? I can't live like this."

"What do you want to do, Alice?"

"I don't know. I'm just so miserable and mixed up right now that I'm crazy," she choked through the tears.

"I'm going to give you a prescription for something to help you sleep. You need a good night's rest and some nourishment. Have a good meal, take two of these pills I'm prescribing and go to bed. Can you do that, Alice? Maybe you could call your mother. It might be good for you to have some company for a while."

Angie handed the prescription to Alice. "You can get this filled at the Owl Drug store on the Avenue, go straight there. They'll be expecting you. I'll call them right now."

CHAPTER 44

Dewey Slick hadn't heard anything much from his younger brother Harold since he had joined the Army two years ago. But, today was his unlucky day. He answered the phone on the third ring.

"Hello."

"Hey Dew, this is Junior."

Dewey felt like his worst nightmare had come to light again.

"Thought you were in the Army?"

"Yeah, well, I was. Now I'm not. I'm out."

"Honorably?"

"Fuck you, Dewey!" he snarled.

It was quiet for a few seconds.

"What do you want, Harold?"

"I need a pad for a few days 'til I start working."

"Then I suggest you start speaking to me with a little more respect."

"Well, la-dee-dah Dewey. How about you treating me with a little respect?"

Again, there was silence.

"Where are you, Harold?"

"At the bus station on 2nd and Chelan."

Dewey knew that his older brother probably loathed having to beg for a place to stay.

"I've got a suitcase and a full sea-bag or I'd walk."

"I'll come and get you," Dewey said flatly.

On the way down to pick Harold up, he thought about how to make his expectations for his "guest" in the small rental cottage clear. He wouldn't tolerate any verbal abuse or nonsense, not in his own place.

There was no greeting or handshaking.

"I see you still have this old piece-of-shit Hudson."

"I should have let you catch a cab."

Harold put the duffle bag in the trunk and his suitcase in the back seat. They drove up Orondo Street, past Miller, and finally arrived at Dewey's cottage. They hadn't exchanged a word.

"OK Harold, I have some rules for while you're here. One: no girls in my cottage. Two: you can drink beer as long as you don't get abusive. Three: I work and I need to get at least seven hours of sleep, so keep the radio down, and four: try not to piss me off, cause I'll kick your ass out if you do."

"You sound like my fucking C.O. in the Army."

"That's the way it is Harold. You can take it or leave."

Harold looked around the place. There was a sink, a small cabinet above it for dishes, a frayed two-seat divan, and a single picture of a sailing ship that had probably been there since Moses was a pup. It had tilted and the wall behind it was lighter, cleaner, than the rest of the wall.

There were two tiny bedrooms, each just large enough to fit a single bed. The closet was no larger than a broom closet, and the bathroom was more like a stall than a room. Just a toilet bowl, sink, a single towel ring and, of course, a shower.

"Cozy," Harold sneered.

"There's a sleeping bag in the storage shed behind the cottage, you'll see it."

Harold put his sea-bag in the corner and his suitcase in the small bedroom, the one with no bed in it. He found the sleeping bag in the shed and brought it to the bedroom. Elvis was singing 'Blue Suede Shoes' in Dewey's bedroom. Harold tapped on the door.

"You got any beer, Dew?"

"In the fridge. The fridge is in the back of the landlord's house in a small shed." He gave Harold directions and told him to bring one for him too.

Harold found the fridge and returned with two beers.

"So what are you going to do for work?"

"Thought I'd go to Great Northern Railroad and try to get my old job back."

"What'd you do down there?"

"Mostly box car maintenance."

"How's the pay?"

"Well, two years ago, I was making $1.90 an hour."

"Not bad."

"You still a grease monkey?"

"Yeah. I make $2.83 an hour and I'm getting a raise next month. Ever thought about becoming a mechanic?"

"Nope, don't like all the grease and oil. You don't like me, do you, Dewey?"

Dewey stood and studied the empty beer bottle in his hand. "Want another?"

"Sure."

He walked out the door and returned with two more, handed one to Harold and sat down.

"I don't know how to say this Harold, so I'm just going to say it. We grew up with the meanest son-of-bitch I've ever known and the little bit that I know of you sounds like you've become just like our dad. Me, I grew up with Mom's brother. Maybe not mean like Harold Senior, but he wasn't a warm stove in the winter, either. Hardly ever spoke to me. I could have been a fly on the wall far as he was concerned. I felt like the geranium somebody gave him one Christmas. It dried up and he just left it sitting in his window. I bet it's still in that very spot.

We're like two lost souls, Harold, two lost souls. We're missing things in our life, don't know what, but we're different from other people. I'm surprised you haven't noticed."

"Hey, Dewey, I'm no lost soul. You might be, but I'm no goddamn lost soul." He took a long pull on his beer.

Dewey studied Harold and knew Harold would never understand, and he didn't feel like expending the energy to try to explain it.

"You just don't know it, that's all."

"Hey, come on Dew, let's talk about something else. So do you have a girlfriend?"

"I have a friend that's a girl, that I see once in awhile."

"Do you fuck her?"

"See what I mean, Harold? You're such a shit. You're just like Senior. An asshole!"

"Should I have said, do you engage in sexual intercourse with your friend? Would that have been better?"

"No, that's not any better! It's none of your business."

"You're my brother, I thought I could talk to you about anything. That's what brothers are for."

"We have the same father and the same last name, but we're hardly brothers."

"Fuck you, Dewey."

"Are you trying to piss me off? Do you think you can kick my ass?"

"No, I'm not trying to piss you off and I probably can't kick your ass, I'm trying to be your brother, that's all."

"Well, let's get something straight here, Harold. I'm your brother in name only. As far as I'm concerned, we are just acquaintances. You don't really know me and I really don't know you. Let's leave it like that."

Harold shook his head.

"All right Dewey, I guess that's the way it's gonna be."

There was a knock at the door and a voiced called, "Hey, Dewey, could I speak to you for a moment outside?" Dewey opened the door and faced his landlord tentatively.

"Are you taking on a room mate?" The tall landlord asked with some authority in his voice.

"No, this is my brother. He just got out of the Army and is going to be here just a few days."

"So he's just visiting?"

Dewey nodded.

"All right Dewey, sorry to have bothered you."

"What was his problem?" Harold asked contemptuously.

"He wanted to know if you were moving in. He's the landlord Harold and that's his right."

They finished the beer and Harold offered to purchase more the next day.

"Could I borrow your car while you're at work? I'll go check out Great Northern."

"OK, but you gotta get up early. I have to be there by 6:00 and get off at 3:00. Hope you have some money cause you'll have to put gas in the tank. Probably take about three dollars to fill her up."

"I have some money saved up, so I'll fill her up."

Harold was tired and decided he needed to get some sleep.

"Thanks for letting me crash here, Dew."

Dewey peered at his older brother.

"See you in the morning."

CHAPTER 45

Kelli Finnigan had called Dewey at work and set up an appointment to meet with him at the police station. He was already waiting outside the glass doors as she arrived early.

"Did you know that most people are late for appointments?" Kelli greeted.

He had observed her as she approached and thought she was a knockout.

"No, I didn't. It's probably my only virtue. I'm almost always early."

They went inside and Kelli located a small conference room.

"How come you don't wear a police uniform?" He asked.

"I'm a detective and as such, mostly wear street clothes, to use the police vernacular. I want to thank you for meeting me, Mr. Slick. I appreciate your cooperation." She had opened her note pad. "The last time we talked, I asked you if you knew Lili Jo Zilke."

She was watching him closely.

"Like I said before, I think I may have heard the name, but but I just can't think where."

"Have you ever been on Okanogan Street?"

He looked at her curiously, and grinned slightly, "I'm sure I have."

"Are you aware that your car was seen in the area where Lilli Jo lived?"

"My car?" He tried to think why his car would have been seen on Okanogan.

"You mean driving by somebody's house on that street?"

"It was seen parked near the woman's home."

He opened his eyes a bit wider, surprised.

"There must be other '47 Hudsons in this town, Miss Finnigan?'

"Are you sure you didn't know Lilly Jo personally?"

"No way! I don't know her," he stated adamantly.

He thought about her question. She had phrased it, "didn't know her."

"What did you mean didn't know her?"

"You don't remember going into her house the night of May 11, 1954?"

"No, no way." He stood up, trying to contain his anger.

"Sit down Mr. Slick," she ordered.

He squinted down at her, angry and confused. He sat down quietly and folded his arms across his chest.

"I don't know what you're trying to do to me, but I don't know this Zilke woman."

Kelli referred to her notes and wrote something down.

"Mr. Slick, I would like you to come in next Saturday morning at 10:00."

"What for?" he challenged.

"I want to put you in a lineup," she said calmly.

"A police lineup? I'm not getting something here, why would you want to put me in a police line-up?"

"You should know why."

"Well, goddammit, I don't," he said, raising his voice.

"You sure?"

"I'm not sure you can make me do that, either."

"Well, I think I can. I have enough probable cause to get a warrant for your arrest. Then, I can put you in the line-up. Do you understand that?"

He stood and stared at Kelli.

"How…what probable cause? I wasn't there!" he reiterated earnestly.

"Will I see you Saturday morning at 10:00. Mr. Slick?"

He certainly didn't want to get arrested, and he believed her when she said she could make it happen. He nodded warely.

CHAPTER 46

It was Saturday morning close to 10:00. Oren and I had arrived and been directed to Detective Finnigan's office.

"Morning guys, I'm glad you're here. This is very important."

"So, what do we do, I mean, exactly?" I asked, full of nervous excitement.

"This is what's called a 'lineup'. There will be five people. Since you two saw the person you think might have been in her room that night, you're going to look very carefully at each one, and see if you see him."

"Will he see us pick him out?" Oren asked.

"No. They can't see you because you will be in a separate room looking through a one-way mirror. You can see them, but they can't see you."

Kelli led us downstairs and into a small room with a large window that looked in on a well-lit room with height measurements marked on the wall.

I sneaked a peek at Oren; we both smiled nervously. I thought, *I can't believe were actually doing this thing.*

"Here they come, guys. Now, don't be nervous. They can't see you. Take your time and look at each one before you pick one. If you see the man you saw that night. Don't say anything out loud, we want to be sure that you don't influence each other. Understood?"

We nodded numbly.

"The officer will have each one step forward and say, 'you remember me?'"

In a few minutes five men marched across the floor and turned to face the boys. They were all about the same height and with similar coloring. Each man, in turn, stepped forward and repeated the same words until all had spoken.

"OK fellas, don't answer out loud. When I ask you, I

want you to put a number on this paper." She handed each of them a sheet of notepaper and a pencil. "If you see the man you saw in Lilly Jo's bedroom, write his number on your paper," Kelli instructed. Oren and I each scribbled a number on our notepads and handed them back.

"Are you positive this is the man?" Kelli's eyes flitted back and forth between Oren and me.

We nodded.

Both of us had picked Dewey Slick.

"That's the guy with the '47 Hudson, right?" Oren asked Kelli.

"His name is Dewey Slick, and yes, he drives a '47 Hudson."

"You were right all along, Oren." I turned to Kelli, "He was pretty sure from the first time he saw him driving down Okanogan Street."

"All right guys, thanks for coming down. We really appreciate your time and your involvement." Kelli solemnly shook each of our hands.

"So now what happens?" I wanted to know.

"Well, we have a suspect and the Chief will contact the District Attorney to see if it's enough to warrant an arrest."

"You mean it's not for sure, yet, that he will be arrested?"

"That's right."

"You mean, even though Oren and I saw him in her house that night, it's not enough?"

"I'm afraid not. You didn't actually see him kill her."

"No."

"Just let us do our work now. You've been a bigger help than you know, but we've got to take it from here. I've got your phone numbers and I'll be calling you again soon."

CHAPTER 47

Dr. Angie Lansing had been asked to sit on one of the panels, 'New Concepts: Homosexuality,' at the Hilton Hotel in Seattle, where psychiatrists and psychologists had gathered for the Northwest Conference of Therapists.

She knew her opinions were in the minority and would possibly be called into question by some of the more rigid, more traditional thinkers. She left the large conference room and headed straight for the adjacent restaurant for a much-needed cup of coffee. Early this morning she had been a little nervous, but once the discussion had started her nervousness disappeared.

"What can I get for you, honey?" The waitress asked as she set a glass of water on the table.

"Coffee, please."

"Anything else?"

"Not right now, thanks."

She reached down for her brief case to pull out a notepad.

"Excuse me, Miss…"

Angie looked up to find a large, not tall, but massive man with thin, tossed, graying hair, wire glasses, a bulbous nose, and ashen visage, wearing a rumpled blue suit with a loosened blue and white tie.

"Lansing."

"I thought it was Lansing, but I didn't want to embarrass myself with the wrong name," he said in a heavy, gravelly, but gentle voice. "May I sit down?"

"I'm sorry. I didn't get your name."

"Of course, I apologize. My name is Dr. Bernard S. Waxman, but please call me Bernie."

"You here for the conference?"

"Yes."

He stood gazing down at Angie, as though waiting for

her permission to sit.

"I'm sorry Dr.---please sit down, Bernie."

"Thank you."

"You disagree with my views on homosexuality."

"Quite the contrary, Miss Lansing. I've come to praise you." He gave her one of his rarely seen grins.

"Coffee for you, sir?" the waitress asked as she set Angie's cup on the table.

"Please."

"You're a proponent of the progressive view?"

"I definitely am."

"Where do you practice, Dr. Waxman?"

"Bernie, and I practice in New York."

"I'd be interested in your theories, Bernie."

"I'd say they run parallel with yours, from what I heard this morning."

"Truly?"

"Yes. You see, I'm an old man now and it's taken me quite a few years to learn all that I've learned on this subject, and here I am sitting with a very young psychiatrist," he gestured with his hand, "who already knows all that I know. Yes, I've come to applaud you.

"There are no good studies, because all these nincompoops are afraid to take a chance by disputing conventional wisdom, and I use the term 'wisdom' advisedly. They're waiting for that pioneer, a frontrunner to take the first steps across the thin ice covering this particular pond. You might just be that person, Miss Lansing. I guess what I'm trying to say is I've developed a line of communication with several very prominent people, homosexuals of both genders."

"What kind of prominent persons?"

"Well, I know a senator in one state that I won't mention, a superintendent of schools, a police chief, a National Football League player, mayors of three major cities and several show business celebrities."

"I see, so your view is that their prominence supports the premise that they are not mentally ill."

He grinned guardedly, "I'm not saying anything."

"I'm sorry Dr. Waxman, but I believe you just told me you have a professional relationship with several upstanding, responsible individuals. Are you afraid I might quote you?"

"Would you quote me?"

"No sir. I wouldn't. I'm just encouraged by your progressive views."

"As I am with yours, Miss Lansing."

"How about treatment?" she asked.

"Where do you practice?"

"Wenatchee, Washington. It's a small rural community of about 18,000 people."

"Do you currently have homosexual patients?"

"I have one who recently discovered she had 'different' responses to the opposite sex than her friends and was terrified. I'm working with her now."

"I'm a little surprised you would have any patients. It's been my experience people in small communities are more inclined to stay 'in the closet.' How'd you get involved?"

"Her mother called me."

"And you convinced her you were not a proponent of the prevailing philosophy?"

"Somewhat."

"I believe just like you, Miss Lansing. It's not a mental illness."

"Would you be interested in having dinner with me, sir?"

"I'd be delighted, Miss Lansing."

"By the way, it is Mrs. Lansing," she smiled.

"I'd still be delighted, - - - Mrs. Lansing."

CHAPTER 48

Rufus Applewood kept hearing a ringing in his ears. It would stop, then start again. He opened his eyes and looked at the clock. Could it really be 2:00 P. M? He must have fallen asleep. The bell rang again. it was the doorbell. He leaned forward and rocked as fast as he could and finally was able to stand awkwardly. He forced one leg in front of the other, to the door, and opened it just in time to see Tony at the end of the walkway.

"Tony!" he shouted.

I turned to see Rufus waving to me from the doorway, and jogged back to the porch. Rufus had already returned to his chair.

"Come in my boy."

"I'm sorry Mr. Applewood. I thought we had settled on 2:00 P. M. today---was that wrong?"

"No, no, it was 2:00, I'm sorry. I just dozed off for a minute."

"I woke you up, didn't I?"

"I think I sleep as much during the day as I do at night."

I hadn't seen Rufus Applewood for about two years and was concerned at the difference in his appearance. He seemed more stooped over, and looked very tired. He really did not look well. Much weaker, frail. Rufus kept his curtains closed, Which I thought was pretty depressing. He needed light in this house, and maybe some music. Rufus was looking up at me and he seemed embarrassed.

"I thought maybe you had forgotten your old friend."

"No, I'm sorry for not coming around. I called you a couple of times, but never got an answer."

"Could you get me a glass of water from the kitchen? Should be some clean glasses on the right side of the sink, first cupboard above the counter. Let the water run for about thirty seconds, please."

I hurried to the kitchen and returned a minute later with his water. "Here you are Mr. Applewood."

"So, now I'm Mr. Applewood, again."

"Forgot, Rufus."

"You and Oren have been getting some coverage in the sports section of the paper lately."

"I didn't think you read the sports section."

Rufus raised an eyebrow, "This may be hard for you to believe but I was once, long ago, a pretty good forward on a darn good basketball team in high school."

"Really? Tell me about it."

"Not much to tell. Had a center by the name of Joe Schremmer. The most natural gifted athlete I ever saw. Truly remarkable boy man. He was definitely a pro playing with amateurs."

"Pro?"

"Figure of speech, my boy. He could play any sport he tried. Tennis, pitched on the baseball team, state champ as a sprinter, quarterback in football. He could throw that football a mile. All natural. Other than the practices after school, he just did them. He was a six footer and weighed around two hundred pounds."

"What high school?"

"Louis and Clark in Spokane."

"Did he go on and play for one of he universities?'

"No, don't think he played any sports after high school."

"Aw, come on Rufus. He just quit?"

"He probably could have been a Rhodes Scholar, bright as a flash bulb. Went to a small college, got his teaching credential, then taught there till he retired. At least that's what I heard. Don't know for sure."

"And you were a forward on his team."

"Yup, and a pretty good one, too."

"Imagine that. You never cease to amaze me, Rufus."

"I knew you'd be impressed because you're a jock, but I'm more impressed that I went on to college and became a lawyer. You see, no one in my family had gone to college before me. Anyway, you didn't come to talk to me about my high school days. What's on your mind my boy?"

"I'm glad you shared that story with me Rufus, you've given me a new outlook on some of these older guys around town. I mean, I knew the coaches were athletes, but some of the men you see, just regular guys, were probably good athletes."

"You'd be right."

The odd thing about Rufus was that he never seized to amaze me. It's true, there is always more to the person we know by name, but very little about the real person. How he became the person he is now. I found myself liking Rufus all the more, because there was so much more about the man I didn't know, and it would surface at the oddest times. I wonder what other gem I will discover about Rufus.

The room got quiet, neither of us entirely comfortable raising the issue that was on both of our minds.

"I see the police have a suspect in the Zilke murder."

"Yeah, they do. I wish I could tell you more about it Rufus but Detective Finnigan has told us to keep our mouths shut."

Rufus scrutinized me closely.

"You do remember that you hired me to be your attorney, do you not?"

"That's right! Does that mean we can discuss the things we've talked to Detective Finnigan about. I mean, you and me, Rufus, without getting in trouble with the police."

Rufus forced himself to stand and then stood precariously looking down at me. His hands shook discernibly and he placed them in his robe pockets. He walked toward one of the bedrooms or maybe the bathroom. I heard water running in the sink. Rufus was splashing water and clearing his throat. He came back to his chair. He had washed his face and combed his hair, or at least attempted to make his hair lay down on his head. Why had he gone through all the trouble to wash his face and comb his hair for me, or was it for him? Was it because he had brought up the fact that he, Rufus, was his attorney, and now he had to appear to me to be representative of the court? Rufus was a strange man, but he was a good man and he was smart.

"So many people see things that are wrong, but never say anything. You and your buddy, Oren, were eye witnesses to something you know was wrong. "

"Actually, we were cowards, Rufus, no matter how politely you word it. We were cowards."

We gazed at each other eye to eye.

Rufus nodded slowly, "Yes, there was some lack of courage on your part, but you're undoing that wrong, now."

"I suppose so."

I told Rufus about the police line-up and how we had picked out Dewey Slick as the man we had seen in the room the night of the murder. We were ninety-nine percent sure. I sat back in my cushioned chair.

"Not a hundred percent sure?" he questioned.

I stood and walked across the room, then back.

"You know, Rufus, we were sure it was the guy. But then again, there was something that didn't seem right---you know, that doubt. Like when my brother and I clean the church and we unlock the outer door to the vestibule. Then when we leave he always asks if I locked it up. Father O'Sullivan wants it locked at all times. Anyway, I'm always sure I locked it but when he asks, I have to go rattle the door to confirm it is locked, and it always is. But there was that little doubt about it. Well, when the Detective asked us if we were positive about it being Dewey Slick. The first time we were sure, but after they asked us a bunch more questions, then that one again, I felt like I had to go rattle the door."

"Thus, the ninety-nine percent sure."

I nodded.

CHAPTER 49

Oren and I were walking down Methow Street on our way to Mills Brothers Clothing store.

"I almost swung at him, Oren. What an ass." I seethed as we headed out again. we met the Simmons twins coming out just as they reached the door.

"Hi Tony, Oren," they said almost in unison. They stood outside the door.

"Who's buying something at Mills Brothers?" Taffy inquired.

"Oren's looking for a belt."

"Don't buy it here. Go to Penny's, I'm sure it'll be cheaper," Taffy whispered. "Or Sears," Taffy called over her shoulder as they turned to leave.

We checked the price in Mills Brothers, then walked to Penny's. The twins were right. The price was better here.

"Remember the '49 Olds the Gwynn twins had?"

"Black, right?"

"I think it just drove down the Avenue."

They leafed through the belts looking for prices.

"One twenty nine," Tony grinned.

Oren got his belt and we walked across the street and by the Cascade Hotel.

"Ever get a hair cut in there, Tony?"

"No way, he's too expensive, I think he charges a buck or a buck and a quarter. Where do you get your haircuts?"

"My aunts."

"No way."

"Where do get you yours?"

"Ed's Place on the Avenue, 50 cents."

"That's a good price."

"My dad used to give us haircuts. Wow, was that a chop job, and it hurt like you wouldn't believe. Tears would be running down my face along with the hair, and believe me, they were tears of pain. He had these clippers that you squeezed to cut the hair and sometimes they didn't cut so it pulled your hair out. Sometimes, he got to close to your skin and the clippers would grab your skin. It was sheer, no pun intended, torture to get a haircut from my dad. Those squeeze clippers were designed for torture, not haircuts, no doubt about it. We all had bloody necks when he got through with us."

CHAPTER 50

Harold Slick, Jr. had run out of options and was going to have to take the job his train-car supervisor had offered him. He didn't look forward to working on a section gang, but it was essential he move out of Dewey's small cottage. Harold needed his privacy. He was reading the paper when Dewey arrived.

"You didn't happen to kill some girl up on Okanogan Street a couple years ago, did you Harold?

"What are you talking about?"

"I think I got picked out of a police line-up Saturday. They didn't hold me. I'm not really worried, cause I didn't kill the damn girl. But I'm pissed off to be involved, when I'm not involved. Fucking police have a way of putting innocent people in prison."

"What makes you think you got picked out of a line-up?" Harold asked.

"She doesn't want me to leave town, that's how."

"Who the hell is 'she'?"

"The fucking detective, that's who. Haven't you been listening?"

"The detective is a she? A woman? No shit?"

"Only thing I can think is that somebody out there looks like me and guess who that might be, you bastard! And I'm the one on the hot seat."

"How'd they get your name?"

"It was my damned car!"

"That piece of shit---that green and black beetle? You gotta be kidding," Harold laughed.

"This is not a laughing matter, asshole. It's not your ass on the hot seat, but I have a feeling that maybe it should be."

"I didn't do anything, Dewey! Stop yelling at me. How'd they get to you from the Hudson?" Harold queried.

"I'm not sure. Kelli came down to where I work and asked

me if I drove a '47 black and green Hudson. She told me my car had been seen on Okanogan Street by the house where some woman got killed."

"So the detective's name is Kelli? What's her last name?"

"What, you writing a fucking book, Harold?"

Dewey pulled the card out of his wallet and threw it on the small table. Harold picked it up and studied the name carefully.

"They can't get you for something you didn't do. So why worry?"

"Cops make mistakes just like anybody else. That's why."

"If you got picked out of a line-up that means somebody thinks you're the killer."

"Wow? You're some kinda genius, dumb-nuts. I already told you all that."

"So, somebody was there? Somebody saw?"

"Exactly, Clouseau."

"Whoa!" Harold was trying to hold back a laugh.

Dewey glared at him, then allowed a grin to break through. They laughed out loud, the tension somewhat relieved.

"There must be more than one black and green '47 Hudson in this stupid town. Why you?"

"That's what I'm trying to tell you. I'm innocent. I know I am, but you can't tell the damn hardheaded cops that. They're not listening."

"What about a lawyer?" Harold asked.

"What about it?"

"Can't you get a lawyer?"

"How the hell am I going to pay a lawyer, shithead?"

"Hey, I'm trying to help here, quit calling me names."

"Tell me how I'm going to pay for a fucking lawyer, Harold you tell me."

"Call one."

"Who? I don't know any."

"Any lawyer, and ask about how you pay or how to get a

free one I don't know. Maybe you can hell I don't know. Just call one and ask. Where's your phone book?"

Harold scanned the yellow pages. "How about Anderson, John, Attorney at Law, 3417. You want to call him?"

"The phone's in my bedroom."

Harold sat down on Dewey's bed with the phone book open on his lap and dialed the number.

"Law office."

"Hello. May I speak to Mr. John Anderson?"

"One moment please."

"This is Mr. Anderson's secretary. May I help you?"

"Like to speak to Mr. Anderson, please."

"I'm sorry sir, he's out of town right now. Would you like to leave your name and number and he'll get back to you?"

"Ah, well, ah, no thanks." Harold hung up. "He's out of town."

"He's out of town."

"Isn't there another one in the damn book?"

"Hey, quit yelling at me asshole, I'm trying to help you. Here's an Applewood, Rufus, Attorney at Law," said Harold.

"Applewood! What the shit kind of name is that? Rufus, Dufus. Oh my God, Dufus Applewood," lamented Dewey.

"Hey, dumbshit! He might just be a damned good lawyer."

"Yeah, yeah, Rufus, Dufus."

"Well, do you want me to give him a call?" asked Harold.

"Sure give Rufus a call."

Harold dialed the number and waited. The phone rang seven times before a gruff voice answered.

"Hello."

"Is this Rufus Applewood, Attorney at Law?"

"It is."

Harold put his hand over the mouthpiece. "Do you want to talk to him?"

"No, you talk to him," Dewey whispered.

"Yeah, thanks."

"Are you seeking the services of an attorney?" Rufus asked.

"Yeah, at least I think I am," replied Harold.

"May I ask for what purpose?"

"Well, actually it's for my brother."

"Does your brother have some kind of problem, or merely a query?"

"A what?"

"A question."

"Oh, yeah. He's not sure. That's why he wants to talk to a lawyer."

"Is he in some kind of trouble?"

"Yeah, but he's innocent."

"And he needs the representation of a lawyer?"

"I think he does."

CHAPTER 51

He had been thinking about the girl in Apartment 2 and considered driving up to see if he could see what her little dwelling was like. As he looked in the mirror, he was happy with what he saw. His mother had always called him 'Pretty Boy,' He kind of liked it and tended to call himself 'Pretty Boy' too in his own mind, never out loud.

Dear ole Mom had always thought he was some kinda sissy. How wrong she had been! She was always nagging him to play with the older boys on the block, but he didn't like the older boys. They always picked on him, called him a little faggot. He had asked his mother what a faggot meant and she had just laughed at him. He'd gone to the library and looked it up. When he discovered what it meant he almost cried, then he got furious. *I'll show those bastards*, he thought.

Well, those punks should see me now, they'd see just how wrong they were.

He combed his hair back and turned off the light in the bathroom. There was that stirring in his body and he felt like having a beer. Opening the refrigerator, he gazed in to find only an almost empty bottle of milk, three eggs and two bottles of coke. No beer. He thought he would stop at Peppy's Tavern. He had never been there before.

The tavern was located on a hilly street with a 30% incline. He strolled up to the indistinctive watering hole and pulled the door open to find a very small, dimly lit, smoke filled room, where there were only seven bar stools. When the door opened four men and a single woman watched him as he stepped in. They all just stared and the woman dragged on her cigarette as she sized him up and down. She sat on the stool furthest from the door, and she leaned forward to expose her long white legs to him, then leaned back on her elbow, which allowed her ample breasts to jostle the buttons on her tight white blouse. Her lips were deep red and seductively beguiling. She turned back to the bar, but gave the man a last peep at one of her best assets, the long white legs that reached to a very short skirt made even shorter because it had crept up on her when she turned.

Pretty Boy took notice and sat down at the opposite end of the short bar. He peered into the long mirror and their eyes met. She drew on the long white cigarette, held her breath and smiled lasciviously. The smoke rose up lazily and she sipped on her beer, licked her lips, turned her head and continued to smile. Pretty Boy gave each patron a cursory scan and his gaze fell on the man sitting next to her. The punk quickly looked down into his beer. *Not her husband or boyfriend*, he thought. The bartender stepped in front of him.

"Give me a Lucky Lager," Pretty Boy ordered.

The bartender brought the beer and went back to whispering to the man on the third stool.

The patron on the bar stool two seats away had left a cigarette in the ashtray, and the smoke was spiraling directly into his face.

He coughed. "Would you mind butting your cigarette? It's making me cough," he snarled. The regular looked at the stranger and after a quick scrutiny turned and said something to his friend and they left. Pretty Boy was laughing inside. He was remembering his mother's words and wishing she was sitting next to him right now. He had become a man that could scare other men off just by looking at them. He was big and strong and that was all he wanted. He had often wondered if the man his mother said was his father really was his father. She had known so many men it could easily have been someone that spent the night in her bed.

He had grown so much larger than the man his mother said was his father, and he didn't look like him at all. She was such a bitch. Why couldn't she have been like other mothers?

When he was growing up, he didn't know there was a difference. He thought all mothers were like his. It was only after he got to high school and made the football team that he learned differently. After practice one evening he went to his friend's house for dinner. His friend's mother had been kind and polite, and treated him like an adult. She spoke to him sincerely and listened when he talked. She was gentle and sweet and loved her son. She openly kissed and hugged her son to his dismay, but he would have loved that from his mother.

The woman from down the bar slid onto the seat beside him and the bartender brought her beer. She brushed her right leg against his left and excused herself. She was prettier than he thought when he first saw her. He could smell the faint aroma of Canoe through the cigarette smoke, the perfume his mother used to wear. Suddenly it was his mother sitting next to him and he smiled. She put her right hand on his thigh and squeezed it gently.

"Hey!" He pulled away violently. The others looked over at them.

She looked at him, her eyes large with confusion and a little fear. She started to slide off the stool.

Pretty Boy put his hand on her arm and asked quietly, "Do you like James Taylor? They're playing one of my favorites. Sit back down and I'll buy you another beer."

"What was that all about?" she asked petulantly as she resumed her seat.

Pretty Boy looked down at his beer and smiled ruefully.

"Just for a second there, I thought you were my mother," he said without a smile.

The door opened and a large man walked through the small entrance, stared into the mirror at the wincing blonde and then at the man she was with.

"I don't belong to you, Charles?" she shouted at the mirror. "You don't own me."

Pretty Boy took in the big malevolent presence in the doorway. He didn't need trouble, that's for sure. He turned around, casually threw a bill on the bar. He paused at the door and said quietly to the large man, "I don't poach, buddy. Didn't know. No harm done," and stepped out the door.

CHAPTER 52

Rufus knew he was talking to someone who knew nothing about attorneys. Someone who had very little education, who obviously thought profanity was polite conversation, had little or no money, and probably wasn't employed.

"Sir, you have the upper hand here. You obviously know my name. Would you be so kind as to give me yours?" he requested.

"Yeah sure, well, I'm callin' for Dewey Slick."

"Dewey Slick, S-L-I-C-K," Rufus spelled it out, "and you're a family member?"

"Yeah, I'm his brother."

"Would you like to set up an appointment so Dewey Slick can tell me about his problem?"

"Now wait a minute, are you going to be charging us for this?"

"Mr. Slick- "

"Harold, call me Harold," the voice cut him short.

"There is no charge for this conference," Rufus replied.

"So what do you mean about a conference?"

"Well, Harold, if Dewey has a problem, our meeting will be to discuss the nature of that problem, then determine if he wants to secure my services as an attorney. And I will, at that time, determine whether I want to represent Dewey."

"Uh, well, let me see," Harold stammered

"Harold, you need to discuss this with Dewey. If he is in need of an attorney he will need to decide if he wishes to pursue this matter and then call me back for an appointment."

"Yeah, yeah, let me talk to Dewey and we'll call you back."

"That will be fine."

Rufus Delroy Applewood set the phone down and pondered the short conversation. Why in the world would he be considering thiscase, whatever it was? He had nothing to prove, had more money than he needed. His mind was still sharp, and if it weren't for this dreadful disease, he would still be practicing. But why take on a hooligan that probably didn't deserve his expertise?

Like a moth to a flame, he knew couldn't help himself. Why do people climb deadly mountains? He knew why. His daughters would be adamantly opposed to this venture and would state so, probably quite loudly.

He would call the doctor and see about getting a prescription for the new drug that would control his hand tremors. He hadn't been interested when the doctor first told him about it, but now well now he just might find himself back in a courtroom.

"And I've got to stop drooling all over myself," he said out loud.

He stood and started for the bathroom to wash his face when the phone rang. He turned around slowly and sat back down, grabbed the phone too hastily. It slipped and hit the side of the end table. He placed the phone to his ear.

"Hello."

"What the fuck was that?"

"Excuse me," Rufus said indignantly.

"Uh, what was that noise on the phone?" Harold said much more politely.

"My apologies, I dropped the receiver on the floor."

"Oh, OK. Well, Dewey and I talked about asking you to help him, but we want to know what you're going to charge him."

"I'll be doing it pro bono no charge."

"What's this per bone thing?"

"Pro bono, it's free, no charge, Mr. Slick."

"What do you mean no charge?"

"It's free."

"You're not going to charge him one penny?"

"That's right."

"How come?"

"Well, do you want me to charge him?" Rufus asked rolling his eyes.

"No, no, hell no."

"Would you like to set up the appointment to discuss what I'm going to be doing for Dewey?"

"Well, he works Monday thru Friday, but he's off Saturday and Sunday."

"Saturday would be fine, Mr. Slick."

"Harold."

"Would Saturday be all right, Harold?'

"Yeah, sure, what time on Saturday?"

"Ten o'clock."

"Ten o'clock is OK, then, we'll see you Saturday."

"Do you want to know where to go on Saturday?" Rufus inquired.

"Oh, yeah, sure," he said laughing.

"It's the Doneen Building, on the corner of Wenatchee and Kittitas Street. I'm on the menu out front, Applewood. Got that? Applewood. My office is on the 2nd floor, room 210. My telephone number is 3353."

Harold repeated the address and the telephone number. He had Rufus spell the Doneen Building again.

CHAPTER 53

Alice arrived at Dr. Lansing's office promptly at 3:00 P.M. with her mother in tow. They were standing outside her door waiting while Angie conferred with her secretary. She finished and approached the two with a friendly smile.

"Mrs. Baker, I presume?"

"Dr. Lansing, how wonderful to meet you face to face. You're smaller than I imagined, but I'm sure you carry a big stick."

"You know what they say about small packages, Mrs. Baker," Angie responded, as she winked.

"No offense, Dr. Lansing, just stating an observation. And I might add, we Alice and I, are grateful for your professional interest in her ah, turmoil, for the lack of a better word."

Angie nodded and turned to Alice.

"How are you, Alice?"

"I'm a lot better. I don't know if it was the pills you prescribed for me or that my mother was coming to stay with me, that allowed me to sleep. Maybe, in conjunction, the two things gave me a new perspective."

Angie offered coffee or water, which they politely declined.

"Could we just talk for the hour, informally, maybe using first names? Would that be all right?' Jane asked politely.

"I think that's a good suggestion," Angie responded.

"May I speak openly?" Jane requested.

"Please do."

"Alice has spoken about you very affectionately. She feels some progress can be made with regard to, I believe the common term for her...uh condition, the one you might hear in public is queer."

"That's interesting you would bring up that particular term. I was recently at a conference in Seattle. There was an open discussion led by some prominent psychiatrists from around the country, most notably from New York, the hub of well-known doctors in this field. I met a progressive psychiatrist from New York who has the same opinions as I do. His ideas parallel mine in that he believes homosexuals are not mentally defective, nor are they mentally ill.

He has personally observed and treated many gays and lesbians who function in the real world in prominent positions, such as governors, policemen, nurses and doctors. He believes they are proof it is not a mental illness."

"Oh my gosh, Dr. Lansing, that's wonderful. You mean homosexuality is not a sickness?" Alice asked.

"That is what I, and several others, believe."

"I'm just thankful to know, if I am a queer "

"Homosexual. Let's not use the negative terms anymore, Alice."

"So, it's final. I'm a homosexual, Angie?"

"We haven't clinically proven that."

Alice raised her eyes to her mother and then to Angie. "Well, it's just good to know if I am, that it doesn't mean I'm evil or retarded or sick."

"Honey, I've never felt there was anything bad about you, I just didn't know what was troubling you." Jane said.

"Part of the problem is, there is not enough research data on homosexuality. The fear of exposure adds to the scarcity of information," Angie stated.

"So what does one do who is afflicted with this thing?"

"Many, maybe most, 'live in the closet,' to utilize the current euphemism. According to the psychiatrist from New York, it's pretty hard, for obvious reasons, to formally proclaim you're a homosexual when you've been elected to the governorship of a state."

"What obvious reason?" Jane queried.

"In the Governor's situation, he could possibly be recalled for not declaring he was a homosexual before he ran for

Governor, even though that isn't a legal requirement. If he had been brave enough to declare he was a homosexual *before* the election, he probably wouldn't have been elected."

"Can we move on to my more immediate problem, Angie?" Alice asked almost apologetically.

"The Zilke situation?"

Alice nodded slowly.

"Have you told your mother?"

"Everything."

"I see. Jane, do you think Alice should contact the police department and tell them she was in the Zilke apartment on the evening the young lady was murdered?"

"Well, Alice didn't kill her."

"That's a given."

"She'll be thoroughly interrogated and she'll suffer greatly." Jane said, concern on her face. "I don't know honey, do you think you could handle all that?"

They looked at each other, each considering the impact of telling the P.D.

"How much time do we have left, Angie?" Jane asked.

"We've run over a little, already."

They all stood and walked to the door.

"I'm sorry. Could I discuss this with my mom and let you know next Friday?"

"Do what you feel right doing, Alice."

Jane walked over to Angie and hugged her warmly.

"I am so glad we picked you to help Alice. It must have been God's will. I'll probably be here another week or so. We'll discuss this thing and fill you in next Friday."

"Jane, it can only get better." Angie assured.

She closed the door and sat at her desk. Jane's mental state was significantly better. Her mother's visit had had made a huge difference.

CHAPTER 54

Detective Kelli Finnigan tapped on Patrick's office door and entered.

"Kelli, how's it going?" he asked as he leaned back in his chair and placed his hands behind his head.

She proceeded to narrate the events as she checked her notes. She informed him of the boys' presence at the Zilke residence, and the reasons for their proximity to the window. The reason behind their reluctance to come forward with the information was embarrassment, both public and personal. They are both Catholic alter boys, hence afraid of the confessional. Anyway, the boys did not see the actual murder.

"But this Dewey Slick person was in the house on the evening of the murder. The boys saw him in there, and can verify that, right?"

"Well, they're 99% sure," she replied.

"What? 99% sure, what does that mean?"

"I think they're just afraid to be wrong and put the man behind bars. They both said it was him without hesitation…but…"

"What about the possibility that someone else was in the house that night?" Chief speculated.

"Well, there is a possibility there was someone else in the house, but we're not positive. I interviewed that woman, Patrick and I'm not sure we can depend on her. I have some reluctance in believing her, and I don't think she would be a good witness. It's her problem with dementia, the old age thing, where you don't remember well. She was coherent and lucid when I spoke to her, but her daughter says she has good days and bad days. On the bad days she…Kelli shrugged her shoulders.

"What have you got in your hand, Kelli?"

"Oh yes, one more bit of confusion to add to this crime scene," she said, placing an enlarged picture on Patrick's desk.

"What is this?"

"It's a picture of the ground outside the window where the boys were standing when they were peeping in that evening."

"So then, these are the boy's prints that I'm looking at?"

"Well, most of them are the boy's Chuck Taylor All Stars prints, but there is a part of shoe print that isn't accounted for, right here." She pointed.

"Do you have any idea whose print it is?"

"Not yet, but I went down to the crime lab and talked to the technician. He thinks it could belong to a policeman. The edge looks like the sole of the police issued shoes."

"Humm, how about Brees or Troop, the previous detectives on the case?" Patrick asked.

"I thought the same thing, Patrick, so I checked it out. They both wore civilian clothes and shoes. Brees wore a pair of cordovans and Troop wore a brand of loafer from Carl's Shoes. Neither could have left that print."

"A policeman, humm. Kelli, you're doing a good job. Keep it up and you're going to solve this case. Now, about this young woman that could have been in the house that evening. Let's throw that around and see where it takes us?"

"Why would a young lady, that we'll say was in the house and maybe witnessed a murder, not come forward with that information?" Kelli asked.

"She didn't see anything? She was in co-hoots with the perpetrator? She's afraid?" Patrick watched Kelli closely to gauge her feelings about his suggestions.

"She didn't see anything, does sound plausible, because if she had seen anything, she would be dead too."

Patrick nodded.

"Cohorts doesn't sound reasonable because of the statements by the witnesses. If Mildred Dern is to be believed, she saw a single woman leave the house and then stand under her willow tree. Supposedly they spoke. I personally think cohorts is not a viable premise."

Again Patrick nodded.

"'Fear, yes, that could be the reason she didn't come forward. If this person is not coming forward because of fear, she is probably having problems sleeping, eating, just doing everyday things."

"I believe you're right on target, Kelli. It just occurred to me, do we have any other suspect? I mean besides this Slick fellow, no pun intended."

"Right now, he's the only one."

"Is he a local fellow? Does he have brothers or sisters, extended family? How much do we know about him?"

"I know he lives alone, his father was killed in a railroad accident, his mother deserted him years before. No sisters. A brother in the Army. That's it. I'll drive up to his house tomorrow and see what else I can find out."

CHAPTER 55

The next day, Saturday.

Kelli parked in front of a two story older home that was obviously well kept. It was white with blue trim, recently painted. She saw some paint drippings on a large daisy bush as she walked behind the house to a small white cottage. There was a narrow strip of grass on either side of the sidewalk that led to the door. She knocked three times. The door opened and a man who favored Dewey standing there, looking at her inquisitively.

"Well, well, well. Who are you?" he purred.

"Detective Finnigan," she replied stolidly. "Who are you?"

"Oh, you wanna talk to Dewey?"

From behind Harold, Dewey said politely, "Detective Finnigan, come in."

She entered the very small front room and looked around. There was very little space in the tiny dwelling.

"What can I do for you Detective Finnigan?" asked Dewey.

"Is this your brother from the Army?"

"Oh yeah, this is Harold."

Harold was leaning on the door with his arms folded across his chest.

"Hi," he said, as he opened the door to go outside.

"Would you mind staying, Harold? I'd like to ask you a few questions."

"Sure, no problem."

Dewey placed a cigarette to his lips and started to light it.

"Would you mind going outside, Mr. Slick, to smoke that cigarette?" She requested.

He peered and seemed annoyed she would ask him to go outside of his own cottage to smoke.

"No, I guess not," he said, grabbing his lighter and walking to the door. "I'll be outside."

"Thank you, Mr. Slick."

Harold walked over to where she was standing.

"Is there another chair available?" she asked.

He walked to his bedroom, came back with a small stool and sat directly across from her. She pulled out small notepad and fumbled around for her pen. He expelled gas noisily at that moment. "Ooops, sorry about that," Harold said smiling.

Kelli stood. "Maybe we should all go outside," she instructed angrily as she jerked the door open. "Are you currently employed?"

"I'm not working yet, but I have a job offer from my former employer, Great Northern Railroad. Why?"

"I'd like for you to come and see me at the police station at 10:00 A.M. this coming Monday."

"Why, am I under suspicion for something?"

"No."

"What if I say I don't want to come down there?"

"Now why would you want to say that, Mr. Slick?"

Harold focused his eyes on Kelli. She didn't flinch. He blinked.

"I guess not."

"Fine, I'll see you on Monday at 10:00 A.M." She handed her business card to him. Kelli walked away briskly, knowing Harold would be watching her.

CHAPTER 56

"I'm here to see Detective Finnigan, Harold Slick declared to Mary Corley at 10 a m on Monday.

"Your name sir?"

"Harold Slick."

Mary led him to Kelli's office.

"Hello Mr. Slick, please sit right here," said Kelli as she waved him to a small conference table, "I'll be right with you."

Harold sat down and brought his left ankle to his right knee.

Kelli carried her folder over to the table and sat down across from him. "Would you like a cup of coffee Mr. Slick?"

"No, and call me Harold. I get nervous when people call me Mister anything."

"Fair enough. You must have just gotten out of the Army?"

"A while back."

"Over a month ago?"

"Not quite a month," said Harold.

"When did you join the Army?"

"You mean the exact date?"

"Yes."

"May 13, 1954."

"Are you certain about that date?"

"I'm sure. Everybody says it's an unlucky number, but the recruiter said it was his lucky number."

"OK, so May 13th, 1954 was the day you joined the Army."

He nodded.

"Do you remember where you were on Wednesday, May 11th, 1954?"

"Now, how in the hell would I remember that date? That was a long time ago."

"You remembered May 13th, 1954. This is just two days earlier."

"Yeah, well, that was on my discharge papers and my

departure I.D. card, that's the only reason I remember it."

"Have you ever driven down Okanogan Street?"

"What kind of question is that? I've lived here almost all my life. I guess I've driven down that street a few thousand times."

"You know a woman by the name of Lilly Jo Zilke?" Kelli locked her eyes on Harold's and held them till he looked away.

"Never heard of her."

"Did you strangle her, Harold?"

Harold stood abruptly, knocking the chair over backward.

"What kind of bullshit question is that?" he snarled between clenched teeth. "I don't know that girl and I didn't strangle her, god damn it."

"Sit down, Harold!" Kelli commanded.

Harold stared down at her, rage in his eyes.

"Harold, sit down," she demanded and pointed to the chair.

"Fuck you!"

She started to stand and his right arm raised up to slap or slug her. She blocked it with her left forearm, stepped in, and with her body weight behind it, swung a straight right to Harold's midsection. He staggered back, hit the wall with a thud and slid to the floor. She started toward him, but he wasn't getting up, not for a while, anyway. The door opened and Mary Corley peeked in to see Harold on the floor.

"Is everything all right in here, Detective?"

Kelli gazed at Mary, surprised at herself. It all happened spontaneously and without thought. It was a Kung Fu trained reflex.

"I'm all right." Harold shook his head and attempted to stand. "I just tripped over my chair, I'll be all right," he said sheepishly.

Kelli nodded to Mary. Mary grinned wryly and closed the door.

They sat down at the table again.

"I want you to know something, Harold. I can be a real bitch if I want to be and you don't make points by swearing at me. I don't like profanity. You understand? I can't keep you from using gutter language, but I can put your feet to the fire, if that's what you want it's up to you. If you can't think of good word to use just grunt and I'll try to help you out."

Harold sat quietly, peering at the floor.

"Do you remember where you were on May 11th, 1954, between 7:00 and 9:00 P.M.?"

No response.

"Well, Harold?"

"I'm thinking! Maybe a movie, I just don't remember for sure."

"A movie. Do you remember the name of the movie or what it was about?"

"Detective, I really can't remember."

Then it hit him. That was the night he had gone to that girl's house. His memory of that night was sketchy. He remembered smoking some reefers and he had consumed at least a pint of White Horse Scotch. So that was May 11th. He vaguely remembered going into a house. It might have been on Okanogan Street, but he couldn't recall for certain. That girl is dead, oh my God. No wonder the shit is flying around poor Dewey. He's going to kick my ass if he finds out I was there.

But I didn't kill her I don't think I killed her. I must have gone inside the house, but not for sure. The whole thing is hard to remember. I wonder if I'm talking myself into believing I was in that house. That damn scotch! That shit made me crazy. Reefers never did that to me.

"Harold, where were you just now?"

"What do you mean, where was I? I'm right here."

"I called your name three times before you acknowledged me."

"What?"

"Your mind was somewhere else for a few seconds. Where were you?"

Kelli was certain she had bumped his memory and Harold had remembered something in those few seconds. He had remembered something and now he was trying to be elusive.

"What was the girl's name?" he asked timorously.

"Lilly Jo Zilke," she repeated as she observed every tiny movement Harold made. She could see he had remembered something and was trying his best to keep her from seeing it in his face. He put his left hand to his cheek and over his mouth as he pondered something; he knew something, she could sense it. He fought even the slightest movement of his body, trying to stay still and impassive, like a rabbit a few feet away from a fox. The slightest movement would give it away. He squinted in thought and Kelli observed the twitch.

"Did you remember something, Harold?"

He forced his eyes back to Kelli and responded.

"Maybe my brother Dewey mentioned the name, I'm not sure."

"So, you have heard the name before?"

"I believe Dewey mentioned the name."

"Have you and your brother discussed Lilly Jo at all?"

"Some."

"In what context?"

"You mean, why have we talked about her?"

She nodded.

"Well, Dewey knows he's innocent, but he believes there are lots of people in jail that are innocent and that's why we discussed the Lilly Jo thing, and we called a lawyer for him."

"He's getting a lawyer?" she asked.

"He's thinking about it."

"Do you know a local lawyer?"

"We called one yesterday and we're going to go see him next Saturday. His name's Appleway. We called him for Dewey, but I guess I need to talk to him too."

"Who?"

"Appleway, Rufus," Harold repeated.

"You mean, Rufus Applewood, don't you?"

"Yeah, that's right, it is Applewood. Do you know if he's a good lawyer?"

"I've heard he has a good reputation in the community."

"Do you think Dewey needs a lawyer?" she questioned.

"He didn't do nothing wrong," Harold said indignantly.

"How would you know that, Harold?"

"Dewey doesn't really like girls," he snickered, "always been kind of scared of 'em."

"What about you Harold, do you like girls?"

"I didn't do anything wrong."

"Do you like girls, Harold?"

"They're all right, I guess. Yeah, I like girls."

Harold was thinking about the strangling thing. Dewey was definitely going to need a lawyer and he was beginning to think he might be in need of a lawyer himself. He was pretty sure he hadn't killed the girl. Still, he couldn't remember a lot about that night, just bits and pieces. He was beginning to sweat and he could feel his face flushing.

"What are you thinking about, Harold?" she purred as she wrote in her little pad.

"I'm not thinking anything." Annoyance flavored with defensiveness colored his tone.

"I think you were, Harold. I could almost hear the wheels turning in your head."

"This woman on Okanogan is dead?" he asked.

"Where have you been for the last," she checked her watch, "forty minutes?"

Kelli could see something was confusing him. He wasn't a bad looking guy, other than his crude, coarse, disgusting language and crass behavior. She was confused that he wouldn't know Lilly Jo was dead. That's what this whole thing is about, the numbskull.

"Whose idea was it to get a lawyer?" she asked.

"I think it was mine?"

"Because?"

"Because he knows he's innocent and because someone said they had seen his car around the street where the dead girl lives. At least that's what he said."

"Did he tell you why his car was parked on Okanogan on that particular evening?"

"He doesn't remember ever parking his car on that street."

"Never?"

"I thought you asked him all these questions already?"

"I did, but now I'm asking you, Harold."

"Detective, I'm getting confused about what I've said and what Dewey has said and I'm getting rattled. I'm having trouble keeping things straight. How much longer are you going to quiz me?"

Kelli placed her pen down, crossed her arms over her chest and sat back.

"I want you to go home and think about where you were on May 11th, 1954. OK, Harold? Make it good, cause I'm going to check it out. You can go now. I'll call you in a couple of days. You let me know if you leave Wenatchee for any reason." She handed him a business card. "If you move out of Dewey's place, I want to know right away and where your new residence is located."

"Yeah," he scowled and left.

Kelli was thinking about the Slick brothers when she remembered she had snagged her nylon earlier. She stood and pulled her dress up to see if there was a run in her nylon.

Mary Corley walked around the corner just in time to see Officer Dan Dupree standing close to the partially open door to Detective Kelli's office. When Dan looked up and saw Mary, he turned quickly back to the stairwell and left. Mary went over to see why he was looking, no, peeking into her office. Kelli, was just then pulling down her dress.

"Hi Kelli, are you all right?" Mary asked.

"Yeah, I think I need to get a new pair of nylons."

"Oh."

"Did you want to tell me something, Mary?"

"No. The reason I came over here was because Dan Dupree was peeking into your office, I wanted to see what he found so interesting."

"Officer Dupree was peeking into *my* office?"

Mary nodded.

"Hummm." Kelli sat down and folded her hands on the top of her desk.

"Close the door, Mary. I want to ask you something."

Mary checked the hallway, in both directions, and closed the door.

"What's the story on Officer Dupree?" Kelli asked.

"Is this confidential, Detective Finnigan?"

"Hey, Mary, this is Kelli. Right now, we're talking girl stuff. Please. I get funny vibes from that guy sometimes."

"Well, Chief Allen used to call him the 'noisy one' cause he only spoke when spoken to. Patrick calls him the 'quiet one,' for the same reason.

"OK, he's quiet. What else?"

"He's divorced, no children, originally from Omak or Okanogan. Came here from Chelan, no girlfriends, that I've heard of, doesn't mix with the other officers and pretty much stays to himself. His work is OK, but not spectacular. He's a good policeman, I guess. Never heard otherwise."

"That's all police jargon, Mary. What do you_think of him?"

"Me, personally? I don't know Kelli, I mean…"

Kelli rolled her eyes, shook her head and gave Mary an

exasperated smile.

"Go get your bible, Mary."

"Bible?"

"Yes, your bible, so I can swear on it that I'm not going to repeat anything that you and I discuss in this room."

Mary inspected Kelli's eyes seriously and Kelli stared back and then they burst out laughing.

"He's not my type of guy, he's he's, almost creepy, you know, when he looks at me, it gives me the creeps. There's something about the man that makes you uneasy. I guess, I can't really put it into words." She grimaced. "I'm not real good with words, Kelli."

"You know Mary, that pretty well sums it up for me too. He is kinda creepy. I'm not sure I've ever talked to the man other than to say hello. I have caught him staring at me, but that, in itself, is not unusual when you work in a male dominated environment. I don't have time for men in my life, right now. I'm too busy with being a cop, and for your information, I am straight. Mary, I'm pointing that out because in the PD I came from, I heard the whispers and sometimes deliberate slurs because I didn't have anything to do with all the passes and taunts they threw at me. Some men just don't get it. Of course, I'm generalizing. Not all men are like that."

"I think I understand, Kelli. You are a beautiful woman and most women would love to look like you, but that's only part of it. You're also a career woman and very good at your job. It must be very difficult for men to see you as a police Detective. A lot of people still think a woman's place is in the home, having babies and fixing dinner for her man."

There was a knock on the door.

"This conversation was just between us Mary, and will go no further."

Mary stood and winked at Kelli.

"Come in."Kelli called.

"I heard all the laughter in here and thought I'd come join in," Patrick said with a big smile.

"Just girl talk, Patrick," said Mary.

Kelli winked conspiratorially, "Thank you, Mary. You've been a big help."

"How's the Zilke case going, Kelli?" Patrick inquired.

"Pretty good sir. I had Harold Slick in here today and we had a pretty good interview. I think he knows more than he's telling, tho."

"So, does that mean we have a Dewey and Harold Slick, now?"

"That's right, you don't know about Harold, the brother."

"You'll have to bring me up to speed on him, Kelli, but not right now. If you need assistance, let me know, and I'll assign Detective Charles, to you. His request."

"Would you be pulling him off anything important, Patrick?"

"He's got a couple of assignments, nothing major, and he asked if you were in need of assistance on the murder case."

"I'm all right for now, Patrick, but that can change anytime."

"I'll let him know."

Kelli looked down at her note pad and saw the name Mildred Dern. Detective Daryl Troop had interviewed this woman who said she had seen a man come out of Lilly Jo's house. She picked up the phone and dialed.

"Hello, Mrs. Alexander, this is Detective Kelli Finnigan. Would you mind if I came by to talk to you and your mother?"

"I guess that would be all right, Detective, what's this about?"

"Oh, I'm sorry Mrs. Alexander. It's about the Zilke murder a little over two years ago."

"My gosh, they still haven't solved that poor girls murder? There's still someone out there lurking about. I thought they would have taken care of that by now."

"We've been trying. I'm the lead on the case currently and I'd like to come by for a few minutes."

"That will be fine, Detective Kelli. I'll tell my mother you're coming by."

"I appreciate it, see you in about 15 minutes."

CHAPTER 57

"Wow, you're prompt Detective Kelli," Mrs. Alexander said as she opened the door. "Let's go into the kitchen, my mom's waiting there. Would you like a cup of coffee?" She led her to a chrome table and chair set.

The top of the table was speckled black and cherry-red, and the cushioned seats of the chairs matched. Kelli could smell the fresh coffee brewing and a sweet fragrance of something baking, something good. An older woman with her hair pulled back into a ponytail sat at the table. She stood as Kelli walked in.

"Hi, I'm Mildred Dern," she said and smiled enthusiastically.

"Kelli Finnigan, Mrs. Dern."

"Would you like a cup of coffee?"

"Only if it's already made, Mrs. Alexander."

"I've got some fresh chocolate chip cookies just coming out of the oven," Mrs. Alexander offered.

"Oh no, my absolute favorites. Coming here is not going to be good for my figure."

"I don't think you have anything to worry about it, Detective. You look very fit."

"Thank you."

They sat and had cookies and coffee and talked about Wenatchee in general until Kelli directed the conversation to Lilli Jo.

"Now, I never saw anything. It was Mom, here, that saw people at Lilli Jo's house."

"All right. Mrs. Dern, tell me what you saw two years ago, on May 11, 1954."

"Excuse me Detective, I just want to tell you this first," June Alexander interjected. "Two years ago, when this thing happened, Mom's memory was getting bad, you know, sometimes she couldn't remember things. But then, other times she could be razor sharp, remember everything. Well, the doctor, told her to start walking more, eat plenty of fish you know, for memory. Well, Mom walked all over the neighborhood and ate salmon, or halibut, or trout every day. Her memory started getting better. Honest."

Kelli acknowledged Mrs. Alexander's update on her mom's condition, and turned to Mrs. Dern. "Well, let's see what you can tell me about that night, ma'am," Kelli asked. "So how many people did you see come out of Lilli Jo's house, Mrs. Dern?"

"Three, all total."

"That's not what you told Detective Pool two years ago."

"That's what I saw, three. One young lady, I think, I mean, I think she was a young woman, not old. Then I saw a tall man come out and then I saw a stout man come out about a half hour later."

"Why would you say a half hour later, why would you remember that?"

"Well, I had seen the young woman come out and then the tall man came out and then June here, called me into the house to watch the Art Linkleter Show for a half hour. Well, after that, I didn't want to watch the next program so I went back outside. After a few minutes, I saw the stout man come out, that's how I know it was a half hour later."

"Did any of these people see you?"

"No, they didn't. Wait that's not true, I did say something to the young woman. Right June? I did say something to her."

Kelli looked to June, who added, "Well, I heard her talking to someone when I went outside to call her in for the evening. I don't recall what she said, but I do remember hearing her speak. I remember asking her who she was talking to outside. She said a young lady. That's right, she said a young lady was standing by the willow tree in the front yard, that's where she saw her."

"Maybe you could show me the tree?"

June ushered Kelli out of the kitchen and through the front door.

"Well, this is the tree, "Mildred said standing by the very large weeping willow tree.

"Why were you standing by the tree here?" Kelli asked.

"Well, I wasn't standing by the tree until I saw the girl come out of the Zilke house. You see, I was sitting on the front porch," Mildred said as she walked back to the front porch. "Here, I was sitting right here, just enjoying the evening, just looking at anything that moved, I guess. It's pretty quiet but occasionally one of the neighbors walks by or someone comes out to water their lawn or garden. Anyway, she comes out walking real fast. So the minute I saw her, I run to the tree just as she crosses directly toward me. I walked up so I was behind the tree and she couldn't see, like this," Mildred peeked around toward the street, "and she walked right up to my tree. See how close I am to the sidewalk?"

"So you saw her up close?"

She nodded.

"She was crying, Detective. Yup, she was crying, not sobbing tho, real quiet like."

"You mean whimpering?"

"Yeah, kinda, you know those sounds you make when you're crying but trying not to let anybody know."

"I think so," Kelli nodded. "What about the tall man?"

"Well now, that's the one I didn't see very well. He came out and got in a car that was parked down the street a little ways and he left."

"What kind of car?'

"Don't know."

" Do you remember the color?"

"Didn't see it real well, just heard him slam the door and drive off."

"Humm, back to the girl, do you think you would know her

if you saw her again?"

Mildred shook her head slowly. "I really don't think so. Didn't see enough of her face, cause she was crying."

"Mrs. Alexander, could we go back in the house now?"

"Sure, Kelli, I've still got coffee."

"I'd better not, but thanks."

"Tell me about the stout man," Kelli asked, pencil in hand. "Wait. What did the girl look like?"

"She was pretty tall "

"Six feet?" Kelli interjected.

"Maybe, five feet eight or nine. She was tall for a girl, you know."

"Hair?"

"I think it was dark, not sure though."

"Was she wearing a coat or a sweater?'

"Maybe a form fitting sport coat. Could have been a red sweater and slacks. The slacks were dark grey, I think, maybe charcoal."

"Shoes?"

"Didn't see her feet."

"Did you say she wore a hat?"

"Didn't say, but I think she was wearing one of those black Navy Watch caps, those kind that fit tight on your head. But some of her hair was sticking out by her forehead, and down her neck."

"Was she thin?"

"Hard to tell. In the dark and with what she was wearin', couldn't tell. But if I had to guess, I'd guess on the thin side."

"Good, Mildred. Now tell me about the stout man."

"June, could you pour me a cup of your black coffee, honey?" Mildred asked.

"You sure you should drink a cup?" June asked as she stood.

"I'll be all right, hon."

Kelli cozied up to the table and put her notepad directly in front of her, pen poised.

"What do you mean by 'stout man'?"

"Well, he was about as tall as George, June's husband, but thicker. He was kind of wide, bulky, more…more massive. No…just thicker."

"How tall?"

"I think he was maybe five feet ten or eleven - - maybe."

"Uh huh. What color was his hair?"

"I think he had dark hair."

"Light or dark skinned?"

"Could have been Indian."

"American Indian?"

"Is there any other kind?"

"Well, there are Indians from the country of India."

"I was thinking of the Nez Perce that live up by Okanogan and Omak. There's a few living in this town, you know."

"I've heard that."

Mildred looked over at Kelli pensively and nodded. "That's right, but I don't think I've ever seen an Indian from India here."

"How old do you think he was?" Kelli continued.

"Looked to be - - - maybe fifty."

"Did you notice if he wore glasses? Did he limp?"

"Wasn't limping from what I remember, and what was that other thing? Oh, glasses. I don't recall seeing glasses, but wouldn't be surprised if I just didn't notice."

"Do you remember anything about his attire?"

"Attire?"

"What he was wearing?"

"I think it was all black."

"A black shirt and trousers?"

Mildred nodded.

"Could it have been a uniform of some sort?"

She thought for a few moments.

"At the time, I sure didn't think anything about a uniform, but now that you've said it, I guess it could have been. Maybe, like a Catholic priest wears?"

"I suppose it could have been a Catholic priest's attire."

"Are you Catholic?" Kelli asked.

"No, we're Presbyterians, and our minister wears regular clothes."

"Can either of you think of any company that has black uniforms?"

They shook their heads thoughtfully.

"Can you think of anything else that might be important?" Kelli queried.

Again they shook their heads.

"Well, I must say, you have a wonderful memory Mrs. Dern."

"I think it's all the fish I'm eating and all the walks I take during the day, lots of exercise. Just like the doctor ordered."

Kelli stood and put her notepad away and walked to the door.

"You both have been very helpful. Thank you for the cookies and coffee Mrs. Alexander."

CHAPTER 58

Sometimes he could still hear his mother's sharp criticism from when he was young, like when she had been watching out the window when he pushed that snooty little girl off her bike and sent her home crying. She called him into the house and beat him for being a stupid oaf. That little girl had been calling him a big dumb oaf. To this day he hated that word.

He had hated his father too and was glad when he left.

He thought about the time he had seen one of the neighborhood boys who played football, and had snidely called the sport a sissy game. The boy, who was three years older, had beat him up to show him it wasn't a sissy's game. Then when he went home and told his father what had happened, and his father called him a dumb oaf and beat him again for being so stupid.

He looked at his watch and estimated it would take about fifteen minutes to get there. He stood and poured the rest of his coffee down the sink, rinsed his cup and walked out the front door. He sat in his car for a few seconds, thinking he shouldn't go there too often. He wasn't a dumb oaf. He was smart now, he giggled to himself. Not only was he smart now, he was big and strong. He was somebody.

There was a car already parked in his usual spot, so he drove around the block. *Maybe he should just go back home*, he thought. Just as he turned the corner, he saw a lady get into her car and drive away. "Timing is everything," he said out loud as he parked.

The apartment house where she lived was a block down, but because of the precipitous incline of the street he was looking almost straight into her window. Of course, he would still need his trusty Bushnell binoculars.

He reached into his glove box, took them out and rested them on the steering wheel. He looked around to see if he could see anyone. Not one soul in sight.

The window was dark. He looked at his watch. Maybe she went to bed early tonight. He bit his lower lip nervously and tapped his heel on the floorboard. He would give her one more minute.

Two minutes passed and he put the binoculars back in the glove box, started his car and put it in gear. At that moment the light came on. He hit the brakes and backed up, grabbed the binoculars and focused. There she was. He settled in to watch as she started to undress. She always made him dizzy.

Through the binoculars, she looked like she was just ten feet away. He could feel himself getting aroused. He felt as though she knew he was watching her and maliciously driving him crazy. He could see her breasts and the small patch between her legs. The light went out. He was breathing hard and sweating. He reached down, turned the key, and the engine purred to life.

CHAPTER 59

Rufus Applewood had set his alarm for 4:30 A.M., but woke up at 3:55 and decided he would go ahead and get an early start for his meeting with Dewey Slick. His condition required ample time to shower, shave and clothe himself. He would fry a couple of eggs and have toast and glass of orange juice. Then a short walk would be essential to get his legs loosened up and he would be ready for the meeting.

He paid half of the rent for a small, two-man law office he shared with another lawyer. His condition had forced him to downsize his workload. Though, his mobility was impaired, his mind was still sharp and intact. He would inform their mutual secretary of his meeting with Mr. Slick.

Rufus straightened his law degree from Gonzaga University, pulled out a contract form for Mr. Slick to sign when, and if, he agreed to take the case.

He looked at his watch. His potential client should be arriving soon, he thought. It felt good to be doing something in his field; he was actually kind of excited. He was working. He grinned and rubbed his hands together.

"All right!" Rufus said out loud.

There was a soft knock on his office door and Carol Wise, the secretary, poked her head inside.

"Are you all right, Mr. Applewood?"

He smiled and nodded.

"Mr. Dewey Slick is here to see you, sir."

"Thank you Carol, would you send him in and bring us some coffee, please?"

He stood and waited.

"Ahhh, Mr. Applebox?" Said Dewey as he stepped inside.

"Applewood, Mr. Dewey Slick, I presume?"

"Sorry about that sir."

Rufus gazed at the tall, unpretentious young man. *He called me 'sir'. Somehow it seems awkward coming from him,* he thought. *He seems tenuous and out of his environment. He's looking at me like I, doddery old Rufus Applewood, might, in fact, be intimidating him.*

"Please come in and sit right here," Rufus said as he gestured toward an oak chair with a soft chocolate brown cushioned leather seat.

"You can call me Rufus, and if you don't mind, I'll call you Dewey while we're in this office."

"Yeah, sure, you're the lawyer." Dewey agreed.

"Now, why do you feel you need my services?"

"Last Saturday I think somebody picked me out of a police line-up."

"Why were you in a line-up?"

"I don't know why!"

Rufus frowned and studied Dewey's face. He wondered if he really wanted to get involved with this cabbage head. Would it be worth the effort to work through the evasions and half-truths?

"I drive a '47 green and black Hudson, and some woman was killed on Okanogan Street. The detective said my car was seen there."

CHAPTER 60

Alice Baker called her councilor, Dr. Angelina Lansing, and they made an appointment to meet today, Tuesday, at 1:00. Alice arrived early and seemed tentative and anxious.

Dr. Lansing was clearly thinking about something else when Alice started talking to her in the hallway as they walked to her office. She stopped and looked at Alice. Alice stopped talking.

"I'm sorry Angie, I feel like my spring is wound too tightly."

"Why don't you sit down and tell me about it."

Alice began to relax, just a little, as she sat on the love seat and thought about what she wanted to say to Dr. Lansing. The drive over here had taken some of the wind out of her sails. Now she wasn't so confident about what she wanted to say. It sounded insane. Maybe the old psychiatrist's theory about homosexuals was true. Maybe they were mentally ill. She sure seemed to fit the picture right now.

How could she tell Angie she was thinking seriously about abducting that Slick slime and putting a bullet in his heart, or his head, or better yet, both?

Angie sat down at her desk and finished whatever she was doing and then came over to Alice. She sat on the chair, crossed her hands in front of her, and focused on Alice.

"They have the killer in jail," Alice said quietly.

"Lilly Jo's killer?"

Alice nodded.

They sat quietly. Angie could hear the cuckoo clock ticking and looked up at the time.

"Mom thinks I'm preoccupied with Lilly Jo's murder and sometimes I think she's right. Sometimes it's all I can think about. I only knew her for a few minutes and yet she has possessed my mind every since. What's my problem? Why can't

I go on? I seem to be stuck in a thirty minute time period. Angie what's wrong me? I'm in this thing. How do I get out of it?"

"I don't know exactly what to tell you. You met someone you liked instantaneously. You felt a kinship, like she might be like you and-"

"Sorry to cut you off, Angie. *Was* she like me?"

"If she was everything you said about her, beautiful, intelligent, independent, pleasant, and honest you shared many traits. The paper was very nice to her and substantiated what you had told me about her. I believe she was a lot like you."

"She was a a?"

"Alice I'm not altogether sure you're anything but a little mixed up."

"But I thought we had discussed that I was a a homosexual."

"You could be, I'm just not sure you are. And even if you are, it doesn't mean you're bad. Alice, where are we going with this?"

"That seems to be part of all this. I'm not sure who I am and I'm confused by the feelings I had for Lilly Jo. I mean if I really cared for her, or if I'm just feeling sincerely sorry for losing a brand new friend in such a violent way."

"Is it important for you to know that?" asked Angie.

"I think so, don't you?"

"Did you have friends in Spokane that you felt this way about?"

Alice thought about the question. She did have friends, girls she liked, and they ran around together. They talked about boys, teachers, music, and openly about a variety of subjects that weren't discussed with their parents. But there was something special about Lilly Jo. Something she couldn't put into words.

"I've always had friends. My house was a place where the girls could gather and talk. I think I've grown up in a normal peer and family atmosphere. Do you think I might be reading too much into what happened to me two years ago?"

"What do you think?"

"Angie, sometimes I have this dream where I'm in a small row boat out on the Pacific Ocean without the proverbial paddle, and the wind is blowing, the sky has opened her rain clouds. Rain falls heavily, the boat rocks wildly over two-foot waves and the horizon is falling further and further away. I'm all alone in the boat, helpless. I'm cold and wet and the terrible fins of sharks appear cutting the water around the small boat."

Alice stopped talking, rocked back and forth and cried. She hugged herself tightly.

"Angie I've had some terrible thoughts lately. I'm not sure I should share them with you. They're just thoughts, no substance oh, I'm sounding crazy even to myself." She covered her face with her hands.

Angie was tempted to go to Alice's side, but recognized Alice had to do this thing herself.

The room was still and quiet except for the tic tock of the cuckoo clock on the wall next to the window.

"I suppose I should go." Alice looked up at Angie through red swollen eyes.

"You still have twenty one minutes."

"Angie, am I doing the right thing by coming here and talking to you? Sometimes I feel like I'm losing it by coming here. Like I'm not handling my problem, like I'm trying to make it your problem. Does that make any sense?"

"Alice, you've just started therapy. I think you're making progress. Maybe not as quickly as you would like, but you are progressing."

"Coming here seems to magnify my problems, make them bigger than they are. Then again it might just be the seriousness of my current situation. If I had never met Lilly Jo at that table in Kresses that day, I wouldn't have ended up in her house the night she was killed. To this day, I can't believe I walked in uninvited and got caught up in this," her voice trailed off. "Sometimes I sound like some raving crazy person. I'm starting to scare myself."

"You're not crazy, Alice. You are confused, and you have a right to be. You were just starting to try to find your identity, and you suffered a severe trauma. You witnessed a murder, the murder of someone you liked. I think I would be a little off balance if that had happened to me, too."

"You mean that?"

"Of course I do."

Alice looked long into Angie's eyes.

"I think I believe you. I'm really not going crazy?"

"The death of your friend has had a devastating impact on you, and to add to that, you were a witness to her actual death."

"Well, I didn't actually see her killed, but I know it was that man, Slick, the one they had a picture of in the paper."

The two surveyed each other in silence, each waiting for the other to speak first. Silence.

The cuckoo clock announced cuckoo, cuckoo for two o'clock.

"Saved by the clock," Alice said as she stood.

"You don't have to set up an appointment. Next time if you feel you need to talk, just call me."

CHAPTER 61

Rufus Applewood got up early and thought of all the things he had to do today. He had an agenda, which he had composed the night before. He took his first pills at 6:00 A.M., two hours earlier than usual. His logic was that he would be in need of all his extremities in the middle of the day, so taking the pills early would allow him to be more mobile during the afternoon. The medicine's effect normally lessened in the late evening hours. The doctor had told him that the medication didn't work that way. But Rufus had decided he was the one who took the stupid pills every day. He knew how they worked, probably better than that doctor.

He looked at the list of witnesses and decided to check which ones he would call.

1) George and Nelda Plant he would pass,
2) Mrs. Danielle Stumply pass,
3) Josephine Beach, pass.
4) Oren Brown and Tony Marinquez, he would see.
5) Mrs. Mildred Dern he would see.
6) Alice Baker, he would see.

There. He was done and he felt better now that he knew what he had to do. He was practicing law again and he felt ten years younger. Maybe this was what he needed, the smell of a courtroom battle in the air, the sound of the judge's gavel, the stinging words of a rebuttal, the sneer of the opposing counsel, the anticipation of the twelve jurors. He was alive again. His eyes welled. He extended his hands out in front of him. No tremors. He stood and danced around the oak table. One of his slippers caught the foot of one of the chairs and he fell. He lay there looking up at the ceiling. Had he ever been on the floor of the kitchen before? he wondered. He started laughing. When his laughter finally died down he rolled to one side and got both hands on the wooden parquet floor, brought his legs up towards his hands and stood, surprising himself.

"Yes!" he shouted, slightly dizzy from standing up so fast. He sat down at the table and clasped his hands together. *You're not 25 anymore, so don't push it, Rufus.* He chuckled again. He decided he would shower and call the "will see" people from his list to schedule interviews.

CHAPTER 62

Alice Baker was lying in her bed thinking about Lilly Jo. She peeked at the wind-up clock on the nightstand 2:18 A.M. She guessed she had slept, but was now wide awake. Her mind kept going back to Lilli Jo's house, and what she did, and how she had run away and left her to be killed.

Angie had said there was no fault. She didn't know if the man was Lilly Jo's boyfriend, or a relative, or friend. How could she know? She couldn't know! So what was the problem?

No matter what she did, it seemed like it always came back to the fact that Alice had been there, less than twenty feet from her friend when he, *the beast*, went in to kill her. She had been there, right there! How could she have run away like that?

She turned over and practically laid on Mandy, her new Beagle puppy. The dog snored softly completely unaware she had almost become a pillow. Alice scooted over, rolled to her back and clasped her hands behind her head.

She heard a siren way off in the night, and the big cat down the block yowling at...whatever it is cats yowl at.

Alice was listening to the night sounds. She heard a car door close and then another. It must be the guys across the street, she thought, and glanced at the clock again. It was 2:29. Eleven minutes had passed. The taverns close at 2:00, no doubt the reason for their arrival. She sat up and draped her legs over the side of the bed. Mandy raised her head and peeked at her from behind barely open eyelids.

"Don't get up Mandy, I'm just going to get a drink of water."

She shuffled slowly to the kitchen sink, turned the water on and reached for a glass.

What was that? She froze and strained to hear. Was that the front door knob turning? She turned from the sink and stared at the doorknob until her eyes lost focus. Nothing. She filled her glass, took a drink, and went back to the bedroom. The drawer in the nightstand drew her attention. Inside was a .38 caliber pistol. *There is no denying it, one feels more confident when there is loaded gun at hand*, she thought. The down side, her grandfather used to say, was that you could kill someone with good intentions just as easily as you could someone set on doing you harm.

She slid into bed and thought about the Slick character. Imagine that, having a name like Slick. *It should have been Slime*, she thought. *I'd like to put some lead in your ass, Slick*. It was her last thought as she fell over the edge into slumber.

The next morning, she let Mandy out into the backyard, went to open the curtain on the window by the door, and as she did she distinctly heard the doorknob turn. She paused, went to the door and turned the knob. It rolled back easily. She opened then closed the door and the knob stuck. She touched it lightly and it rolled back. She did it again and again the knob stuck.

"That's it!" she said out loud, "That's what I heard!"

She went to her purse, dug out her small address book and found the mailing address she had plucked from Detective Finnigan's purse. She showered, slipped into jeans, a white blouse, and deck shoes, kissed Mandy on the snout and told her to guard the apartment. She picked up the brown bag of kitchen trash and headed out the front door to the garbage can at the side of the house. When she opened the lid to the circular gray can there, on top of her trash, was the big black cat she thought she had heard the night before. Headless.

Alice gasped, dropping the bag of trash and the lid. The metal lid clanged loudly against the receptacle. Her neighbor came out to see what the noise was all about.

"Ma'am? What's wrong? What happened?" he called as he ran across the space between their apartments. Alice pointed to the garbage can. He edged over and peeked inside.

"Oh my God! That sure looks like Velvet, the neighbor's

cat." He replaced the lid. "Why would somebody kill their cat like that? Why would anybody do that and put it in your garbage can?" he asked incredulously as he put his arm around Alice's shaking shoulders and tried to calm her.

"Sick! Somebody sick!" Alice managed to squeak out, but she knew. She was absolutely sure she knew who had done this cowardly, barbaric thing.

"Do you want me to call somebody? Maybe the police or the dogcatcher?"

"Please, yes, call somebody, sir. I live in apartment two over there," she gestured toward her apartment. "I have to go now. I have to go," she choked out as she turned to head for her car.

"Excuse me Miss, ah, what's your name?" he called out.

She turned to look at him, wondering whether she should say.

He noticed the apprehension and spoke softly. "They will want to know your name."

"Alice, Alice Baker. I'm sorry, but well, strange things have been happening, and I'm uh.."

"Don't worry. The dogcatcher is part of the Police Department. It'll be OK, and I'll keep an eye on things till they get here."

Her eyes welled with tears. "Thank you." As she turned to cross the street she realized she had no idea who he was. "Sir, I apologize for being well, anyhow may I know your name?"

He approached Alice slowly, and extended his hand, "Glenn Morgan, Alice, and I'll let you know what the authorities have to say about this, you know."

Alice managed a half-hearted sad smile, and continued on to the two toned, blue and white '54 Buick Special her parents had given her when she came to Wenatchee.

She drove up Orondo, past Miller, and over to Millerdale where she found the address she was seeking. Her interest was in the cottage at the back of the property.

There was a baseball park a little further down on Millerdale. No one would pay any attention to a car parked there. It was still early, so she walked down to the address, crossed the street and strolled by as though she was just out for a leisurely walk. A car had passed by and was parked just ahead of her. She crossed the street to avoid any contact. As she got closer to the address she could see the cottage behind the well kept home. Her heart pounded with the awareness of his proximity. *That's where the beast lives*, she seethed mentally.

Alice cased the place for the following three days and knew what she had to do. She knew when the brother left for work, and when *the beast* used the car and when he picked up the brother from work. She knew *the beast* didn't have a job.

CHAPTER 63

Rufus Applewood received a call from the prosecuting attorney informing him that they had probable cause and would be arresting Harold Slick Junior for the murder of Lilly Jo Zilke. Rufus inquired if they had anything new on the case that he should be aware of. He was told they had a new witness that would corroborate the existing witnesses statements, and add a new dimension. Rufus told the D.A. he would bring Harold Slick Junior in to the local jail the day after tomorrow, which would be Friday. He wanted to give Harold a chance to get all his business together and prepare to be in jail for an indefinite period of time.

Rufus was a little nervous. He hadn't been involved with any law practice now for a few years, at least not Criminal Law. He had done some probate and divorce and even some immigration work, but not Criminal Law. As he walked up to his office, where he would be meeting with the people he had called in for interviews, he began to drool. He extracted a clean white handkerchief from the inside pocket of his suit and wiped his face thoroughly.

I can't get stressed now or I'll start shaking. He stopped and looked down at his right hand. No discernible tremble. He could feel the beads of perspiration on his brow and some under his arms.

"No stress Rufus," he said out loud to himself.

A young man coming down the stairs looked around for someone else and asked, "Did you say something, sir?"

"I apologize, I was talking to myself."

The man raised his eyebrows and headed for the door.

Rufus pulled himself together and headed for his office, where he went over his interview schedule with Carol Wise.

CHAPTER 64

"Mrs. Dern tell- "

"Would you mind calling me Millie or Mildred? She interrupted, "I'm nervous enough just sitting here, and I would feel better if you did."

Rufus put his notes on the table and looked across the table at her.

"Thank you, Mildred, I'd like that. And you can call me Rufus. The truth be known, I'm a little nervous myself."

"Why would you be nervous?"

He pulled out a yellow writing tablet and pencil and laid them on the surface in front of him.

"I haven't been involved in a Criminal Law case in a while, and I'm nervous because I want to do the best job, the right thing for all concerned. I suppose you could say I'm a little rusty. My corporeal image is shaky. This is possibly my last hurrah. I want to do it right. Legally and morally."

Millie nodded and her eyes twinkled like she had decided that she liked Rufus.

"Would you mind telling me what you saw on the evening of May 11, 1954, Mildred?" he asked.

She told everything she could remember about the evening with very few interruptions from Rufus. They finished the interview then discussed their mutual interest in trees and flowers.

"So you're the lawyer that's going to defend the man they have in jail for for--"

"Yes, Mildred, I am. I hope I'm doing the right thing. Well, I believe I am. It looks bad for him but I believe he is innocent and I plan on proving in a courtroom."

"Well, for your sake, I hope you're right. You seem like a good man."

"Thank you, Mildred, that means a lot to me. You won't be

disappointed if Harold Slick is proven innocent?"

"Not if he's innocent, I won't."

Rufus stood, thanked Mildred for coming in and for her willingness to do her civic duty.

He sat for a few minutes and thought about all that Mildred had said. He looked down at his notes and was pleased. The door opened and his secretary stuck her head in to announce Oren Brown and Anthony Marinquez had arrived. The boys were ushered in and seated across from Rufus.

"Nice to see you Tony, and I feel like I know you, Oren. I took in a couple of your home games this past year." Rufus extended his hand across the table and shook ours. We chatted about sports for a while and Oren started warming up to Rufus. I knew Oren would like Rufus if he got a chance to meet and talk to him.

"Tell me about the evening of May 11, 1954, as you saw it, please," Rufus urged gently,

Oren started and told about the garden and the light. I spoke up at different points in the story and we took turns telling what they had seen. No we were not aware at the time, that there were other people in the room. No we had not spoken to anyone except Detective Finnigan.

Rufus put his pencil down and sat back in his chair. His right hand, the writing hand began to tremble ever so slightly. He pulled his hand back.

"Do you need to take a pill, sir?" I asked quietly.

Then the old man started shaking and drooling like some condor, he thought.

"Good observation, Tony my boy. I'll do just that, please excuse me, I'll be right back."

"Rufus is all right," Oren whispered to me.

"What'd I tell you?" I countered righteously.

"Yeah, yeah."

Rufus came back eating an O'Henry candy bar.

"Sugar seems to help. Don't know why, maybe it's all up here," He tapped his temple. "I'd share, but it's the only one I had, guys, my apologies."

"No problem," we said in unison.

"Thank you for coming in and giving me your perception of what you witnessed."

We shook hands all around and then we left.

Rufus was a little weary, but the stimulation of working again was energizing him. The pills were doing their job. At least he wasn't trembling. He was just now aware he was drooling again, and thought he should go wash his face.

Rufus checked his list and saw that Alice Baker was his next interview. *This should be interesting*, he thought.

When he returned, he found Carol chatting with a very attractive brunette. She was tall, pretty, and appeared quite tentative. She peeked at Rufus suspiciously as he walked to the table. She was young and not very confident. She definitely did not want to be here.

"Thank you for coming in today, Miss Baker. My name is Rufus Applewood, and I represent Mr. Slick, the man charged with the murder. I'm sorry for your loss, and sincerely appreciate you coming in today. I know how hard this must be for you."

Alice stood just inside the door and stared down at the floor.

"Would you like to sit down at the table here?" he asked as he pulled out a wooden chair.

She did not take the cue and remained standing. Rufus returned to the other side of the table and sat. He opened the tablet to a fresh sheet and waited.

"You're at liberty to tell me what you saw that day, Miss Baker. The District Attorney has probably told you that the defendant has a right to what's called 'discovery.' All that means is that we are entitled to view, or hear the evidence the state has accumulated," he said as he watched her.

Alice nodded grimly, sat down with purpose and confidence, and examined Rufus. "Why are you defending this, this murderer?" Something had awakened in the pretty young woman, now she had fire in her eyes and she was bitter about something not yet known.

"It's the law. If not me, then it would be some other lawyer. It's a basic right. We all have the right to an attorney, guilty or innocent. We are all innocent until proven otherwise." Rufus felt his body react to the first signs of stress and he feared he would begin to tremble. He certainly didn't need that at this moment.

"I saw him do it." Alice said emphatically and then clasped her hands over her mouth.

Rufus was bewildered by her outburst. He sat dumbfounded.

"Would you like to tell me about what you saw, Miss Baker?"

She began to cry softly and leaned over on the table with her hands over her face. Rufus had brought three handkerchiefs with him and he fetched one from his suit pocket, walked around the table and placed it next to her.

She looked up and saw what he had done. "Thank you." She wiped her eyes and sat up straight.

He was still standing next to her when he began to shudder, just enough that Alice noticed.

"Are you all right Mr. Applewood?"

He returned to the other side of the table and sat. He knew he had to relax or he would be in trouble soon. He checked the clock on the wall above the door. He still had another hour before he could take his next pills.

"Are you well? Would you like me to call your secretary?" Alice persisted.

"I believe I'm all right. Thank you for your concern. Maybe we should terminate our interview. I think I need to go home. I need the sustenance of a good dinner. Would you object to rescheduling our meeting? I really need you to finish telling me everything you saw that evening, Miss Baker."

Alice stood, walked around and laid the hanky on the table, then leaned over and wrote her telephone number on the legal pad. "Call me when you feel better. I hope I wasn't the cause of your discomfort." She placed her hand on his shoulder, squeezed it gently, turned and walked away.

Rufus eyed the telephone number and then wrote down the words, I saw him do it. *Why would she perjure herself?* He wondered. He lifted himself from his chair, gathered his pencils, legal pad and handkerchief then moved cautiously outside, still thinking about Alice Baker. Maybe, she wasn't perjuring herself, maybe he was wrong. He was nearly to the exit door when the secretary shouted.

"Are you finished for the day, Mr. Applewood?"

"Forgive me, Carol. Yes I am."

CHAPTER 65

Alice watched from her car on Millerdale Avenue as Dewey Slick got into a green and black Hudson and drove off to work. She knew the schedule. Harold, *the beast,* would be alone in the cottage. The owners of the home in front both worked and left earlier in the morning. She checked her watch. It was time to go.

She stepped out of the car, walked to the passenger side and pulled out the brown grocery bag. She walked with resolve to the front of the large house and followed the narrow cement walkway to the back door of the Slick residence. Her heart was pounding. She could hear it in her ears. Her gray sweatshirt and Levi's were damp with nervous perspiration. The sunglasses she wore were misting. She was here and she wouldn't change her mind.

She bit her lower lip and knocked. She listened for any sound from inside. Nothing. She thought she should leave. Should she knock again? She wanted to turn and go, her confidence was draining away by the second. A small drop of sweat ran down her neck. She turned and started to walk away when the door opened.

"Yeah, what do you want?" Said a gruff voice.

Alice turned and forced herself to walk back to the door. He must have been asleep. He was disheveled and was wearing only a white t-shirt and boxer shorts.

"May I come in?" She asked.

"Dewey's not here," he snarled.

"Then you must be Harold, Harold Slick?"

"So? Who are you?"

She reached into the brown bag and pulled out a pistol target and handed it to Harold.

"You were in the Army so you must know what that is."

"Yeah, so what about it?"

"Do you notice the grouping?"

"Someone is a pretty good shot with a pistol."

"That would be me. " She pulled the pearl-handled pistol out of the bag and aimed it at Harold as she backed him up into the tiny living room.

"What the fuck?" he yelled.

"Save the expletives for your friends, if you have any, cause I don't like a foul mouth." She pulled out a hemp rope, threw it at Harold and told him to sit in the only chair in the room. Alice pulled out a pair of handcuffs, told him to turn his back and placed the cuffs on his wrists. She then took the rope and tied each leg to a chair leg, then ran the rope around his mid section until he was completely immobile.

"So who the fuck are you, you bitch?"

She looked into his eyes and changed her pistol to her left hand and slugged Harold on the right cheek so hard the chair almost tipped backward. Blood oozed from his mouth and dripped on his white t-shirt. She shook her hand.

"You swear at me one more time and I'll put a bullet in your foot. Do you understand me Harold?"

They stared at each other until Harold finally looked away.

"Why did you kill Lilli Jo Zilke?" Alice hissed.

He was furious she had gotten the drop on him, and he refused to look at her.

She had him handcuffed, tied and she had her .38 in her hand, she felt invincible.

"I was in the house the night you killed her, Harold. I saw you walk into her bedroom. Do you deny that?"

"How how, No, that can't be. What-"

Alice interrupted his stammering, "Yes, Harold. It can be. I was there."

"I didn't kill her, I didn't even know her. I admit I was in the house that night, but I don't remember killing her. I didn't kill her, I swear."

"You don't remember killing her? What does that mean?"

she shouted.

"I'd been smoking reefers that night and I had a lot of Scotch, which I never had before. It made me a little crazy, but I don't remember killing her," Harold insisted.

"Just because you don't remember doing it, doesn't mean you didn't do it. What were you doing in her house that night?"

"I don't remember exactly where I was when she said 'hello' to me, maybe Sears or Penny's, and she smiled at me when she said it. She was tall and beautiful." Tears were threatening to overflow from his eyes.

"And?"

"And I followed her home, and then every once in a while I would watch her through her window at night. I knew she was living alone. Why would I want to kill her? I thought she was beautiful. I know it looks bad for me, but I didn't kill her and Mr. Applewood is going to defend me."

"Does he know you were in the house that night?"

"Yeah. I didn't even know her name until Dewey was questioned by that woman detective."

"Why are you lying to me, Harold?"

"I'm not lying to you. Applewood says it's all circumstantial. I don't remember killing her and nobody saw me kill her. To this day, I don't even know how she was killed. Do you know how she was killed?"

He's lying, Alice fumed internally. She thought about her friend, her beautiful friend, moved over to Harold and put the pistol against his temple.

"You know you killed her, you animal, and now I'm going to do the same to you." She pulled the hammer back and it clicked in place. "Do you know how to pray, Harold? Because now is the time to do it."

He started to cry, tears rolling down his face."I didn't kill her, I swear, I didn't kill her. I don't want to die for something I didn't do, and I didn't kill her. You have to believe me, I didn't do it, I swear."

Alice blinked and a tear rolled down her cheek. She would be as bad as him if she pulled the trigger. What if he was telling the truth? She would be taking the life of an innocent person, even if it was a low life like Harold. Alice raised the pistol above his head and lowered the hammer. She couldn't do it. Even if he was guilty and she knew he was, she couldn't do it. She reached in her jeans and found the cuff key. She removed the cuffs and placed them in the bag.

"Harold, I want you to give me your word you won't try to keep me from leaving if I untie you."

"I don't like what you did to me. I didn't kill that girl," he growled

"I'm not altogether sure you didn't. Harold so do I leave you tied up?"

Reluctantly, he agreed, "You have my word. I won't try to stop you from leaving."

She untangled the knots on the rope and began unraveling it, then stopped and walked to the door.

"You'll be able to finish the rest by yourself. I'm leaving and you won't be seeing me again, not till the day I testify against you in court."

She slipped through the door and jogged to her car. She sat in her car for a few minutes to see if he would come out looking for her. He didn't. She pulled the .38 from her waistband, took off the black watch cap and sunglasses and put them all in her brown bag. Would he call the police? Could he recognize her without the cap and glasses? Somehow she didn't think he would call the police. Did she feel better? Not really. She had thought she could kill the monster, but she couldn't.

Alice drove directly to her apartment and had just stepped out of her car when she heard her name called. She turned to see a man in a pea green uniform walking toward her.

"Miss Baker, I'm Jeff Morrow, Animal Control. Could I

ask you a couple of questions?"

"I guess this is about the cat in my garbage can. I really don't know anything about it except I was surprised to find it in there. The neighbor said the poor little thing belonged to the other family that lives on the other side of him. That's about all I know."

"Did you hear anything unusual that night?" he asked as he wrote on a small pad.

She considered saying something about the doorknob, but she might have turned it herself. *Not important*, she thought.

She shook her head. "Not really."

"Somebody killed that cat and put it in your garbage can. It could be a coincidence or somebody could be trying to tell you something, Miss Baker. I'm not saying this to alarm you, but maybe you should stay extra alert and consider this is as something, rather than as nothing. Be safe rather than sorry. Lock your doors at night. I will report this to the police department and they will keep an eye on the neighborhood. But if you hear or see anything unusual, you call them. Have a good evening, Miss Baker, and stay vigilant."

She walked to her apartment, his words replaying in her mind. *Some one killed that cat and put it in your garbage can; stay alert; someone trying to tell you something; stay vigilant.* She was thinking how ironic this situation was. Here she had been out, fully intending to kill someone today, and now she felt like someone was trying to kill her.

CHAPTER 66

Detective Finnigan read the report Animal Control Officer Jeff Morrow had left for the police department. She looked at the date at the top. *This happened last week. Last week? Cat in trash last week but left there until yesterday,* she thought. Kelli thumbed through the Rolodex on her desk and plucked Alice Baker's card out. Alice answered after the first ring.

"This is Detective Finnigan, will you still be home at about 10:30?" she asked as she glanced at the clock on her desk.

"Yes. Is everything all right?"

"I think so, but I'd like to stop by for a few minutes."

"I'll be here, Detective."

Kelli drove to the Zilke residence to touch bases with Amet and Kara. She arrived early and the three discussed the latest information on Lilly Jo's trial that was set to begin in two weeks. She informed them who the Deputy District Attorney was going to be and who was defending the man they had arrested.

They were glad the end was nearing and they could put the death of their daughter behind them. They wanted to take a trip back to Turkey and visit old friends in Istanbul. Detective Finnigan took her leave and headed to her next appointment. She was feeling good about her work. The case was coming together and her spirits were high. Her only worry now was Alice Baker.

She drove up Sunset Street and parked. On her way to Alice's apartment she checked out the location of the garbage cans and walked over to where they were located. She took the lid off the can and looked in. She checked the distance from the Baker apartment and felt in her bones whoever did this was trying to scare Alice. Just then, the door opened and Alice walked out.

"I think the Animal Control Officer took the cat away when he was here, Kelli."

They went into Alice's apartment and sat.

"How concerned should I be about this, Kelli?"

"You should be very concerned. Persons don't go around killing cats and putting them in garbage cans as a normal thing. I think you should keep your eyes open. Don't take anything for granted, and don't take any chances."

"You don't think it was some nut?"

"Well, you got the nut part right, Alice. But no, I don't think it was random. I think someone did this to intimidate you. That person viciously mutilated that cat and put it in your garbage can for a reason."

"Maybe the neighbor did it, the one that called Animal Control."

"Not according to Animal Control Officer Jeff Morrow. He interviewed the man and the owner of the dead cat. Apparently, Glenn Morgan had a special fondness for the cat, and would take care of it when the owners were away. No, whoever killed that cat is a bad man, a sick man. Alice, I want you to lock your doors at night and keep that .38 at your bedside. If someone enters your apartment you'd better be able to use it."

"Wow Kelli, you really are concerned."

"I'm not trying to make more out of this than it is, but you should be concerned. Go about with your regular routine, just keep alert and if you hear or see anything different, I want you to call dispatch, and then call me, even if I'm at home or it's 3:00 A.M. Promise me you'll do that."

"I promise Kelli."

CHAPTER 67

He drank the first Lucky Lager beer in three long swallows and threw the bottle in the trash, reached in the fridge, and grabbed another. He went to the cupboard and looked for a bag of unshelled peanuts. *Damn*, he thought. He had picked up salted ones when he wanted unsalted. He frowned. Unsalted was better for you, didn't retain the liquid in your body. He placed the bag on the counter and selected a glass bowl for the shells. He walked over to the soft cushioned chair and set the bag and bowl on the small end table and turned the floor lamp on. He placed the bag of peanuts between his legs, opened the bag and shelled a few peanuts, then took a drink of his beer. The man smiled as he thought about the stupid cat. That bitch was probably still crying about it and, no doubt, still wondering who?

He placed the bag on the end table. Too salty. He tipped the beer up and guzzled it down. He wiped his mouth with the back of his hand, laid his head back on the soft cushioned chair, and closed his eyes. He could feel the effects of the two quick beers. It felt good. Relaxing like this was something he didn't do anymore.

"Sunny," she said quietly.

He laid still, not sure he had heard anything." Sunny!" He didn't like her calling him Sunny.

"Sunny, you dumb oaf you better leave her alone," she said, shouting at him now.

His eyes snapped open, but saw only the shadowy ceiling. Was the room moving?

"Sunny!"

"What? I know you're not here, you bitch. Why are you doing this to me?"

She laughed, that nasty laugh he hated, the laugh that made him feel dirty and small.

"I'm big and strong, you can't make me cower any more,

you pig. I know what you were doing with all those men. You weren't a good mother; you were a pig, a slut, a common whore. I didn't know you were bad then because well, I just didn't know. But now I do. I should be laughing at you." The room was quiet again. He leaned his head back and looked up at the ceiling.

"You think just because you wear a uniform now, it makes you something special?" she whimpered. "All I ever wanted was to be happy. You think I liked what I did? I had to feed and clothe you. How was I going to do that without…you got fed, didn't you? You didn't go to school naked did you?"

"You're not telling me you did all that for me, are you? Is that what you're trying to sell me? All that laughing and drinking and your bed squeaking all night long because you were thinking about me? Is that what you're saying? I am special because I wear a uniform. You thought I would never amount to anything but I am something. Why didn't you go to work and do something? You didn't have to do what you did. You liked what you did! Didn't you? Didn't you?" he shouted.

The neighbors next door heard the muffled shouting of a man.

"Who's he talking to?" the woman asked her husband.

"Whoever it is, he's been doing it a lot lately."

"I've never seen anyone go into his house," the woman said as she pulled the curtain to one side and looked out the window.

"I don't think there's anyone else in there. The first time I heard him I thought he was talking to the television or someone on the phone. Now I think he's talking to someone in his head."

"Oh my God, and he's-"

"I know."

"I bet his boss doesn't know he yells to himself." She let go of the curtain and walked back to the kitchen.

"To be fair, maybe someone came when we weren't

looking. Maybe somebody *else is* in that house," he said as he sipped his coffee.

"I don't know, the only light I can see is a dim lamp in the front room. The rest of the house is dark. He's a spooky man."

"Hey, what happened to the 'he's handsome' thing?"

"He is handsome, but he's also creepy. Can't he be both?"

They stopped talking when they heard his front door close, and they rushed to the front room window to peek out.

"Where do you think he goes at night?" she mused as they watched him get into his car.

"Maybe he's got a girlfriend, or has a beer or two at the Igloo or the Elks Club. Who knows?"

"I suppose he could have a girlfriend. He is good looking, but I really can't see him doing the other things. He seems to be more of a loner."

"Yeah, I think so too. Those guys seem to hang out with their own kind, although he doesn't fit the image. I don't think I've ever seen anyone at his house. Have you, Elda?"

She paused and thought for a few seconds, picked up Fig bar and took a small bite.

CHAPTER 68

He turned on the windshield wipers and drove straight down Miller Street until he reached Washington, made a left, then up to Sunburst. He turned right and drove slowly past the Detective's house, then stopped in the middle of the street and scrutinized the house for lights or movement. The passenger window was wet with raindrops and visibility was poor.

"What house are you looking for?" He turned and saw an older man with an umbrella, who had appeared from nowhere, right next to his car.

He rolled his window down a little. "I think I'm on the wrong street, thank you."

"This is Sunburst."

"Yeah, this is the wrong street." He drove off slowly, checking the street in his rear view mirror, but the man had disappeared into the night. What was that old guy thinking, walking around in this rain? He should be inside.

But what bothered him most was how he had let his guard down like that. He drove to the corner and turned left and then right again. He reached First Street, turned right, then left on Miller to 5th, then up to Sunset Street. It was raining harder; visibility was only about 20 feet. He pulled to the curb and parked.

He was barely able distinguish Apartment #2 through the heavy rain. The wind picked up and forced sheets of water against his car. It slapped the metal like a huge paddle, and it swayed his vehicle. He had seen this all before and knew the rain would subside soon and he would then be able to---suddenly there was a squad car driving slowly down the street in his direction shining it's mounted light at the cars. He felt a surge of adrenalin jolt through his body. The squad car was about three cars away.

"Lie down on the seat you stupid oaf!" she yelled. He

placed his hands over his ears. "Lie down, lie down," she repeated. He lay down and hugged the front seat. When the light illuminated the inside of his car, he stopped breathing. The big engine idled. Was it stopping? What was he going to say if the officer came to his door? He whimpered piteously and buried his face in the seat. He felt like he had been holding his breath forever.

"Mama, I'm afraid. I'm scared. Help me mama, please help me."

He jolted awake and it was quiet, where was he? The seat was wet where his face had been. He raised his head slowly and peeked out. It was dark. Then he looked at his watch and saw the time. Maybe he was a stupid oaf like his mother used to say. He started his car and he drove home slowly.

CHAPTER 69

Two weeks earlier, Oren and I had waited for Alice Baker to come out of Applewood's office. We shared, what we had seen that evening. She, in turn, told us what she seen and done. She seemed somewhat relieved to know she had not been the only one who had witnessed something that night. We were drawn to each for comfort, and were reluctant to part company.

We went to Clausen's Drug Store and sat at one of the small tables by the fountain.

"This is where I met Lilli Jo just a little over two years ago, at this very location, maybe the very table." Tears fell to the tabletop and we were uncomfortable, but deeply touched by her grief.

"It must be a girl thing," she said with a brief sigh.

"Well, we didn't know her, you know, like you did. We just saw her…ah saw her," Oren glanced at Tony for some help.

"I'm ashamed to say this to you because you're a girl, but we saw the most beautiful woman we had ever seen and we saw her, ummm, naked. She was beautiful. I guess that must be a boy thing."

"I guess I can understand. She was beautiful, but not just to look at, she was beautiful inside too. After we met we just talked for a little while, but I felt like I had met the nicest person I had ever known. For two years, all this has festered in me. What happened to her is the cruelest thing I've ever known. It just shouldn't happen to someone that nice," Alice said.

We sat reverently as if in prayer for a few seconds, each lost in our own thoughts.

"Alice, what did the Detective tell you that made you feel vulnerable? Isn't that the word you used, vulnerable?" I asked her.

"Well, a few nights ago Kelli, came to my door. She told me that a prowler had been seen in the area where I live and she thought he might be looking for me, or watching me."

"Who would be looking for you?"

"Harold Slick is the only one that comes to mind," Oren thought out loud.

Alice seemed to give that some serious consideration.

"How would he know who you are, Alice? I know you said you saw him, but you didn't say anything about him seeing you. Did he see you that night?" I asked.

"I don't know, maybe he did see me," she said.

"We didn't see him kill Lilli Jo, and you didn't see him kill her, because you left first. You said you heard voices so she must have been alive, right? I don't think he saw you, Alice," Oren offered.

She pulled a handkerchief from her purse and dried the tears that ran down her cheeks.

Oren and I were baffled by her reaction, and exchanged glances. I reckon Oren thought he had said something that made her cry.

"Alice, maybe he did see you. I was just guessing. You're not mistaken."

Alice took a deep breath, then she told us how she had obtained Harold Slick's address, gone there and tied him up. Tears were rolling down her face as she told the story.

"But I just couldn't do it. I couldn't pull the trigger. Your assessment was correct Oren, he didn't see me in the house that night. He didn't even know I had been in the house until I told him, and that was after I had him tied up."

"Are you all right, Miss?" the Clausen manager asked Alice as he stood over their table, his hands on his hips. "These boys giving you a bad time?"

"I'm fine sir, just a little emotional. These boys are my friends, but thank you. It was sweet of you to be concerned," Alice assured him.

"You sure?"

"I'm sure." He left, not completely convinced.

"I'm sorry I lied to you, but I was so ashamed," Alive explained.

"You held a gun up to Harold Slick's head?" I whispered.

"A real gun?" Oren grinned, his eyes bright.

"Yes, a .38 Special - S&W." She explained her ability to use the pistol, and about her grandfather who was retired from the Spokane Police Department.

"So you're a pretty good shot?" Oren asked.

"I'm a qualified expert with the .38 at 25 yards. Of course, that was over a year ago, but a few days ago I was at the local firing range with Detective Finnigan and she thought I was pretty good.

"The more we talk, the more concerned I am that Detective Finnigan might be right about someone stalking me. Stalking is my word; she said someone might be looking for me."

"Do you have someone who could stay with you?" Oren wanted to know.

"My mother. But then I'd have to tell her why, and I don't want to worry her or put her life in jeopardy."

Oren and I exchanged glances, nodded and stood.

"We'll be right back, Alice. We need to talk." I said seriously.

At this point in the story Oren and I had gotten to like Alice and we felt she kind of liked us, for real. It was a swell feeling. Which reminds me the word swell was *thee* word in the fifties. She was swell girl, we were swell guys, it was a swell car. Everything was swell. Anyway, we'd gotten a little braver and we wanted to help Alice.

A few minutes later we returned.

"Would you like us to stay with you, Alice?" Oren asked.

She looked in shock at us, but it was a nice kind of shocked, like she was touched by our offer.

"That is so kind of you, but I couldn't let you do that. What about your parents?"

"I'll tell my aunts I'm staying with Tony, and Tony will tell his mom he's staying with me. We do it all the time for real, I mean. They never call each other, they trust us," Oren smiled roguishly.

know, everything is swell.

"I don't know guys. What if something bad happens? I'd feel responsible, and I'd never forgive myself."

"Aren't you a qualified expert with the .38 Special?" Oren teased.

Slowly, all three of us smiled, then burst out laughing.

CHAPTER 70

Alice Baker opened the door to a smiling Angie Lansing.

"Thank you for allowing me to come over, Alice."

"Oh Angie, I'm so glad to see you, and it is I who should be thanking you. The boys knew you were coming so they're going for a walk while we talk. But first, I'd like to introduce them to you."

Oren and I, who had been sitting quietly, stood simultaneously and Alice made the introductions.

"I commend you two for your concern for Miss Baker," Angie said.

"She's pretty neat, ma'am. It's a blast staying here," Oren enthused.

"Yeah, we saw her target practice shot chart and she's quite the marksman or markswoman."

"Oh, so you're proficient with a pistol?" Dr. Lansing eyeing Alice warily.

"She sure is. Even Detective Finnigan thinks she's good."

"I heard somewhere that you two play basketball for the Panthers."

The boys nodded shyly.

"Well, it was nice meeting you. But now I would like to chat with Alice. I promise to be brief."

We told her it was swell to have met her, and headed off to let them have their girl time.

"They seem very nice, Alice. I'm glad you found some friends."

"Angie, they are nice. This is going to be their third night here with me. We've had some interesting discussions, talked well into the night."

"Oh, really?"

"Come over and sit, Angie. I'm so glad you're here."

There was definitely something different about Alice Baker.

"You wanted to tell me something?" Angie inquired.

"Yes, yes I did, but for a second there, I had reservations. The boys and I have discussed everything sports politics, religion, policemen and teachers, the full gamut. Sometimes our differing opinions put some 'chili into the stew,' as Tony put it.

Over these past few days, we've bonded. We almost cut our fingers like the American Indians used to do when they became blood brothers. We just talked and talked." The exuberance faded and her eyes dropped to the floor. She took a deep breath and continued, "And I just blurted out to Tony and Oren that I was a homosexual."

Dr. Lansing studied Alice's face. All she saw was a contented expression.

"I think I see the question in your face, Angie, and I understand. Should I have told the boys that I was homosexual?" Alice paused, and continued thoughtfully, "I really believe what they said afterwards. They were curious like I was when I didn't know. But it was all right with them; they were sensitive to my feelings with their questions; they were true gentlemen.

"Angie, Oren and Tony are my buddies. We'll probably be friends for life. And I'm comfortable being me whoever 'me' turns out to be.

"Oh, and we went to Tony's house and had lunch with Mrs. Maringuez and some of Tony's brothers. They're a little roudy, but really nice. I had a great time. Angie I have friends."

"Alice, I'm happy for you. I hope you do understand that not everyone out there in the world is so…accepting. I'm just reminding you to be cautious. You made a bold statement to Tony and Oren that very easily could have turned out badly. Alice, just know there are a lot of people out there just like you, and many who are just as confused. Please be careful in whom you confide.

"Now I'm preaching. I'm glad the boys were here today.

Please tell them goodbye for me."

Alice gave Angie a big hug and thanked her again for coming over to meet the boys. She was happy again, felt good about herself, and was comfortable in her own body at long last.

CHAPTER 71

Pretty Boy was dressed in his dark blue outfit as he sat in the large cushioned chair and drank a Lucky Lager. He had listened to KPQ's weather report and knew there would be some dark clouds out tonight, but no rain.

Harold would have to turn himself in tomorrow. Good old Mr. Rufus had set it up. So he had to do tonight what he wanted to do a couple of days ago. He had driven by Apartment #2 and noticed the lights were on in the front room. He went home to bide his time.

"Sunnny," she said quietly.

"Leave me alone, I wasn't thinking about you, so leave me alone."

He stood and went to his bedroom, pulled out his secret notebook, then came back and sat.

"How come you've got your dark clothes on tonight?" she taunted.

"I'm not going to talk to you."

She began to sing, "I've got you under my skin," and then hummed the rest. He didn't say a word.

He went into the bathroom, splashed water on his face and stared at his dripping reflection and into his own brooding dark eyes. She was there, looking over his shoulder. Angrily he turned the faucet on again, leaned over and splashed his face again. When he straightened up and looked into the mirror, she was gone. Good riddance, his tortured mind shouted. He went into his bedroom and picked up the dark blue watch cap and placed it on his head, then admired himself in the mirror.

"I bet I know where you're going, Sunny."

"Leave me alone!" he shouted.

CHAPTER 72

Elda, the neighbor turned the television volume down so she could hear more clearly.

"What's the matter Elda?" her husband Fred, inquired.

"You didn't hear that? He must be in the bathroom, cause I heard him say 'leave me alone.'"

They listened but heard nothing more.

"Are you sure it wasn't the TV?"

"I'm sure Fred. Just cause you can't hear, doesn't mean I can't."

"Sunny, you can't shout me out, you should know that by now. What's more, you're the one that summons me, you dumb oaf." She began laughing and the decibel level of her screeching hurt his ears.

He covered his ears with his hands, bolted to the kitchen, snatched his keys off the counter and ran to the front door. Tears were cascading down his face as he closed the door behind him and rushed to his car. He sat in the relative comfort of his car and thought about what he was going to do.

"What's he doing, can you see anything Elda?"

"Looks like he's just sitting in his car."

He saw a couple on the sidewalk coming towards his parked car. As they got closer, he turned his head away so as not to show his face. He could see the old busy bodies in his neighbor's house as they gawked at him with the curtain pulled to the side. *Mind your own business,* he thought.

He turned the ignition key and the engine whirred to life. He drove, not yet thinking about where he was headed. But he did know where he was going. He steered the car to Miller Street, careful to keep to the speed limit. A police car passed, going the other way. He followed its tail-lights in the rear view mirror until he couldn't see them any more. He turned left on Washington Street, still traveling at 25 miles an hour. Suddenly there was a red light flashing behind him. *What did I do wrong? I didn't do anything wrong. What gives?* He pulled his car to the curb and waited for the policeman to come to his door. A big shot of adrenalin had been pumped into his system. He was perspiring, his mouth was dry, and his hands were clammy on the steering wheel.

"Oh, it's you," the officer said as he shined the flashlight on his face. The officer took notice of the dark clothing the man was wearing, but then, he knew this was an odd bird. "You've got a tail light out on the passenger side."

From the patrol car came the dispatcher's amplified announcement, "Car 14, Car 14, domestic disturbance at 314 Berg Street." The officer told Pretty Boy to get his light fixed and jogged back to his car, made a U turn and drove off with his red light flashing.

The man sat in his car, shaking and barely able to breathe, his grip on the steering wheel so tight his knuckles were white. He bolted out of the car, ran to the curb under a large English Maple and threw up. His legs were weak and unsteady as he leaned against the tree, his forehead against the bark. He pulled out a clean handkerchief, wiped his face, and walked unsteadily back to his car.

He was tired all of sudden, just needed a little time to rest. He saw a man walking a dog in his direction down the dark street. He started his car and drove up Washington, then Eliot to Madison, where he paused trying to decide whether to park up or down on Madison Street. It was important to think things out in advance, and this was a serious consideration. What if he had to leave in a hurry? He parked headed up the street. He sat for a while to let his eyes become accustomed to the dark. When he was sure there was no other living thing in the area, he opened the car door, carefully stepped out of the car, and gently pushed the door closed, quietly.

The black moccasins he had purchased at Buster Brown's were perfect for his nights out. He felt like an Indian moving quietly over the cement walkway.

"Sunny?"

He stopped and slammed his hands over his ears, grimaced and gritted his teeth. He wouldn't listen to her. He would not listen to her. Pretty Boy removed his hands slowly from his ears. She was gone! He did it! Always knew he could, and now he'd done it.

He moved easily down the street until he was on Sunburst. He held his breath and listened. Nothing. Just him. As he approached the front of the house he thought about her long, shapely, white legs as she had inspected a run in her nylons. She never gave a thought that he could be watching her.

He felt he was almost invisible in the night, and he laughed quietly. That was it, he had never thought about it before, but he must be invisible at night. Stealthily he glided between the two houses and stood next to the bedroom window. Muffled voices could be heard coming from the adjacent home, then the bedroom light went on. *If they open the blinds they'll see me,* he thought. He quickly took the four steps across to the lighted window. Someone started to open the window and he heard the voices.

"Don't open the window, honey, what if there's a murderer out there?" she slammed the window closed.   Pretty Boy grinned.

He tiptoed his way to the side of the Detective's home, where he found the other bedroom. He froze.

There was a beam of light moving erratically from tree, to ground, to yard, and back. It disappeared, he heard voices, and then it was quiet again. *It's nothing,* he thought. His attempt to open the window, then the backdoor were unsuccessful as both were locked up tight. If the front door is locked he would leave.

It was.

Damn, he thought as he jogged to his car, opened the door quietly and sat. Glancing at his watch, he determined it was still early.

Embolden, he drove East on 1st Street until he reached Miller, then left on 5th to Sunset and left again. This was his destination. Poking along at 5 miles per hour he observed Apartment #2. No lights, no neighbor's lights, and no barking dogs. He drove to the next block, quietly exited his car and walked briskly to Sunset Street and Apartment #2.

He surreptitiously crept along the side of the building and tried the back door. Locked. He moved quickly to the side of bedroom. He tried to push the window up. Damn, everything was locked. He moved to the front of the apartment, tried the handle of the screen door and it opened quietly. His huge hand tried the doorknob. The door opened. He looked to see if there was a chain on the door. No chain. He opened the door slowly until there was enough room for him to slip in. He stood by the door waiting for his eyes to acclimate to the complete darkness. He was trying to remember which room he had seen the light on in on his previous trip to #2. He could distinguish a bathroom and two doors that probably lead to bedrooms. Did she have a roommate? She hadn't mentioned one. He squatted down and felt the floor; he was standing on a throw rug, not a carpet. The floor was wood. He moved slowly across the room until the floor groaned. He stopped. He broke out in a cold sweat and his heart beat faster. He heard someone talking, probably to a dog.

"I'm sure it's only one of the boys going to the bathroom, Mandy," a girls voice said, hardly audible.

"Sunny, you're in trouble?" his mother said quietly.

He stared at the door where he had heard the voice. The sweat ran into his eyes and it stung. He blinked and brought his forearm up and wiped the sweat away. He eased forward until he was directly in front of the bedroom door.

"Sunny!"

"Shut up, you bitch!" the man shouted out loud.

The door opened and Alice Baker was face to face with a large, angry man standing there with wild eyes. He hadn't even noticed she was there until the little dog bit his ankle. He screamed out in rage and kicked at the dog.

Oren and I were in the extra bedroom. I was having a hard time falling asleep.

The floor creaked. I crept across the room, eased the bedroom door open, and saw the silhouette of a large man standing by Alice's door.

I woke Oren and mimed the strategy of tackling the intruder. I would go low and Oren would go high. We opened our bedroom door, just as the man screamed. Then Alice opened her door, Mandy attacked his ankle and was barking like a real guard dog.

Pretty Boy was still screaming when Oren and I hit him simultaneously. Our momentum carried us all into Alice's room. I hit my head on the doorjamb and it dazed me. Oren landed on top of the intruder and they wrestled on the floor. The man was strong and managed to pull himself upright with Oren hanging on for dear life. He pushed Oren back so hard he bounced off the wall and crumpled to the floor.

Alice had picked up her .38 Special from the nightstand and was fumbling with the phone, trying to dial with the pistol in her hand. At the same time, she was keeping an eye on the struggle. The intruder turned and took a step toward Alice. Without hesitation she shot at his leg. It was a direct hit. He screamed in pain and fell to the floor. He shouted "Mom!" and began to cry. He looked up as if praying, stood, turned, grasped his leg, groaned, whined, and scrambled toward the door, raised the hand that had been covering the bloody hole in his leg and placed it on the white wall, leaving a bloody handprint. He raised his right arm and used it like a battering ram. He hit the screen door with such force it flew off the hinges, and he limped off groaning in terror.

Alice dialed the operator, then dropped the phone on the bed and rushed to us, where we sat, dazed by the blows we had taken.

"This is the operator, hello, this is the operator, hello, can you hear me, hello, this is the operator."

"Send the police. Send the police!" Alice screamed as she helped Oren to stand. Oren stumbled over to me and helped me up, then we fell on Alice's bed. She picked the phone up. "Please send the police," she pleaded.

"I'm ringing the police. What is your address? What is your name?"

"My name is Alice Baker," and she gave the operator her address.

"Police Department, emergency."

"I just shot an intruder and he's escaping as we speak. Send the police," she screamed. She hung up the phone and asked us if we were all right. We nodded and she went looking for little Mandy. She found the little dog lying on her side. Mandy raised her head to look at Alice. Alice gently picked up the dog and brought it around the bed, laid her down and crooned reassurances to her. Oren and I ran to look outside to see if the intruder was still in the area.

Pretty Boy was limping along the Sunset enroute to his car on the next block. He turned the corner just as a patrol car barreled toward him. He stopped and hid behind a large Blue Spruce Douglas Fur and watched as the car sped by him down Sunset. He continued down the next block and finally reached his car, unlocked the door and slid into the driver's seat, grimacing from the pain in his leg.

He assessed the wound as well as he could in the dark. He had to stop the flow of blood from the hole in his thigh. Another police car rocketed by with its red light on. He looked around for something he could use to stop the bleeding and found a Pendleton shirt neatly folded on the back seat. He grabbed the shirt, leaned to the glove box and felt around inside for the jackknife he knew was there. He found it and cut a strip of material from the shirt, all the time keeping an eye on the street. A patrol car stopped at the corner. He put the knife down, threw the shirt on the passenger seat, and reached in his pocket for the car keys. No keys!

"You dumb oaf," she said sarcastically.

Then he remembered he had them in his hand when he opened the door. They were already in the ignition. He breathed a sigh of relief.

The patrol car at the corner turned left and started up the street slowly shining its spot light on the cars parked along the street.

He turned the key. The engine came to life. He pushed the shift arm to Drive and quickly made a U turn. He had to get away from here. His eyes locked on the rear view mirror as he accelerated down 5th. The headlights of the patrol car that had been going the opposite direction appeared behind him. Now they were after him. *He felt light headed, probably from the loss of blood*, he thought.

"You're in trouble now Sunny," she said in a singsong fashion.

He came to the intersection of 5th and Wenatchee and wondered which way to turn. Left would take him to the North end and toward Cashmere, and right would have him going South, toward the bridge.

"The bridge Sunny, the bridge," she shouted from the backseat.

"I don't want to go to the bridge," he whimpered.

"Yes you do, Sunny. Yes you do."

He turned right and drove only a short way as he drifted across the white line and almost hit the only other car on the road. He felt weak, but strangely his leg didn't seem to hurt anymore. He knew what was happening to him, but there was nothing he could do about it. As he raced down Wenatchee Avenue, he could see the steel structure of the bridge across the Columbia River up ahead. He focused his eyes on the rear view mirror and could see two squad cars chasing him now, their sirens wailing. He began to feel sleepy, euphoric. He started across the bridge, began to slow down, and finally stopped midway on the structure. He looked in the rearview mirror and saw that the patrol cars had stopped about thirty yards back. The bridge was lighted so he could see the officers with their guns drawn. Detective Finnigan was standing in front of the others with a bullhorn in her hand.

CHAPTER 73

"It's time to give it up. We know you're wounded and you need medical assistance. We've called an ambulance and it should be here any minute."

He stepped out of the car and took off his watch cap. He didn't need it anymore.

"Hey, Dan. Its Dan Dupree!" one of the policemen shouted.

Detective Finnigan looked confused as she raised the bullhorn again.

The ambulance arrived; it's siren blaring as it screeched to a halt behind the police cars.

"Dan, we know you're wounded. The ambulance is here to take you to the hospital."

Dan reached into his car and when he stepped away he had something in his right hand. One of the officers shouted out "gun."

"Put the gun down, Dan. Nobody wants to hurt you, and I don't think you want to hurt anyone." Everyone had taken cover behind cars.

Dan began to talk to someone they couldn't see as he staggered closer to the railing. He looked down at the swiftly flowing river beneath him, then turned and glared at the police that were inching toward him. He raised his right hand and pointed in their direction. They all stopped.

Dan again said something to someone, then used the last of his ebbing strength to pull himself up on the girder and slowly roll over the edge.

The officers rushed to the railing and looked down at the river. It was flowing just as if nothing had happened. Dan Dupree was nowhere to be seen.

"Could anyone hear what he was saying?" Detective Finnigan called out.

"I think he said, 'I'm coming Mother,'" one of the officers

said.

Another policeman pointed to a blackjack lying on the roadway where Dan had gone over the railing.

"He didn't have a gun," she observed sadly as she took in all the blood on the bridge where he had been standing.

CHAPTER 74

Two days later, Chief Patrick Duffy was looking through the journal Dan Dupree had kept about his tragic life. It was well-written and precise. He had a wonderful hand, so the reading was easy, though terrifyingly graphic. The memoir could have been written by a professional novelist. One like Steven King, maybe. He found a picture of Dan with his mother at some happier time. On the surface they had been happy, but who really knew.

"Kelli, Dan was, on the surface, a good police officer. Everything a good officer stood for. He was dependable and smart. We may never know what happened to this man. He was always a little eccentric, obviously. But I never heard him complain about the long hours or double shifts when someone called in sick. He once told me he had always wanted to be a policeman."

Kelli looked up slowly and nodded, "I can understand why. What better cover than a blue uniform and a badge."

Chief Duffy and Detective Finnigan studied all the evidence and verified all of the data they had obtained on Daniel Dupree. There were the footprints from the Grace Hopper rape, and the semen collected matched Dupree's blood type. The handprint left in Alice Baker's apartment, the dark strands of hair found on

Lilli Jo's bed, and the semen found on the bed sheets.

The young lady, Nadine Morrison, that had been raped and murdered in Chelan had been his victim too, thus clearing up that unsolved murder for Detective Jim Rotter.

There was the murder of a woman in Renton that was going to be solved when he called that Police Department. The journal, in his own handwriting, verified it all.

"You know Kelli, I'm going to take back my comment about Dupree going bad on my watch. That man had always been bad. He just managed to fool a lot of people for a damned long time."

Hey, are you two going home tonight?" Mary Corley asked as she poked her head in the Chief's office.

"Mary, what did you think about Dan Dupree? You must have had an opinion about him."

She looked at Kelli and they smiled.

"I tried not to be around him because he was creepy, so I knew very little about him. Thank God," she said quietly, turned and left.

"Mary and I didn't like the man, that's all. He gave off an ominous aura," Kelli said and picked up her sweater.

"By the way, Kelli, I know you went over to see Lilli Jo's parents this morning. How did they take the news?"

"I think that's the reason I do this job, Patrick.

There is no feeling like the one you get from solving a crime and being able to face the family and tell them the bad guy got caught. It makes all the frustrations worth it.

"Since they no longer have their daughter, they asked if I would be their daughter in spirit, and stay in touch.

"See you in the morning, Detective."

Kelli waved over her shoulder without breaking stride.

CHAPTER 75

Six months later, Rufus Delroy Applewood, called me and told him to come to the Windmill Restaurant on Wenatchee Avenue for a steak dinner, and to bring Alice and Oren with me. As we approached the entrance, Dewey and Harold Slick were just leaving. Harold held the door open for us to enter. Oren and I stopped and extended our hands. He looked confused but shook each proffered hand.

"Do I know you guys?"

Oren smiled and looked over at me.

"We know Rufus Applewood," I said awkwardly, and walked into the diner.

The smile on Harold's face evaporated and there was anger in his eyes when he saw Alice Baker with her hand extended to him.

"I was wrong Harold, and I deserve a punch in the face or something. I can only say I'm sorry for what I put you through." He stared at Alice for a few long seconds and then there was a faint but discernable smile on his face as he walked away to join a waiting Dewey.

"Who was the chick?" Dewey asked.

"Just a mistake, an honest mistake," he answered enigmatically.

Inside the diner, the three of us approached a waiting Rufus Applewood.

"I see you met the Slick brothers. I wasn't aware

you knew who they were."

Oren and I looked at each other, smiled mysteriously and sat down at the table.

"What's Harold doing out of jail?" Alice wanted to know.

"Well," Rufus drawled, "he pled guilty to trespassing and burglary. I think I got him a pretty good deal. The judge gave him six months county time, and three years formal probation. One of the conditions of his probation is that he go to psychiatric counseling sessions twice a week. I know he can be helped, if he wants to be, and I think he does. Dewey is willing to help him, as long as he really works at getting better, getting past his past, as it were. But, enough about that! What I invited you down here tonight for is to thank you for performing your civic duty. Whether you know it or not you performed a vital function in our democratic system of justice.

"You probably wondered why I would defend a person whom you three probably thought was guilty. Well, I'm pretty sure I had told Tony during one of our conversations that I had a vision of what happened at Lilly Jo's that evening. Unfortunately, I didn't see the face clearly, but the body configuration was definitely thicker and heavier than either of the Slick brothers. At any rate, with the journal that Daniel Dupree kept and having seen his picture in his uniform, I'm reasonably certain it was him I saw."

Rufus patiently explained to Oren and Alice about

his 'visions'. They were fascinated, though skeptical.

"So now that you're out of high school, I hope you're going on to college." Rufus challenged Oren and Tony.

"I haven't really decided what I'm going to do." Oren admitted.

"I think I'm going to join the Marines," Tony said nervously.

"I'm transferring to Gonzaga, so I'll be moving back to Spokane," Alice told them. "I'm hoping to follow your lead Mr. Applewood and become a lawyer."

Rufus nodded gravely and raised his water glass. "I hope we can stay in contact until we are all gone."

They raised their glasses and hailed, "here, here."

EPILOGUE

Well, that's my story. I did join the Marine Corps and got to see some of the other countries of the world. But there is no place like the United States of America, and there is no place like your own home town and all the memories, some good, some not so good, of the people you grew up with and shared good and bad times with. Wenatchee, Washington will be a part of me 'til I die.

Oren stayed in Wenatchee and became, an electrician, from what I heard a very good electrician.

Alice became an attorney, just like Rufus knew she would. He never told her, but he had a vision of her in court. Thing was, she was wearing the black robe and sitting on the bench with the litigants and their attorneys down in front of her.

Sadly, we lost Rufus a few years back. One night he just went to sleep, and never woke up. I was lucky and got leave to come home for the funeral. Rufus had left me and Oren letters with instructions not to open them until we hit the big 30. We loved that grumpy old guy and we'll hold the letters, just like he wanted. Kelli is now Chief of Detectives in an expanded Wenatchee Police Department. Sometimes we have dinner when I visit Wenatchee.

Jimmy Speed came and went, just like he always had for a couple of years after we graduated, then he just wasn't there any more. At first nobody missed him, because he wasn't always around, but this time, well--- this time he just never came back.

THE SHADE

THE SHADE

Also by Joseph Montoya

    Where is Brian Douglas
    The Innocent
    Mysterious Ways